ALSO BY JESSICA SIMS

Beauty Dates the Beast

Desperately Seeking Shapeshifter

D0029272

BEAUTY DATES THE BEAST

"A world that is both dangerous and humorous. Add a heroine who is plucky and brave and a hero who is sexy and powerful, and you get a story filled with sizzle and spark!"

—*RT Book Reviews*

"The adorable relationship between Bathsheba and Beau drives the story and will leave readers eager for more."

—*Publishers Weekly*

"This page-turning debut . . . possesses humor and a protective male character similar to those of Katie MacAlister. This will likely be a popular series."

—*Booklist*

"A fast-paced story that's got both humor and heat. Beau is a meltingly sexy hero."

—*Romance Junkies*

"What an awesome debut book! . . . If you enjoy shifter books, then this is a must-add to your reading list."

—*Bitten by Books*

JESSICA SIMS

MUST LOVE FANGS

Pocket Books

New York   London   Toronto   Sydney   New Delhi

Pocket Books
A Division of Simon & Schuster, Inc.
1230 Avenue of the Americas
New York, NY 10020

This book is a work of fiction. Any references to historical events, real people, or real places are used fictitiously. Other names, characters, places, and events are products of the author's imagination, and any resemblance to actual events or places or persons, living or dead, is entirely coincidental.

Copyright © 2013 by Jessica Sims

All rights reserved, including the right to reproduce this book or portions thereof in any form whatsoever. For information, address Pocket Books Subsidiary Rights Department, 1230 Avenue of the Americas, New York, NY 10020.

First Pocket Books paperback edition September 2013

POCKET and colophon are registered trademarks of Simon & Schuster, Inc.

For information about special discounts for bulk purchases, please contact Simon & Schuster Special Sales at 1-866-506-1949 or business@simonandschuster.com.

The Simon & Schuster Speakers Bureau can bring authors to your live event. For more information or to book an event, contact the Simon & Schuster Speakers Bureau at 1-866-248-3049 or visit our website at www.simonspeakers.com.

Manufactured in the United States of America

10   9   8   7   6   5   4   3   2   1

ISBN 978-1-4516-6182-8
ISBN 978-1-4516-6185-9 (ebook)

For Ilona

Who always offers commentary on how to fix my plots . . . and never gets mad when I ignore her always excellent suggestions. That's true friendship!

Thanks for being my sounding board for every book.

Chapter One

*W*hen I was a child, my father used to let me stay up late to watch movies with him on Saturday nights. My father had stunningly bad taste in movies. His favorite? *Mothra vs. Godzilla.* I remembered being terrified of the massive, furious creatures that screamed and bellowed as they tore through Tokyo.

Those furious growls and outraged shrieks sounded a bit like what was going on right now in the Midnight Liaisons conference room. No laser beams shooting from eyes, but there was enough snarling to make any human feel on edge.

My boss, Bathsheba Russell, was perched on the corner of my desk, wringing her hands and staring at the front door.

It made it impossible to work, and I shoved my notepad under a stack of papers. "Something I can help with, Bath?"

She glanced over at me, startled, then shook her head. Another round of furious snarls came from the conference room, and she winced as the snarls turned into shouting. "No, I'm sure they'll be here soon."

Well, that was frustrating, and it didn't bode well for my own plans. I cast an oblique look over at my coworker, Ryder. She widened her eyes and gave me a helpless shrug, as if saying, *What can you do?*

Sure, Ryder didn't care if the boss stuck around for an extra hour or two. It wouldn't derail her night like it'd derail mine.

And I needed this night.

I needed every single day I had left. When you're dying, you tend to get a little pissy about wasted time.

The front door opened, and just like that, the conference room got quiet. I could practically hear their shifter ears straining to make out who had just entered. In walked a scowling, lanky young man, hand in hand with a pretty, but frightened, redhead. The girl stared at me fearfully, then looked at Bathsheba as if she'd been about to pounce.

"We're human," Bath said in a dry voice. "The ones you need to be scared of are in there." She gestured at the now-too-quiet conference room.

The boy braced his shoulders and pulled the woman under his protective arm. She went willingly, her face utterly pale. Poor thing. They marched forward toward the conference room.

"They look like they're heading to a funeral," I whispered to Bath.

"They might be," she whispered back. "Vic wants to kill him."

She flushed when the boy paused in front of the conference room and turned to glare at us.

No one said a thing as the conference room door opened. They stepped in. Closed the door. A pause.

And then tempers exploded all over again.

"How dare you turn a human?" roared Vic. The snarl of the tiger alpha's voice rose above all others. "What the fuck were you thinking?"

"There's no one for us," the man shouted back. "There's no women my age. There's no women, period!"

"Then you use this goddamn agency and find yourself a date," Vic roared again.

"Let's calm down," Beau said firmly. The Alliance leader, a were-cougar and Bath's husband, was usually cool and in control of every situation, but he didn't sound calm now.

Vic gave another ear-shattering roar, and I heard the gulping cry of the woman.

"She's still thinking like a human," Bath said in irritation, getting to her feet. "And they're going to scare the shit out of her. I'm going in there."

As she moved toward the conference room, I took off my glasses and pretended to check them for smudges. Act calm. Easy. No problem.

But my heart was racing a mile a minute. My head throbbed with the adrenaline rush. I ignored it, just like I did all the other physiological symptoms lately. I didn't have time to mess with them.

Ryder pointed at her computer monitor, indicating that she was going to send me an instant message.

I turned to my screen and waited.

Yikes, she sent. *It sounds like they might be in there awhile.*

I typed back quickly. *What exactly is going on? Did that guy really turn a human?*

Yup, she sent back. *I got here just as they were shoving Sara out the door. You know how B protects her. Ramsey, too.*

Sara was Bath's quiet, delicate sister; she normally hung around the agency until her mate, Ramsey, a were-bear, picked her up in the evening. It seemed that Sara was a werewolf and everyone had known this but me. Humans, always the last to know. But since I worked at a dating agency that catered exclusively to the paranormal, it made sense that someone on staff would be, well, paranormal.

I glanced over at Ryder again. More than *one* someone. Sara was just out of the closet, but Ryder was still in hiding. I put my hands on the keyboard. *So do you have the scoop?*

Wellllll, Ryder typed. *From what I've been able to overhear, it sounds like ol' Johnny fell in love with his girlfriend, and Uncle Vic in there did not approve. So Johnny turned her and decided to ask permission later. Can you believe that?*

That was bad. Really bad. Humans weren't supposed to know about supernaturals unless they were allowed into the Alliance first. And every human who'd been allowed into the Alliance was currently in this office: me, Ryder, and Bathsheba.

For a supernatural (or "supe" as we liked to call them) to reveal their true nature to a human was against the rules. To reveal their true nature and then turn a human into a shifter was worse than bad. It caused all kinds of problems. What if they broke up? What were human parents supposed to do with a were-tiger daughter? Who was going to explain why their cute little Lola had to use a scratching post and went gonzo when the catnip was rolled out?

By revealing his true nature to a human, Johnny had endangered everyone in the Alliance. The network was built on a tenuous trust of the other species, and now that had been broken.

And it was going to play havoc with my plans.

As the yelling in the other room increased, I pulled my notepad out again and looked at the list I'd been working on.

<u>Potential Supernaturals</u>
Were-anything
Vampire

I frowned, displeased at how very short it was. Perhaps I was forgetting something? "Hey, Ryder?"

"Hmm?" My coworker dragged her gaze away from the conference room, where it had gotten awfully quiet again.

I tapped my pencil on my desk, thinking as I

stared down at the list. "Can you think of any supernaturals that can turn someone?"

"Turn someone?"

"You know, *turn* someone," I said. At her suspicious look, I pointed at the conference room, where a low rumbling argument between two men could be heard, interspersed by an occasional higher voice that was probably Bathsheba, trying to interject some common sense into the argument.

Ryder shook her head. *"Bad timing,"* she mouthed. *"Let it rest."*

But I couldn't afford to let it rest. I stared down at the paper, thinking, as the voices now rose in the conference room.

"This is abominable!" Vic shouted. "A disgrace!"

Ooo, *abominable* made me think of yeti. Were-yeti? I wrote it down and put a question mark next to it. Then I scratched it out. No one in their right mind wanted to be a yeti. Gross.

I chewed my eraser, thinking. Fae? They were born, not made, but they were also secretive. Maybe they knew something—

The bell clanged against the glass of the front door, signaling that someone had entered the office. I looked up, putting a smile on my face . . .

And sighed with dismay at the sight of the man strolling in. Joshua Russell, my least favorite client ever. "Hi, Josh," I said in my most bored voice.

He grinned, making a beeline for my desk.

Damn it. I sighed and pushed the notepad under a stack of reports again, then focused my attention on the tall, sexy man standing in front of my desk. My gaze was just at crotch height, which made things a bit awkward when I was trying to ignore the man.

Suddenly a large, perfect rose appeared under my nose. "For you, beautiful."

I pushed it aside. Some flirts never changed. "Nice try, Josh. I'm human, remember?"

"Yes, but you're an Alliance human. That's different," he said with a devastating grin that would have knocked the panties off any were-cat in the area. "Different is good."

"I have a pollen allergy," I lied in my stiffest voice and gave him a prim look.

He sighed as if defeated, but sauntered over to Ryder's desk instead, presenting her with the flower. She looked up from her reports, grinned at him, and took the flower with a wink.

Good. Maybe he'd leave me alone now.

Like the other big cats his entire clan was infamous for, Joshua Russell was a mix of power and playfulness. I studied him under my lashes as he chatted with Ryder, leaning over her desk. His brown hair was cropped short, just barely a buzz under his black Russell Security baseball cap. There was an attractive hint of scruff on his strong jaw, as if he'd forgotten to shave. Like all of the Russell werecougars, he had strong, masculine features. Where his brother Beau's features were a little more refined, more stern, Josh's seemed to be made for laughing. He had a ridiculous dimple in one cheek that flashed now and then, and his eyes were an unfair shade of blue, framed by lashes thick enough to make any woman jealous. His shoulders were big and brawny, and when he wore a tight shirt—like he was today— you could see the outlines of his pectorals and the bulge of his biceps. Yet these almost paled in comparison to his deliciously tight ass, which was currently pointed toward my desk. I stared at it. What a shame that such a beautiful piece of male flesh was attached to such an overt horn-dog.

He glanced over his shoulder just in time to catch me staring at his ass. I flushed and averted my gaze, but not before I caught his grin.

Damn it.

I sighed inwardly as he strolled back to my desk and dropped into the chair across from me. I shot him an irritated glance. "Can I help you with something?"

"I think I caught you checking me out, Marie."

"You did not," I said stiffly.

"It's fine if you can't admit it." He leaned forward and whispered, "I'm told my ass is quite bite-able."

I leaned toward him in return. "Your mom doesn't count."

Josh grinned, then sniffed the air and slid my notepad out from underneath the pile of paper.

How the hell had he known that was there? I tried to snatch it back, but I was too slow. Josh held it aloft, then stood, reading it aloud. "Potentials— vampires, were-anything, fae. Yeti?" He glanced over at me. "Grocery list?"

"I'm helping a client decide who to date," I said, holding my hand out for the pad.

He waved it at me. "You're not being very choosy for your client here. Were-anything?"

"Just give it back," I snapped. "And tell me why you're here so I can get you out the door and get on with my life. Do you need a date? There's a shock."

"Ah, a date," Josh said, dropping the list onto my desk and slouching back in the chair again. He gave me a thoughtful look, those long lashes over his gorgeous eyes making him look sleepy—or sexy—or both. His gaze was intense, but his smile was disarming. "You think I should? I'm still avoiding the last girl."

I snorted. The last girl he'd dated hadn't been too thrilled when Josh had never called her back. She'd called me to gripe about it, since I was the one that had paired the two of them.

I reached for the list again and he pulled it out of reach, waggling his eyebrows at me. Ugh. Determined, I got up, moved around the desk, and snatched the list back out of his hands.

As I stalked back to my chair, I eyed him. "You should try dating someone more than once. Don't quote me on it, but I hear that's how you have a relationship."

He didn't seem deterred by my waspish tone. "And you're the relationship expert? How long have you dated your boyfriend?"

I had no boyfriend. "I don't date."

"All the more reason you should date me. I'd change your mind."

"I *especially* don't date clients."

"First time for everything."

Criss, I cussed mentally in my mother's French. Talking to him was like running in circles. I turned to my computer and began to type in his profile number. He came in so often that I had it memorized. At least, that's what I told myself. "How about a were-jaguar?"

"Too pushy. I like girls that are a little tart but melt in my arms."

I rolled my eyes. Oh brother. "Harpy?"

"Pottymouth."

"Dryad?"

"All they want to do is hike. I'm more of a 'curl up in front of the fire and get to know each other' kind of guy."

I'd just bet he was. "Fae?"

"Too delicate. I like a girl I can grab."

Oh, you are a pig. "Vampire?"

He touched his nose. "Not a fan of the dead smell."

I turned from my keyboard in exasperation. "Why don't you tell me what you're looking for, and I'll see if we have a profile that might match that description?"

Josh skimmed a finger in lazy circles on the surface of my desk. "I didn't say I was here for a date. Unless *you're* willing, of course."

"Then why *are* you here?"

He gestured at the back room, where the sounds

of arguing still continued. "Heard that Vic Merino was going to be stopping by in a fury, and those tigers like to roar. Thought I'd come give my brother some backup before heading off to work."

My eyes narrowed at him. "So why all the pretense about your dating choices?"

"You tell me, Marie. You're the one who's so quick to try and get me laid."

I gritted my teeth. "Don't you have someplace to be?" *Like, anywhere but here?*

Josh adjusted his baseball cap, and I caught another glimpse of those inhumanly beautiful blue eyes. "No place I'd rather be than right here with you, Marie."

"Go away," I said, turning back to my computer. "I'm busy here."

"Busy with your list? Rounding up yeti for lonely were-women?"

I glared. "Go."

He laughed and leaned forward, his big shoulders looming over my desk.

My skin prickled with awareness and I stared at him, waiting.

His nostrils flared and Josh tilted his head, then looked satisfied with whatever he'd smelled. He glanced back down at me. "Turns out Beau doesn't need me. Sounds like the conversation's over."

He lifted three fingers to the air, then counted down to two, then one.

The door to the conference room opened.

A large man with inky black hair stormed out of

the office. Beau followed, a grim expression on his face. At his heels, Bathsheba tugged on her long, white-blond ponytail, looking nervous.

The tiger clan leader seemed coldly furious, and I avoided making eye contact with him. He was mean looking, like a lot of the larger predator types. His arms were enormous and corded with veins, but his large, brutish features had an appeal. And he looked strong. Really damn strong. Strong was good.

I slid my list out and made a note of "tiger" under "were-anything."

"Calm down," Beau told him. "Let's talk about this rationally."

"Rational?" Vic Merino roared, the veins bulging in his neck. The big man snarled, his shoulders hunched with fury as he turned to glare at Beau. "One of my clan just turned a *human*. Do you know what this means? It means I'm now stuck with a fucking human who can't figure out why she wants to turn into a fucking tiger every now and then. My clan didn't need this shit."

"I'm sure things will be fine," Bathsheba began soothingly.

Vic turned his withering glare on her. "Fine? My clan will be forced to pay reparations to every other clan for breaking the law. Once the other clans find out what mine has done, they're going to bankrupt us. And we're also going to have to pay off her parents to keep them silent. We're fucked." His eyes grew fierce and wild. "My wife is pregnant with our child. You want me to be calm and rational while that idiot is taking food out of my mate's mouth?"

Beau stepped in front of Bathsheba, silently protecting her, his glare fierce. "Don't take that tone with my mate, Vic."

Vic snarled back at Beau, baring his teeth . . . then dropped back a foot, pacing away. "Sorry. Fuck. I'm just a little stressed right now."

I discreetly crossed "tigers" off my list. Yikes. I wasn't sure I could deal with that kind of temper.

A muscle ticked in Beau's cheek. "I'm just as angry as you are. But shouting isn't going to turn her human again."

"And what am I supposed to do? They've got me by my fucking balls and my clan by my wallet. Who am I going to complain to?" He crossed his arms over his broad chest. "She already tried to go to the police once, and we had to shut that shit down fast."

"No human police," Beau said, not moving from his protective stance in front of his wife. "You know what we have to do."

That stopped the tiger's furious pacing. "What do you propose?"

"The law changes today. Here. Now," Beau said with a slice of his hand through the air. "First the trouble with the wolves and Sara, and now this. Things are getting out of control, and it threatens the safety of everyone. Maybe people think that because I've taken a human mate, the rules have relaxed. That's not the case. Bathsheba's life was threatened. Her sister's been under constant attack. If anything, it's proven to me that humans and weres shouldn't mix." The look on his face was grim. "From here on out, we're moving to a no-tolerance policy. No unapproved turnings. Anyone who does? Can join their newly turned friend in permanent exile."

Permanent exile?

"Exile?" Johnny said, echoing my thoughts as he stepped out of the conference room, the redhead trailing behind him, her hand clutched in his. He swallowed hard. "We're exiled?"

"We haven't decided yet," Vic snarled. "Why don't you go show your girlfriend how to control her change so she doesn't make another fucking scene in public?"

The girl flushed a bright red, and Johnny scowled. He grabbed the girl's arm, and they made a hasty exit out of the room.

Beau rubbed his face, seeming decades older. The tiger alpha looked like he wanted to ransack something, and Beau shook his head. "We'll sit on this for a few days before deciding what to do about his disrespect."

"And the girl—"

"Will be included in his punishment," Beau agreed. "We have to be firm on this. If it gets out that someone's gone and changed a human, we're all at risk. Zero tolerance."

"But won't that be seen as hypocritical after

you've taken a human mate?" Bath asked, her voice quiet. "Your men are lonely."

"And the men are not acting rationally. I'm not protecting them—I'm thinking of you, of Sara. Of every single human woman that's going to be hunted and turned into something she doesn't understand unless we put a lid on this." He fixed a fierce gaze on all of us.

No one said a thing.

Beau turned to Bathsheba. "I need a list of all packs and clans that have an extremely low female ratio. We need to make sure the males are kept occupied. The last thing we want is a string of human women turned by men who can't keep it in their pants."

She gave him a blank look. "I'm sorry, were you asking me as your wife, or your assistant?"

I sucked in a breath, expecting someone to explode.

But Beau only chuckled, leaning in to kiss her cheek. "I'm sorry. Could you please help with this? I promise I'll look at those resumés for an assistant once things calm down."

She gave him a mollified smile and nodded. That was the thing I never got used to with shifters. They preferred it when their women talked back.

"But—" Johnny began.

"No excuses," Beau clipped as he jerked around to fix the man in his gaze. His teeth bared, and I realized he was furious. Barely controlled, despite his loving manner with Bathsheba. "No one else is turned, or they'll be exiled permanently."

My heart dropped into my throat, and I very quietly scratched out "were-anything" on my list.

That just cut down my list of available choices . . . considerably.

After all, I was trying to get someone to turn *me*.

Chapter Two

*M*y mother died when I was eighteen. She gradually withered away, going slowly mad from a disease that had the medical people baffled. It's called fatal familial insomnia, and it's exceedingly rare.

I remember thinking nothing of it when I'd wake up for school and find out that my mother had been up all night, watching reruns on TV, unable to sleep. She'd laugh it off and say that she'd nap during the day. No one in my family thought too much of it at first. After six months, my father began to worry. She tried taking pills and medications to help her sleep, but they only made things worse. She went to see specialist after specialist, only to be told that no one could help her. When they made the final verdict—fatal familial insomnia—we realized what was in store for her. She was going to die a slow, painful death, and there was nothing anyone could do about it.

Mother deteriorated more quickly than we anticipated. Within months, she began to see things. When her hallucinations grew so strong that she had a hard time discerning reality, she had to be hospitalized. And from there, she went downhill. We watched, numb, as the illness took her mind and she turned into an insane, brittle husk of the vibrant woman she once had been. My poor, distraught father kept vigil at her bedside, holding her hand even as she slipped away.

How could you die from simply not being able to sleep? The doctors explained that there was something in my mother's genetic makeup that wouldn't allow her to get restful sleep, and it slowly took a toll on her mind. By the end, she was mad with exhaustion, and half the time she didn't recognize me or my father.

It was devastating.

Then the doctors insisted on testing me, since I shared the same DNA. They were interested for scientific reasons, of course. I was interested because I wanted to know if I was going to end up with the same death sentence.

I wasn't prepared to find out the truth: I was a carrier for the same disease. It might hit me but it might not, the doctors reassured me. Most people didn't see an onset of it until they hit their forties, and by the time I hit that age, surely they'd have a cure for it. They patted me and reassured me, and in turn, I patted and reassured my father, who was still reeling from the loss of my mother. Plenty of time yet before his only child might be affected. And there was always a chance that the disease would never kick in.

But I knew my fate as soon as I heard the verdict. I knew that slow, tortured death would eventually come for me.

So I lived with the specter of my death looming over my mind, hovering like a silent reminder that my days were numbered. It colored everything I did. If you knew you were only going to live until forty or so, it'd affect your life, too. I'd always been a fairly withdrawn, silent teenager, but after my mother's death and my diagnosis I withdrew even more. Lost touch with all my friends after graduation and remained solitary all through college.

I saw how much grief my father went through, and I vowed not to let that happen to another person I loved. Caring for someone and getting close to them only brought pain in the end. Much better to go through life alone and isolated so you didn't shatter someone else when you left.

So I didn't date. I got good at deflecting men's attention. I avoided places where men might hang out trolling for women—bars, clubs, singles groups. What was the point? I was going to die horribly in the prime of my life. Every time I met a man I was interested in, I kept seeing my father's face at my mother's bedside. Did I want to do that to someone else?

No, I did not.

So I'd politely turn down any invitation to dinner or a movie. And if I felt lonely, well, there was always my father's company. Dad and I grew even closer after Mom's death, going out to dinner, to movies, to museum openings together. We went on vacation to England and toured castles. I went to poker night with him and his friends. Everything was just fine.

Until my lonely, still-young-at-fifty father met Posey.

I hated Posey.

Okay. *Hate*'s a pretty strong word. I had an intense dislike for Posey. She was the epitome of Southern gentility. She had big blond hair that she wore in an enormous teased pouf of curls. She wore pink. Lots of pink. She sold Avon and wore high heels with her capris. She coordinated her purse with her earrings. And she talked. Loudly. And she flirted heavily with my father.

And he fell for her. The next thing I knew, my dad was dating. Well, good for him. He was so tired of being lonely. And even though I wasn't a fan of pink, loud Posey, my father adored her and he wasn't sad anymore.

That was good. I was busy with my new job at Midnight Liaisons, since my bachelor's in French language wasn't doing much for me, so I was glad that Dad had someone to spend time with. It was when they went on vacation to Vegas that I started to feel left out. And when they went to Hawaii together. And then took a cross-country trip. They were having a blast just being together, and I began to feel even more isolated and lonely. Maybe at twenty-eight, I was letting life get away from me. Maybe I should have been dating, too.

But then I started having trouble sleeping. At first I thought it was stress. After a week, though, I knew. My mother's first symptom had been insomnia, and I was a carrier.

I was dying.

I tried to deny it at first. I saw doctors and had them prescribe sleeping pills. I kept my problems from my coworkers and my dad, sure that it was controllable. I did everything I could to "fix" my sleeping problems. I bought new pillows, and then a new bed. I went to meditation therapy. Hypnosis. Acupuncture. Had sleep tests done.

But nothing worked. My brain wouldn't shut down. Wouldn't go to sleep. The fatal familial insomnia had kicked in.

I panicked at first. I didn't want to die. Especially not as a faceless, dateless, twenty-eight-year-old who hadn't lived enough. I thought I was prepared for the inevitable, only to find out that I was in no way ready for this. It took only a day or so before the realization kicked in—I could use the agency to help my situation.

Sara unknowingly provided the inspiration. I was at my desk, desperately trying to hold myself together by working extra hours. I was setting up a client with a were-jaguar, and Sara was sitting across from me. Suddenly she laughed and instant-messaged me with a dating profile. *Check it out.*

I pulled the link up on my computer: Joshua Russell. Handsome as hell, and judging from his picture, he knew it. "What am I looking for?"

"His dating list. Look at how long that is! You'd think people would see through his flirting, but he gets away with murder."

I clicked on his history, and sure enough, it seemed like Josh had dated just about every shifter in our database. "He's probably riddled with every disease known to mankind," I commented dryly. "They're welcome to him."

Sara snorted. "Man, you're hard on men. And of course he's not diseased, silly. He's a shifter."

She emphasized the last word like it should mean something to me. "And so . . . ?"

"And so shifters don't get diseases. They have crazy immune systems that keep things running like a race car."

And . . . just like that, I had an idea.

I was going to get a shifter to turn me. Maybe a vampire. I wasn't picky.

I was *not* going to die young. Not if I could help it.

Chapter Three

*O*f course, first I had to find someone to turn me. Not as easy as one might think.

I drummed my pencil on my desk now, looking down at my list. No shifters, if Beau's new rule was ironclad. But there were still vampires. They didn't necessarily follow the same laws that shifters did. They had their own set of rules, and even Alliance vampires didn't necessarily follow the same playbook that the shifters did.

And some of the vampires were quite good-looking. I thought of one that had come into the agency recently. He'd been handsome, with sad eyes and crazy hair, but very attractive. Young, too.

"Hey, Ryder," I called across the small office. "Who was the vampire with the sexy, frothy hair? Your client?"

"Valjean," she replied, not looking up from her computer.

Ah, that was him. I entered his name into the database. IN A RELATIONSHIP, the screen said. *Tabarnak.* Damn, that was fast. All the good ones got snatched early. So much for the hot new vampire.

I chewed on my lip, then changed my search criteria to "vampire only" and studied the profiles it brought up.

Maybe I needed someone that was a bit more desperate to date. I wasn't good at flirting, and I had no amazing bed-play to entice a man. I was great at jigsaw puzzles and bingo, but again, not the way to get a man. But if a guy was desperate, he wouldn't mind, would he? I pulled out my compact and studied my face, wondering if it'd appeal to a vampire. "Hey, Ryder? Would you say that I'm cute?"

This time, she peered over her computer at me, her gaze wary. "That's a loaded question. Why?"

I shrugged. "Just curious."

"Well, let me think," she said, getting up from her desk for another cup of coffee. Ryder mainlined caffeine like it was going out of fashion, which was probably why she was so wound up all the time. "I'm going to say no, I'm afraid."

I scowled at her. "You're a shitty friend, you *tête de cochon*."

"See, there's reason number one. Girls with a potty mouth are never cute. Daring, yes. Cute, no. The French is a nice touch, but not quite enough. Number two, you can't be cute if you keep wearing that eyeliner."

I eyed her perfectly made up face.

"I'm serious," Ryder said, stirring sugar into her coffee. "Throw that cheap garbage out. It makes you look like you have massive circles under your eyes."

Well, I *did* have massive circles under my eyes from lack of sleep. I'd thought the eyeliner would distract from it. "So you wouldn't date me?"

At my wounded look, she waved her hand at me. "Get a haircut. Do something with those bangs. Ditch the glasses. For God's sake, wear something other than a T-shirt, jeans, and sneakers. And pluck your eyebrows. After that, we'll talk."

I frowned, then squinted at my reflection in the monitor. My eyebrows were fine, damn it. "Okay, let me rephrase. Do I look cute enough for a desperate vampire to date?"

She sat down at her desk and took a sip of coffee. "I don't know. You're really not much of a people person. What's your blood type?"

"O positive."

"Then yes, that makes you cute to every vampire out there." Her perfect, lovely gaze narrowed on me. "And again, whyyyy?"

I shrugged, then dared to ask a question of the only person I trusted. "If I set up a date with a vampire while I'm supposed to be working, will you cover for me?"

Her jaw dropped.

"With the whole sunlight thing, this has to be at night, and since we work at night . . ."

"It's against the rules," she hissed. "Humans have to be cleared to date through the boss. And you heard what Beau said about shifters earlier."

"I know. That's why I want a vampire. I want one to turn me."

Her eyes widened. "Are you crazy?"

I was starting to think so.

Despite Ryder's protests, I wouldn't be deterred from my plan. I put up a fake profile on the dating agency site and left it vague. My fake name? Minnie Michigo, cousin to the otter clan of Michigos. I'd be in a hell of a lot of trouble if a Michigo came in and found out the profile existed, but I'd cross that bridge when I got there. Anyhow, Minnie's profile stated that she loved vampires, late nights, moonlight, and was open to exploring new avenues. If that didn't bring them crawling out of the woodwork, I didn't know what would.

Sure enough, Minnie got a hit at one in the morning from a vampire. Did she want to go out on a date tomorrow night?

Hell, yeah, she did.

Could Minnie send a picture of herself?

Damn. I ran to the bathroom and quickly took a picture of myself with my phone, removing my glasses and striking what I hoped was a sexy pose, then sent it back.

He accepted. Must have been sexy enough.

I replied quickly and named a spot that wasn't on the usual Alliance list of date hot spots. Nice and safe.

The next night, before going to work, I picked

out a sweater to go with my jeans and put on lipstick. I was date-ready.

Once I got to Midnight Liaisons, I told Ryder I
had a date with a vamp and begged, "Pleaaaase will
you cover for me?"

"No," she said fiercely. "Absolutely not. Not
while everyone's all ultra-pissy about the new girl
shifter. If you really want to date a vampire, and
God knows why you do, do it next month when everyone's got the stick out of their asses."

I couldn't wait a month; I didn't know how long
I had. My mother had degenerated over a year, but
my case had kicked in early. What if its course was
accelerated? I clasped my hands under my chin and
gave her sad eyes. "Pleeeeeease, Ryder?"

"No," she snapped again. I sometimes thought
I was the only one she dropped her effortlessly
chirpy act with. She only pretended to be sunshine
and puppies because it got her places. "Now go sit
at your desk and work. You know, that thing you're
supposed to be doing for a paycheck?"

"Ryder, come on. Just this once. It's important.
Look, I even put on lipstick. You *know* this date is
a big one if I'm wearing lipstick," I told her, main-
taining a perfectly serious expression.

"No."

I sighed, then pulled out the big guns. "Ryder,
this means a lot to me. It's because . . . I'm dying."

She rolled her eyes.

Well then. Miffed, I sat back down at my desk,
staring at the clock. One hour until my date. I

drummed my fingers on the desktop, waiting for the phone to ring, but Tuesdays were always slow.

After half an hour, she sighed and glanced over at me. "Are you going to do that all night?"

"Do what?" I looked up.

"Drum your fingers on the desk?"

I gave her a hopeful look. "Yes?"

"Okay," she grouched. "You can go on your date. But if anyone asks, you went on a Red Bull run and I have no idea where you are. Understand me?"

"You are my best friend ever, Ryder," I said with a grin. "I mean it. We're total BFFs now."

She raised her pinky into the air in our traditional signal. "Hey. I keep your secrets, you keep mine."

I got up and hooked my pinky through hers, sealing the deal. Then I returned to my desk, grabbed my purse, and ran out the door. "I'll fill you in on all the details when I come back, I promise."

"If you're dating a vampire, I don't want the details," she called after me.

I opted to walk to the restaurant. It was a cute little sushi place, picked for its low risk of other shifters frequenting it (too fishy for their sensitive nostrils) and the fact that it was close. It was pitch black outside, the night skies overcast and crisp. That was okay. I liked the night. Always had. There was something so peaceful about being up late when the rest of the world slept.

I snagged a pair of Red Bulls from a corner store to lend credence to Ryder's cover story, then headed over to the sushi place. The restaurant was empty, except for one table in the far corner of the blazingly bright interior. Probably not the best choice for a vampire date. Still, all that fluorescent lighting gave me a good look at him.

He wasn't . . . cute. Well, that was fine. I wasn't picky. I had barely glanced at his photo, because it didn't matter what he looked like—not if it bought me more time here on earth. Perhaps "not cute" was being generous, though. He looked more like Uncle Fester. Weren't vampires supposed to be gloriously sexy? This one was balding, pudgy, and wearing too much black. He was pale, which I expected, and mopping his sweating forehead with *my* dinner napkin, which I did not expect.

"Hi," I said, expecting him to stand at my arrival. "I'm Marie."

He just wrinkled his brow. "Minnie?"

"Yes, that's what I said," I amended quickly.

He studied me for a minute. "You look familiar."

Next time I'd have to change my appearance a bit more. Obviously he'd recognized me from the office. "I get that a lot," I told him quickly and sat down.

He frowned at me, then picked up his drink, sipping it through a straw, and I noticed the distinct lack of fangs in his mouth. I studied him for a moment, then had to ask. "Are you sure you're a vampire?"

He stared at me, appalled. "Are you asking to see my fangs?"

"Maybe?"

"Am I asking to see your tail?"

Point taken. I gave him a tight smile and stuck my hand out. "Let's start this over again. Hi, I'm Minnie, your date for tonight."

He took my hand and clasped my fingers, the most limp handshake I'd ever received. Worse, his hands were clammy.

But I didn't care if he was unattractive; after all, I didn't want to sleep with him. I just wanted him to turn me.

He had a strangely appealing scent, I noticed. Pleasant and warm, like sunshine or fresh cookies. I liked that about him. Unfortunately it was the only thing I liked about him, given that he continued to stare at me.

"And your name is," I prompted.

"Bert. It was on my profile," he said peevishly.

"Hi, Bert," I said between gritted teeth. "So nice to meet you."

He eyed me up and down, then went back to drinking his water.

"So . . ." I said and smiled again, though it felt tight. "How long have you been a vampire?"

"Long enough," he said, looking at me with irritation. "Look, unless you want me to feed on you, I don't know that this is going to work out."

I sputtered. I just got here and he was dumping me? "Excuse me?"

"I'm sorry to say that you're not my type, Minnie. You looked more attractive in your picture."

I stared at him in surprise. This lump was dumping *me*? Really?

"So," he said, swirling his straw in his glass and making the ice clink against the sides rapidly, "we can skip the small talk. If you're looking for a one-night stand with a vampire, I'm your man. Right now I'm so thirsty, I'll drink just about anything that walks through that door." As if to prove his point, his fangs distended. I watched in horror as they pushed past his parted lips, then retracted again.

Oh, *ew*.

"But if you're looking for something long term, I don't think we're compatible."

"I just sat down," I protested. "How do you know we're not compatible?"

And why on earth was I arguing with this revolting creature about my attractiveness?

"I'm a visual connoisseur, Minnie," he said in an utterly serious voice. "And you have a few things working against you. Those eyebrows. Those glasses. And I like women with more assets. You need a bit more donk in your badonkadonk."

"You think I don't have enough junk in my *trunk*?" I said loudly, causing the sushi chef to look over at us with a frown.

Bert shrugged. "A man can't help what he likes. Some men like breasts, legs, or necks. I'm more of a bottom aficionado."

More like a bottom *feeder*. Ugh. Maybe I wasn't all that desperate after all.

I tried one last time. "Before I go, can I ask you how you feel about turning your partner?"

He snorted. "As if. I wouldn't turn you if you paid me."

"Well, I think I'm done here. Good-bye, Bert."

I arrived at the agency a short time later, plunked one Red Bull down on Ryder's desk, and stomped back to my desk.

"Date went well?" Ryder said in a faux cheerful voice.

"He told me I wasn't his type," I said between gritted teeth. "Too much glasses and eyebrows. Not enough badonkadonk."

"*Reaaaallly*." She popped open the Red Bull and added some to her newest mug of coffee. "You should note on his file that he's an ass man."

I snorted. "An ass man who's an asshole."

"Har har, very funny. So are you done with this now?" she asked hopefully.

"No," I said firmly. "Just because the first one was a pig doesn't mean they all are."

"Marie, sweetie, if they could catch a woman on their own, they wouldn't need the agency, would they? All you're going to find are pigs."

But I refused to give up. I pulled open the database and immediately began to search for the next victim.

I would find someone to turn me. I *would*.

Chapter Four

All the same, I plucked my eyebrows. Even I could take a hint.

When I came in the next evening, Sara gave me a wave from her desk, where she was perched on the massive thigh of her mate, Ramsey Bjorn, the biggest, scariest man I'd ever seen. It was odd to see them together, but she didn't seem frightened of him in the slightest. The were-bear held a game controller in his massive hands, and as I walked past, Sara snatched it away. "Let me do it. You're all thumbs."

He growled.

She growled back, the rumble low in her throat.

I set my purse on my desk and sat down, avoiding them. Shifters were weird, and I supposed it was a good thing that they were off-limits. I wasn't sure that I wanted to growl and snarl, and I had an aversion to fleas. Still, the way Ramsey watched her—hungry, possessive, adoring—made me feel a little wistful. Here I was stuck with Bert the vampire who thought I didn't have enough donk in my badonk.

"Oh good, you're here," Ryder said cheerfully, approaching my desk and dumping a stack of folders on it. "Nice brows."

"Shut up," I said, mimicking her cheerful voice.

Sara glanced over at me. "I almost forgot to tell you—Bath has a new project she wants us to work on."

I stifled a groan. When did Bath not have a project? I didn't have time for this; I was busy trying to find myself a vampire. "Oh goody," I said. "What kind of project?"

"You and I," Ryder said, adding another stack of folders to my already towering stack, "are going to call everyone who hasn't used the service in over a year, and ask them to come back because of the *great* dating selection we have now."

I picked up a folder and glanced at it. Not a vampire. Not interested. "So we're lying to them?"

Across the room, Ramsey snorted.

"Not really a lie," Sara said, shutting down her computer and tossing the control into the inbox on her desk. "More like fudging the truth to drum up business."

"I thought business was fine."

"But why settle for this when we can have even *more* business? That's Bath's new motto." Sara stood up and grabbed Ramsey's big hand, dragging him to his feet. "We want to keep things bustling."

I kind of liked it when things were quiet. "So we're just supposed to magically find all these female shapeshifters that need a date and somehow convince them that they need to use our service?"

"Something like that."

The doorbell clanged and in sauntered my nemesis, Joshua Russell. I tossed the folder back down on the stack. "Problem solved," I said dryly. "We'll just have everyone date Josh."

Ryder giggled.

Sexy, irritating Josh winked in my direction and I ignored it, because sometimes I hoped that if I wished hard enough, he'd fall off the planet and disappear. So far, no dice.

"I see my gorgeous Marie is thrilled to see me once again," he said, going to the chair that Sara and Ramsey had just vacated. He flipped it around and straddled it, his grin making crinkles form around those gorgeous, long-lashed eyes. "Don't take her hard words to heart. She has a secret spot in her heart for me. I don't know if you guys noticed, but she always pays special attention when I show up."

Sara giggled.

I hated that man. "*Ostie de tabarnak.* I wish you'd go away."

"No, you don't," he said easily.

"Yes, I really do."

"Quit speaking all that sexy French at me if you want me to leave."

"I'm cussing at you, *tête de cochon*."

"Oh, I know that one! I think she just called you a pig-head," Ryder said with a cheeky grin. "She called me one the other day, too."

He didn't look discouraged in the slightest. "Dirty French words are Marie's way of foreplay. That's how I know she loves me."

I wanted to bang my head on my keyboard in frustration. "Please. Please just go away."

"Now, Marie," he drawled. "If you wanted me to go away, why'd you doll up and look so damn beautiful?"

I flushed. Crap. He'd noticed my makeup for my next date? I had to be more subtle.

I avoided making eye contact with Sara. If she found out what I was doing, she'd tell Bathsheba. If Bathsheba found out I was using the service without permission during working hours, my ass would be out on the street. She might have been okay with it once upon a time, given that she'd used the service to meet Beau, but with the shifter issues going on, *human* was a dirty word right now. Combine that with the fact that I'd need to date during office hours? It was best that I just didn't ask at all. I noticed Ryder looked suddenly busy, as well.

"Maybe Marie just wanted to look pretty today," Sara said lightly. "I don't think it has anything to do with you, Josh."

"Don't be so sure, Sara. It always has to do with me. All the girls want a piece of me," he said with a grin, clearly joking. When Ramsey cast a black look in his direction, he amended it. "Almost all girls."

Sara grinned and slipped a hand around Ramsey's massive waist. She glanced back at me. "We're off for the evening. Bath said to call her if you had questions about the project, and leave her a report in the morning."

"See you," I said casually, picking up the first folder in the stack and pretending to be interested in it. I was more than ready for all of them to leave the office, so I could check whether a vampire had responded to Minnie's profile. And I couldn't do that if they were all sitting right there.

That was the bad thing about such a small, intimate business. My boss, Bathsheba Ward-Russell, was married to the head of the Paranormal Alliance, Beau Russell. The two businesses worked closely together and shared records. That meant that Beau was constantly dropping by the office, which was fine. He was handsome, polite, well spoken, and friendly. But it also meant his cadre of brothers and cousins was also stopping by at all hours.

And that drove me crazy. Most of the Russells were nice enough. Jeremiah was the tall, muscular one who showed up to work on the network from time to time. Ellis, Everett, and Austin worked for the security firm that Beau ran, and they popped by to flirt with Ryder, chat with Bath or Sara, and do background checks on clients. The three looked so much alike that I had a hard time telling them apart, save for the one who had a sleeve of tattoos up one arm. All of them were incredibly friendly and nice to everyone in the office.

Joshua was the thorn in my side. In personality, he was nothing like serious, polite, well-dressed Beau. Josh seemed to live in a plain black T-shirt, ass-hugging jeans, and a baseball cap. It didn't hurt that he was flat-out gorgeous to boot. Tall, muscular, and handsome, with an amazing grin and sinfully beautiful eyes that didn't belong on a man.

He was also a flirt who didn't seem to take no for an answer. You would think women would see right through his overbearing, overly flirty personality, but you would think wrong. They loved his flirting, and loved him, and he had the dating records to prove it.

Until he didn't call them back, of course. And he never did.

And unfortunately for me, Josh generally worked the same hours that I did. As a vampire security specialist, he tended to be up all night. That meant he often stopped by the office on his way to work, and again on his way back from his shift.

Ryder didn't mind. She said it livened up our long shift.

I minded. Which only encouraged him more.

Tonight was one of those nights that I'd been hoping he wouldn't show up . . . so naturally he was here, and he was early.

I shot Ryder an uncomfortable look as Sara and Ramsey left for the evening and Josh stood, flipped his chair around, sat again, and put his feet up on Sara's desk. His self-assured gaze rested on me, as if evaluating me. He always watched me as I worked, and I was pretty sure he did it to annoy me. No supernatural could be that interested in a human woman who told him to buzz off repeatedly.

He was just acting so focused and determined to bother me. Typical.

Ryder moved to the coffeepot, preparing the first of several she'd brew tonight.

"So what's the plan, ladies?" Josh gave me a mildly curious look, raising an eyebrow in my direction.

"Gee," I said, flipping open the folder. Female. Mink shifter. Not my target demographic. "I don't know. I thought tonight I'd go out on a limb and do some work. You know, that crazy thing that people expect in exchange for a salary?" I glanced over at him, hoping he'd get the hint. "That thing *you're* supposed to be doing right about now?"

"My client won't be up for another hour or so," he said casually. "I thought I'd hang out for a few in the meantime."

I had my next vampire date in an hour and a half. That was cutting it close.

"New client?" Ryder asked him, picking up her headset and adjusting it over her blond pigtails.

"Yup. Another vampire being stalked by a fellow vampire. Surprise, surprise." He sounded bored. "So the shifter muscle has to show up and throw our weight around to make sure his new friends get the hint."

"I hope he's paying you a lot," Ryder said with a grin.

"Oh, he is," Josh said. "Premium security for a premium price."

I tuned out their conversation and pulled up the

record of my date on the computer, glancing back at the were-mink's folder as cover. My date, a vampire named Lewis, hadn't yet cancelled. Good. I'd tried setting up another date last night, but the guy had cancelled on me once I'd sent him a picture.

To ensure that my date would show up this time, I'd googled "sexy brunette in glasses," picked a suitably suggestive photo, and sent that one. It had been a little white lie, but I didn't care as long as he showed up.

There were thirty-two vampires in the Midnight Liaisons database. Nineteen of them were currently available for dating, and I was already down by two. I was starting to get anxious. I only needed one, but what I needed seemed to be a pretty big favor. I had to tread cautiously.

The cowbell hanging against the front door clanged, and I jerked in surprise.

"Little jumpy tonight, aren't we?" Josh teased.

I glared at him and didn't dignify that with a response.

A trio of loud, noisy men entered the office and my heart sank all over again. "Just what we needed," I said with a sour look. "More Russells."

Austin pulled up a chair across from Ryder, and the twins sat down at Sara's desk. I didn't know which ones were Josh's cousins and which ones were his brothers; they all looked like they were cut from the same mold. Tall. Muscled. Incredibly good-looking. Dark, thick hair. Same rakish smile. The twins had deep dimples, though, and one had a sleeve of tattoos. Jeremiah was quiet and soft spoken, but he didn't show up around the agency much anymore, now that he was in a relationship with a were-fox. Well, rumor had it that he was in a relationship with a were-fox and another guy, but that was probably just rumor.

"Can I help you boys?" Ryder asked with a slow, sweet drawl. "You dropping by the agency to see me, or were you wanting a date?"

"Always dropping by to see you, of course," Josh said lazily, giving me that sleepy, sexy look.

I ignored him.

Austin leaned back in his chair and yawned, lacing his fingers behind his head as if he was bored. He fixed his gaze on Josh, who hadn't moved from where he was parked across from my desk. "We saw the car out front and figured you were in here setting up another date. Since you're making other plans, Everett wanted to know if that hot little number from the dance was up for grabs."

Josh shrugged, his gaze on me. "Don't know. You up for grabs, Marie?"

"Very funny."

"I'm serious," he said.

I rolled my eyes at him.

"The hot one," Everett emphasized. "Werelynx. With the dress."

"The blonde?" Ellis asked. "With the rack?"

Austin shook his head. "The redhead. The one with the freckles and the . . ." He coughed, getting flustered at Ryder's direct stare. "Uh, sports car."

"For the record, I went to the dance with Jayde Sommers," Josh said. "And we're not seeing each other anymore."

Oh, I was sure that hot-tempered Jayde loved that. She wasn't one of my favorite clients. "Gee, that's a shame," I said in a voice that implied that I didn't think it was a shame at all. "I'm crushed you two didn't work out."

Josh shrugged.

I pulled my keyboard close. "Well, since you're here, who did you want to be fixed up with, since you're no longer seeing Jayde?"

"I was never *seeing* Jayde," he pointed out. "She was just a date once or twice. And I'm not here to get set up with anyone."

"It was the were-tigress," Ellis announced after a minute. "The tall one. Looks like a super-model."

Everett snapped his fingers. "That's the one."

"Rebecca," Josh said with a grin. "Nice girl."

"Not too nice, I hope," Everett said with a frown. "I like 'em wild."

"Nope, not too nice," Josh said amiably. "Nicer than Marie here, though."

"Marie would be a lot nicer if you would go away," I said sweetly. "And if I get you Rebecca's number, can we make that happen?"

"We can," Everett said with a grin. "You get me her number and I'm buying everyone in this room wings and beer."

"How do you know she'll want to date you?

Maybe your brother made her swear off were-cougars forever."

Everett gave me a smug look. "I can be persuasive, though I'm not as smooth as Josh here."

I gave him the number and all the men left, laughing and teasing each other.

When Josh looked back and gave me a wink, Ryder grinned and returned to her computer. "Boys will be boys."

"Those weren't boys. Those were men in need of a hobby."

"Or a girlfriend," Ryder said lightly.

I glanced at the clock. Twenty minutes before my date. I grabbed my purse and headed out the door. "I'm going. Cover for me!"

"Yay, more Red Bull," Ryder said, twirling her finger in the air.

"I'll be back soon," I told her. "Wish me luck."

A half hour after my date's scheduled time, I had to accept the fact that I'd been stood up. I'd sat at a table for two in the small, dark, popular little Greek restaurant, drumming my fingers on the tabletop and waiting.

Câlice.

Why was it so hard to find a damn vampire to date me? I was young. I was single. I was O freaking positive. I'd sent a suggestive picture as Minnie. I was making myself available. What was I doing wrong?

Desperation made me feel suddenly exhausted,

and I rubbed my eyes. I hadn't slept in three days, and it was wearing on me. I wanted a nice, long nap, but that was useless. As soon as I lay down and closed my eyes, I was unable to sleep.

Sleep was torture. I'd lie in bed, exhausted and aching, but sleep never came. It was the most frustrating thing in the world—to know that most people could just turn over and go to sleep while I'd stare at the ceiling for hours, wishing I knew how to shut my brain off so I could get in a few hours of rest.

But I had to keep going. Find a vampire somehow. I got up from the table and dropped a few dollars for the soda I'd downed, ignoring the pitying looks of the waitstaff. I made my way out of the sea of closely crowded tables, pushing through the front door. The parking lot was busy despite the late hour, so I cut around to the back alley. I didn't want anyone to see me leaving, in case a client spotted me and mentioned it to someone at the agency.

Damn, this stung. Was I truly so unappealing? My pride was starting to feel wounded. More than that, my anxiety was skyrocketing. What if I couldn't find a vampire to turn me? What if I died before I could accomplish my goal?

My stomach churning, I ducked my head and walked faster. A text buzzed on my phone and I paused, my heart flipping over with hope. Maybe the vampire was just late? Maybe he'd been held up?

It was Ryder. *Is everything okay? Text me back.*

Sigh. *I'm fine*, I sent back. *He was a no-show. Heading back now.*

I repocketed my phone and glanced up just in

time to see the hindquarters of a large beast slink into the shadows of the alley. I froze. I'd definitely seen a tail, and I was pretty sure I'd seen a paw, but it had been so quick that I doubted my own eyes. Was I crazy?

I wasn't scared, since I worked with shapeshifters, but I was annoyed that I was about to be caught in the act. I studied the alley for a long moment. Run away and assume that the shifter wouldn't report me back? Or be brave and take my lumps? I thought for a moment longer, then sighed, gut-checked myself, and strode forward.

I turned the corner into the dark alley—and ran smack into a naked Joshua. I yelped in surprise, stumbling backward a step even as he reached out to catch me.

"You okay?" His big hand moved to my waist, as if to anchor me against him.

"Fine," I said sharply, pushing away from him and averting my gaze. The glimpse I'd seen of him was . . . well, it was making me feel flushed. I hadn't expected him to be quite so . . . impressive . . . naked. His shoulders were broad and thick with muscle, his stomach flat and delicious, so tight that I'd seen a very nice six pack. I cast my gaze to the ground, and that wasn't any better, because I had a shadowy view of well-muscled thigh and one long, bare foot. I turned and stared at a wall, hating how red my face felt. "What are you doing here?"

"I'm working. Checking out a few scent trails in the area for a client who is convinced he's being stalked by someone. He's not, of course, but that doesn't mean I don't check things out anyhow. What are *you* doing here, Marie?"

"Red Bull run," I told him, falling back on our story line. "Ryder asked for some."

"Really," he said in an amused voice. "Then why is it that your hair smells like olives and feta?"

I looked over at him, startled, and touched my dark curls. "What?"

"Olives. Feta. Greek." He touched his nose and grinned at me, looking tousled and like he'd just gotten out of bed. He gestured back down the front alley. "Were you at the restaurant?"

"No," I said defensively, clutching my purse to my chest. I kept my gaze on his handsome face, not daring to look any lower, since his arms were crossed over his chest and that meant the rest of him was, well . . . open for business. "Of course not. I'm just on break."

"Then why are you slinking away down a dark alley so no one can see you?"

"I like dark alleys," I said defensively.

"They're dangerous. You should be careful."

Getting mugged in an alley was the least of my problems. But I forced out a tight "Fine." I turned and began to march away. "I'm going now."

"Wait, Marie," he said, and I heard him fall into step behind me. *Damn it, damn it.* "What's it worth to you for me to keep my mouth shut about you hanging out at a vampire joint when you're supposed to be working?"

I stopped in my tracks.

He ran into me this time and he chuckled, then moved to the side. I felt his big hand graze my hips, sending a tingle through my body, before he moved away. "Going to make me guess?"

I ignored him, turning to glare at his face. "I wasn't at a vampire joint."

"You smell like Greek food. Didn't you know that Konstantine's is run by a vampire? It's well known in the Alliance that it's a vampire feeding ground."

It hadn't been known to me. I thought our clients liked the place because it was dark and private. Why did no one fill me in on these things?

"So." He rocked on his heels. "What's it worth to you to keep me quiet?"

"Are you blackmailing me?" I gave him an outraged look.

"Only for information," he said with an easy grin. "You tell me which vampire you're in love with and I'll keep my mouth shut."

I hesitated.

He crossed his arms over his chest, waiting.

Criss. I kept my eyes locked on his face. He had me. "How do I know I can trust you?"

He laughed. "You found a naked shapeshifter in an alley who's twice the size of you, standing close enough to rub against you. And you're worried you can't trust me?"

Point taken. "You're not twice my size," I felt obligated to point out. "More like one and a half times."

He put a hand to his chest in mock pain. "You wound me, Marie. Never tell a man he's smaller than he claims."

His motion made my gaze go to his chest, and I noticed the fuzzy sprinkling of hair across his broad pectorals. Odd how that was so appealing. The pectorals themselves were something close to a work of art—flat, hard, and smooth. Like little bricks of man-muscle—

Josh snapped his fingers at me.

I flushed, realizing I was staring at his naked chest. "Sorry."

"So what's his name?"

"I hate you for making me tell," I said, then dug my phone out of my purse, glancing at the note in my calendar. "Lewis."

"Boy, it must be love if you can't remember the guy's name," Josh said, and snatched the phone from my hands, beginning to flip through my calendar.

"Hey," I protested. "Give that back!"

But he began to saunter away, phone in hand. "Let's see. Two nights ago, it was Bert. And Valjean's here, too. Why, Marie, you minx you. I had no idea you were a vampire groupie."

I reached for the phone over his shoulder even though I had to brush up against his naked chest. "Give that back!"

He held it out of reach and turned around, grinning when I lunged against him again. His other arm went to my waist, pulling me close, and I found my mouth inches from his, my body pressed up against his naked chest.

I became instantly aware of his very, very naked flesh. How hard he was all over, how big and strong. He loomed over me, tall, but not overwhelming. Just . . . right. Just delicious. My pulse fluttered in response.

"Why do you want a vampire, Marie?" Josh's gaze dipped to my mouth, as if he was contemplating kissing me. Then he glanced back up to meet my gaze. His voice dropped to a husky, seductive tone. "If you want to play with your wild side, I'm right here and more than willing."

I pushed him away. "I'm not looking for a one-night stand."

He gave me a bemused smile. "Aren't you? Then what's with all the vampires?"

I bit the inside of my cheek, instantly regretting saying anything. Humans weren't supposed to have ongoing relationships with supernaturals. We were okay for a fling here and there, but commitment? Wasn't allowed.

I reached for my phone again. "Just give that back to me."

He held it over my head for a moment longer, but when I wouldn't play this time, he handed it to me.

I glared at him and stalked away. He was far too naked for me to be comfortable, and I'd noticed far too much of his physique for my own good.

"I'm betting Lewis didn't show up tonight, did he?"

I paused. Gritted my teeth.

"I can help you with that, you know."

Damn it. Why did he have to keep talking? And how did he seem to know that my vampire date hadn't shown up? I turned around slowly. He hadn't followed me this time, and now he stood twenty feet away, which allowed me a full frontal vision of his Adonis-like body.

Naturally, I realized this a moment too late and yelped, raising a hand to cover my eyes.

Too late. The vision of Joshua Russell, male perfection in one arrogant, cocky package, was now burned into my mind. Those tight hips, narrow waist, broad shoulders. That small birthmark on his groin just to the left of some very . . . impressive equipment. Great. Now I was going to be thinking about his birthmark whenever I saw him. "I can't talk to you unless you put some clothes on," I snapped.

"Come on now, Marie," he drawled, a chuckle in his voice. "You know shifters aren't shy about nudity."

"This human is!"

"I thought you liked what you were looking at? You were staring earlier."

"*Ostie de tabarnak,*" I spat at him.

"Oooh, the French. Now I know I'm getting somewhere."

"Joshua Russell!"

"Okay, fine, I'll get decent."

I paused, waiting a moment, then moved my

hand and peeked at him again. He stood there, still facing me, still full frontal, hands on his hips.

And he was getting erect.

I covered my eyes again. "You said you were getting decent!"

"Give me a minute to get excited, and I'll be plenty decent." He gave me a sultry look. "You could always take your top off and help things along."

"That is not what I meant! You are a pig, Joshua Russell."

"And you're too shy, Marie Bellavance." He said my name with the flat drawl of a Southerner. "It's good for you to look at a man every now and then. Get that stick out of your ass."

I did not have a stick up my ass. "If you're not helping me, then I am leaving now," I announced again.

"I'll change," he said. "Give me two minutes, and I'll finish scouting the area and grab my clothes. Then I'll follow you back to the agency to make sure no one takes advantage of you."

"Good idea," I said, a bite to my voice. "It would be terrible if I was accosted in a dark alley by a naked man."

He chuckled. "It's only accosting if you don't enjoy it. And you enjoyed it."

"I did not." Even if I had, I would never, ever tell him that.

"I'm changing now," he announced.

I could have turned and walked away. He would have let me, I knew. Josh came on strong, but that was because he assumed that everyone found him utterly irresistable.

But for some reason, I stayed. Partially because I did want to find out exactly what he thought of the vampires avoiding me, and partially because this would give me a good chance to look at his naked body undistracted. I peeked, watching him. Just a little. His buttocks had the most amazing dimple that flexed when he changed, and my pulse sped up in response. But then he sprouted fur and began to contort, and I covered my eyes again.

Not the glamorous side of being a shifter. I winced when I heard bones crack, and I kept my eyes covered, waiting. Long moments passed, and when I was just about to open my eyes and ask what was going on, something furry rubbed up against my leg. I opened my eyes to see a massive dun cougar stalking away from me, his tail lashing slowly back and forth. He sniffed the alleyway carefully and moved forward, then glanced back at me.

I relaxed a little. "I like you much better like this. Quiet and not naked."

He made a chuffing noise that might have been a laugh. And then he began to sniff around again. I paced a few steps behind him as he followed a scent trail, moving along the back alley and turning down another, before doubling back and rechecking the area he'd already gone over.

The back door to Konstantine's opened, letting out a waft of delicious scents. I stopped just as a man in a dirty apron emerged and headed for the Dumpster. He paused at the sight of me, and then Josh, his eyes widening in alarm.

Shit! I'd just been caught with a shifter in cat-form. The Alliance was going to kill me. I was—

Josh meowed, a sad, pathetic, house-cat meow.

"Bad kitty," I said automatically, figuring out his plan. Genius! I smiled at the man standing frozen in the alley. "Silly cat refuses to go potty on the grass."

"*That's* your cat?" He took a step backward, uncertain.

"All mine," I said, and snapped my fingers at my side. Josh immediately came to my hand, rubbing up against my fingers and purring wildly. I scratched at his face, his whiskers, and he began to lick my fingers, and then my palm.

It . . . tickled. And made me a little squirmy, knowing that there was a human brain behind all that licking. What was going through his mind right now?

The man in the apron chatted with me as he tossed bags into the Dumpster, giving side glances at Josh as he made out with my hand while I stood making small talk. The man told me about his pet dog, and how he'd once seen a big cat at the zoo, and asked me where I'd gotten mine. I told him that my cougar was a gift. And Josh was great at obeying. Harmless. Declawed, I added. All this time, Josh kept licking and nuzzling at my hand.

As soon as the man disappeared back into the restaurant, I jerked my hand away from Josh. "Is this the shifter version of first base?"

He chuffed at me again, then turned, batting at my leg with his tail, indicating that I should follow once more. I did, and he took me down a set of alleys, leading me through the backstreets of downtown Fort Worth, before we came to a neatly stashed pile of clothing and shoes.

He paused, staring at me expectantly.

"Time to change?" I asked.

He reached out and licked my hand again.

"I'm going to take that as a yes. Go on, then." I turned around, picked up his cell phone, and clicked on it, payback for his snatching my phone.

Locked. Darn. So much for my chance to snoop. I waited until Josh finished changing, listening to the sound of clothing rustling as he dressed. Then he leaned over my shoulder and neatly plucked his phone out of my hands. "That's mine."

"Afraid I'll get all the numbers of your girlfriends and tell them about how you've been harassing me in an alley?"

"What, and give away all my smooth moves?" he teased. "Let's get back to the agency. I imagine Ryder's waiting. I assume she's in on this scheme of yours?"

She was, and she was going to kill me if I showed up at the agency with Josh.

We walked back to the small strip mall off a service road. Midnight Liaisons had an unassuming storefront, since the last thing we wanted was to draw attention to our business. The lights were on inside, as they were twenty-four hours a day, but the blinds were pulled shut. When I entered the small waiting room, I frowned to see that all four desks in the main office were empty. I glanced over at Ryder's desk. Her purse was still hanging off the back of her chair.

Not good.

I turned to Josh. "Can you wait here for a minute?"

He shrugged. "Or I could sit down and we can talk for a bit and explore this vampire fetish—"

That was the last thing I wanted right now. "Just . . . stay . . . here," I said, placing my hands on his chest and giving him a nudge backward.

He put his hand over mine, as if to hold it. "I know you want your hands on me, Marie, but think of how jealous poor Ryder will be."

I shoved him harder, ignoring the boyish grin on his face. "I'm going to talk to Ryder, and then we're going to head out for a bit."

"We are?" He seemed surprised. "Shouldn't you be 'working' at your 'job'?" He made air quotes, teasing me.

"Shouldn't you?" I hissed back at him. "You're being paid to track something, right? So go track." When he didn't move, I sighed. "Give me two minutes and I'll tell Ryder where we're going. Just wait here." I didn't want him following me in.

I half expected him to follow me in, but he did as I asked. I hitched my purse closer on my shoulder, braced myself, and headed to the back conference room, where I knew I'd find Ryder.

I cracked the door open just enough to see scaly

flesh and curled wings. One misshapen arm shot out, clearly re-forming. The creature turned to me, eyes wild, and I recognized Ryder's bright blue gaze in that awful face.

"Hey," I said softly, forcing myself to ignore the fact that she was turning into a monster right before my eyes. "I'm taking Josh and we're going to go get something to eat. Call me if you need me, okay?"

The hand wavered, shuddered, and clenched. Then she slowly raised it into the air and jabbed a thumbs-up.

I gave her the thumbs-up sign back and shut the door, leaving her to her business.

After all, I knew all about secrets. There were some things you just didn't want other people to know. I swept through the office and brushed past Josh to the front door. "Come on. There's bound to be something open this late."

Chapter Five

There was a time when I'd have been excited about going out to a late-night dinner with a gorgeous man. A time when, if he'd put his hand on the small of my back to guide me down the sidewalk, I'd have shivered with delight. Tonight I had a handsome, gorgeous man with his hand on my back, walking at my side, and it just bothered me. I was filled with annoyance. What did Josh so arrogantly think he could teach me about dating a male vampire? I was the one who worked at a dating agency, after all.

I strode down the sidewalk and tried not to think about Ryder, who was having a bad night. Instead, I focused on my situation, since it was a worse night for me. Josh easily kept up with my angry strides, his big form staying protectively next to me.

He gestured at a nearby restaurant. "How about that?"

I eyed the yellow sign with a frown. "A diner?"

He grinned down at me and I was distracted by how close he was, by his touch on my lower back. "Why not? Open all night."

"It just seems so . . ."

"Casual? It's not a date." His hand nudged my lower back, directing me toward the restaurant's lit parking lot.

My mouth tightened. Of course it wasn't a date. "You don't need to remind me. And since you picked, you're paying."

"Why? It's not a date."

I gritted my teeth. "Fine."

When we got inside, the elderly waitress lit up at the sight of Josh. "There's my boy," she crowed in a voice that sounded as if she'd smoked too many cigarettes. "How are you, Josh darlin'?"

He gave the small, stout woman a bear hug. "I'm pining away with love for you, Carol."

She gave a raspy chuckle and swatted his bottom. "You want your usual?"

"You know I do." He glanced over at me. "I brought a friend. She'll probably want a menu."

The waitress glanced over at me, her nest of overly bleached curls tilting as she studied me, then she squeezed him in a half hug. "You go pick a table and sit anywhere. I'll get your food started."

"You're an angel," he said with a grin.

I rolled my eyes and followed him to a rounded booth in the far corner of the nearly empty restaurant. When I slid in on one side, Josh slid in right next to me. I immediately scooted all the way around to the far end, putting some distance between us.

That seemed to amuse him, which only made me more irritated.

"I see why you wanted to come here. You get free food every night just because you flirt with the old ladies?"

He grinned. "Not every night, and I don't flirt. They just love me."

As if to prove this point, Carol showed up with two glasses of water and a coffee for Josh. She set it down in front of him, tugged his ballcap off his head in a proprietary move that surprised me, then smoothed his hair like a mother. "No hats inside, young man."

Josh gave her a rueful smile. "Sorry."

He looked even more boyish with his hair sticking up wildly. If it hadn't been for the scruff on his face, he would have looked far too young.

"This one's too charming for his own good," Carol said affectionately, chucking Josh's unshaved chin as if she'd been a doting mother—or grandmother.

"He only thinks he's charming," I pointed out. "He just expects everyone else to think it, too."

She chuckled again, that horrible smoker's rasp. "I like this one, Josh."

My face colored, which made Josh grin.

"You want the same thing he's having, honey?" she asked me.

Anything to get her away from the two of us. "Sure. Thank you."

She put a coffee mug down in front of me and filled it, then left with another smile at Josh.

"So that's your schtick?" I said irritably. "To be a charming freeloader?"

"First of all," he said, lifting the coffee cup to his lips, "I pay for everything. Carol doesn't make enough to buy me dinner on a regular basis." He sipped it and then grimaced. "Her coffee is shit, though."

But I noticed he still drank it. Maybe telling her would hurt her feelings.

"And second?" I prompted, opening a few sugar packets and dumping them into my cup.

"Carol works four nights a week. Her husband died three years ago and she lives in a small apartment on the bad side of town. It scares her to take the bus, so she tries to get a ride with friends. I stop in to check on her and give her a ride when she needs it."

That was . . . unexpectedly nice of him. "So she's a shifter, too?"

"No," he said. "Just a lady with no one to look after her. So I do."

I said nothing. Carol swung out of the kitchen with two massive stacks of pancakes and plopped them down in front of us, then dropped a bottle of syrup on the table. I stared at the massive stack. That was a lot of pancakes.

Josh put a hand over his heart and gave Carol a pleased look. "You make my heart melt with your delicious food."

She chuckled again. "I'll be back with the rest when it comes off the grill. Dig in."

As she left, I eyed the pancake mountain, then looked over at Josh. "The . . . rest?"

He leaned in. "You ordered the same thing I get, right? Perhaps you didn't realize that shifters eat a lot?"

I admit it hadn't been the first thing on my mind. "So what exactly did I order?"

"Two club sandwiches, a skillet scramble, these pancakes," he said, pointing. "And a steak."

"A freaking steak? With all this? That's revolting."

"Does that mean I get to eat yours?"

"Only if you want to buy it from me," I said, mashing my fork into the pat of butter on top of the pancake mountain. "That's what I get for trusting a pretty face."

"So you think I'm pretty? Marie, you flirt, you."

"*Voyons*. It's a figure of speech, *tabarnak*."

"And more French. You know that's sexy, right?"

"You know I just called you vile things, right?"

"That's how you flirt."

"I hate you."

"More flirting."

I ground my teeth and forced myself not to reply, since he'd practically consider it a declaration of love. Instead, I focused on swamping my pancakes with syrup, then taking a bite. Delicious. I'd be totally wound up from the sugar and coffee later, but it didn't matter. It wasn't like I could sleep anyhow. I ate a few more bites in companionable silence as Josh neatly cut his pancakes into perfect triangles and ate them without a bit of syrup.

Carol stopped by with the rest of the food by the time I'd eaten three pancakes and was feeling full. Josh, meanwhile, had polished off all of his pancakes and was more than ready for the next course. While I retreated to my coffee, he dug into the sandwiches, scrambled eggs, and steak, chatting with Carol for a few minutes. He asked her how her job was going, and listened attentively when she complained about a coworker who was taking all the extra shifts. He asked about her hot water heater, which hadn't been working properly in the last month, and volunteered to take a look at it. She turned him down with a wave of her hand. He even asked about her cat. Carol left a few minutes later, smiling.

I digested it all in silence. It was clear that Josh knew the woman well and took an interest in her life. That seemed . . . odd to me. Josh was such a love-them-and-leave-them type that I hadn't imagined him to be the kind to chat with lonely elderly ladies.

There was another side to the incorrigible flirt. Either that, or this was all an elaborate ruse to get women to fall into his arms. Take them to a low-key diner, charm them with his relationship with an old, down-on-her-luck woman, then they'd tumble into his bed faster than the speed of light.

Even as I told myself that, it didn't fit. What playboy was going to hang out at a diner with an old woman to talk about her cats?

"So," I said when we were alone again. "You were going to tell me what I'm doing wrong?"

He stopped eating, wiped his mouth with his napkin, and nodded. "First, I need to know the whole thing. How many vampires have you gone out with?"

I hesitated, wondering if I should tell him everything. Well, if I couldn't get a vampire to show up for a date, it wouldn't matter. I had to take my chances with Josh. "I've gone out with three. At least, I *tried* to go out with three. First there was Valjean—"

Josh shook his head immediately. "He's hooked up and left for Europe. You know Ruby Sommers? Pretty little were-jaguar? Sister to Jayde?"

I didn't, but it was clear that he knew all the "pretty little were-jaguars" in town, which made my teeth grit. "I know he's hooked up. Anyhow, we never went out. I went out with Bert."

He laughed. "No way. Seriously? World of Hurt Bert?"

I wasn't going to have any teeth left if I kept grinding them. "He's a vampire, isn't he?"

"Only in the barest sense of the word. The man's a loser. I can't believe you went out with him."

And Bert had told me that I wasn't his type. That stung a bit more right now than it should have. "It was only one date."

He nodded. "Turned you down, didn't he?"

I gaped. "How did you know that?"

"I did a spin of guard duty for Bert last summer. He likes 'em . . ." He gestured, indicating a rather large butt, and then began to jiggle his hands.

"Yes, I know," I hissed, slapping his hands down. "Badonkadonk."

"I was going to say 'big booty hos', but that works," he said with a laugh. "Anyhow, that's why he's single. He's selective, and the dating pool is kind of lean when it comes to that sort of thing. No pun intended."

I rolled my eyes. "Yes, well, number two turned me down, too. He didn't even show up to our date."

He nodded. "I'm not surprised."

"Why are you not surprised? I am."

"Vampires tend to be skittish."

I eyed the Russell Security T-shirt that he wore. "I noticed. So they're paranoid?"

"To the extreme," he agreed, sipping his coffee again with a grimace. "Vampires are a dog-eat-dog society. You look at someone's blood partner the wrong way, and you could find yourself with a contract on your head. You go into someone's territory and set up shop, there's a contract on your head. It's like the mafia with fangs. The smart ones lay low or leave town fast."

That sounded awful. There was so much that I didn't know about vampires, and I was quickly realizing that Josh could help fill in some of the fuzzy edges. "So what's a blood partner?"

"A vampire's mate is called a blood partner. Blood partners only drink from each other. And since vampire women are rare, you'll find a lot more single male vampires, since every female that isn't partnered pretty much has her choice of men."

Interesting. That sounded like it could work in my favor. If vampire females were highly prized, my willingness to become a vampire female would probably be looked upon positively. "So why aren't there many vampire females?"

"Same thing as female shifters, I imagine," he said. "You're marrying into a family that's not exactly the most fun to get along with. And I hear it's quite painful for the victim if the turning doesn't take—or it kills them."

That wasn't a deterrent for me. I was dying anyhow, so I'd take my chances. I rubbed my eyes, feeling suddenly a bit tired. The more I found out about vampires, the less I wanted to become one, but I was low on choices. Very low. "So vampires are skittish and think everyone is out to get them. Is that why my date didn't show up?"

"That's my guess. Either that, or he didn't like the way you looked and had second thoughts."

I scowled. "I look perfectly acceptable."

"You're beautiful," he agreed.

I was momentarily flabbergasted. "I . . . thank you."

"To me," he amended. "Vampires like different things."

Oh, I remembered. Badonkadonk. Still, I felt warm under Josh's flattery and didn't even mind the reminder. "So what is it about me you'd change?"

He studied me for a long moment, the intense scrutiny making my cheeks flush. His gaze swept over my face, then my chest, then back over my face again. A smile curved his sexy mouth. "I wouldn't change anything."

My cheeks felt as if they'd been on fire.

"But we're not talking about me. You're talking about hooking a vampire . . . unless you changed your mind and decided you want me instead?"

Figured that he'd bring the conversation back around to how sexy he was. I kicked him under the table. "I didn't change my mind. Tell me about what I need to do to get a vampire."

"You girls and your weird vampire fetishes," he said with a shake of his head. "You know dating a vampire's not like it is on TV, right?"

"I'm not stupid."

"No, you're not, but I am questioning your taste in men." At my glare, he raised a placating hand. "Fine, then. Let's start with the basics. You went through the agency?"

I said nothing, suddenly nervous. Josh was the brother-in-law of my boss. If she knew that I was using the database for my own personal needs, I'd be fired in a red-hot minute. That was a big no-no, especially since I was only a marginal member of the Alliance.

Of course, Bathsheba had dated through the agency herself, once upon a time. Anytime it came up, however, she was quick to explain that it hadn't been her choice—she'd been blackmailed into it to hide the fact that Sara was a werewolf. She didn't want Ryder and me dating through the agency because the fact that a human had used the service had stirred up a real hornet's nest among the shifter clans. Some wanted to date humans, but more of them didn't want us contaminating the works. I could understand it, even if it was cross with all of my own plans.

Josh sighed at my reluctance. "I'm not going to rat on you, Marie. If I was, would we be here?"

I had no idea. But I supposed I had to trust someone—I was getting nowhere fast on my own, and I didn't have a ton of vampires in the database to experiment with. "I'm in the database. As Minnie Michigo. Were-otter."

The nod of approval came slowly. "Michigo was a good choice. Lots of them in the area."

Strange, how flustered I felt when I had his approval. "That's why I picked them. Plus, they're not a bigger predator that could be intimidating."

He nodded again, his expression thoughtful. "Your no-show could have run a background check and found out that Minnie didn't exist." He pulled out his phone and began to flip through screens.

"What are you doing?" I asked warily.

"Looking up Minnie's profile." Then he frowned, looking back up at me. "No picture?"

"I send it if they ask for it," I said defensively. "Why should looks matter?"

"Because you're dealing with men," he said bluntly. "Did you send a picture to this last guy? Send it to me."

I sent the photo to Josh's profile.

His eyes widened. "What the hell is this?"

I crossed my arms over my chest, feeling defensive. "Just a picture I pulled off the internet. I thought it might convey fun and lightheartedness." You know, all those things I wasn't good at myself. "It's kind of a silly pose, but I thought it might look natural."

Josh continued to stare at the picture, and then back at me. "That's not you, right?"

I snorted. "No, that's not me. She's putting her fist in her mouth, and I can't do that."

"Marie," he said slowly. "That's not her fist. That's not even her body part."

I snatched the phone away from him and studied it for a minute . . . good God. "I . . . oh." A hot flush crept over my face, and I quickly handed the phone back to him. "I thought it was just a silly picture," I said defensively.

He threw back his head and laughed. "Well, I think I'm beginning to see why date number three was afraid to meet you."

"Shut *up*."

Josh only grinned at me. He glanced back down at the picture, shook his head, then clicked his phone off and tossed it on the table. He slouched in the booth, his gaze moving over me.

I internally squirmed. "What?"

"I see three main problems."

"Well, what are they?"

"You sure you want to know?"

Now he was just torturing me. "Of course I want to know," I said, feeling exasperated. "Would I be sitting here in the middle of the night with you if I didn't?"

He winced and clutched a hand to his chest, as if shot through the heart. Those long-lashed eyes closed dramatically. "Marie, that hurts me. Deeply." His tone was playful, but I got the impression that I had actually hurt his feelings.

"You knew why I was coming here," I said. "Either help me, or leave me alone."

"I'll help you, but I have conditions."

"What kind of conditions?"

"If you want to find a vampire, you have to let me help you."

"Isn't that what I'm doing?"

"No," he said. "I mean *really* help you. You work at a dating agency, right? You help clients make a match." He tapped his chest with a finger, and my gaze went to that tight shirt straining over his big shoulders. "I'm an expert on women."

"I'll just bet you are," I said dryly.

Josh tilted his head, as if studying me. "Don't believe me? I think my track record speaks for itself."

"Oh, it says something, all right. It says that you know how to bait the hook, but—"

"Bait a hook?" he sputtered, laughing.

"—but I haven't seen anything that tells me that you know how to have a relationship," I continued, ignoring his laugh. "You never stick around long enough to find out. You like the chase, Joshua Russell. You get a girl, date her, and then you dump her."

"If we're going to compare fishing to women," he said softly, his eyes gleaming dangerously, "I not only know how to bait the hook but I also know how to reel in my catch. If I'm throwing back what I'm catching, it's because I'm after a different sort of fish."

"The one that got away?" I teased.

He laughed, and the tension was gone. "Something like that."

He made his endless string of dates sound so . . . practical. He stopped dating them because they weren't what he was looking for. That sounded very reasonable. Or was I just falling under his spell? I sighed. "All right. So how can I catch a vampire?"

"You need to *be caught* by a vampire. There's a difference, and that's where I come in. I'll help you bag a vampire, but you have to take my advice seriously if this is going to work."

I watched him uneasily. It was a generous offer, and yet . . . "I don't understand. What are you getting out of this?"

"How about the knowledge that you'll be safe?" His lips tightened, and I found my gaze going to his warm, curving mouth, framed by a day's stubble. "You're human, and you're pretty much approaching every vampire asking them to date you. That's not the safest situation, Marie. Get mixed up with the wrong vampire, and you could be in trouble."

Danger hadn't been on my mind, it was true. I didn't care about the consequences. I hated that he was making me slow down and think about them. "So this is your knight in shining armor thing? Like you do with her?" I thumbed a gesture at Carol, on the far side of the restaurant, taking an order from a trucker. "Patron saint of lost causes?"

"No," he said bluntly. "This is about me giving you what you think you want. I don't know why on earth you want a vampire, but you're determined to get one. And since you're fixed on this course of action, I'm going to help you." He picked up his coffee cup, realized it was empty, and reached for mine. "I want you to see that you really *don't* want a vampire. They're not like in the movies."

"I'm not that shallow," I said quickly. When he brought my cup to his lips and placed his mouth directly over where I'd been drinking, a funny flush went through my body.

"All right, then, maybe I'm the shallow one. Because I see your desire to get it on with a vampire and think that maybe, if I show you how vampires really are, you'll change your mind." Those gorgeous eyes focused on my face, making my mouth go dry. A slow, lazy grin began to spread over his face as he drained my coffee and put the cup down. "Maybe you'll go cougar instead."

Somehow I didn't think he was referring to me dating younger men.

Maybe I should have told him the truth. But the words caught in my throat as he continued to grin at me expectantly. The way he was laughing with me, flirting with me . . .

He was treating me like one of the girls he dated.

And call me crazy, but I liked being attractive to him.

"Why me?" I couldn't help but ask.

I wasn't pretty like Ryder, or flirty. I wasn't soft and feminine like Bathsheba. I was all hard angles, dark hair and glasses. I didn't laugh and joke around like Sara. I was acerbic and distant. What did he see in me that made him stay here? Made him more or less offer a one-night stand if I changed my mind about dating a vampire?

"Because," he said slowly, spinning the small coffee cup with his big fingers, "I've never met anyone as alone as you, Marie. You hold everyone away from you with that icy frown. You need a thawing."

He leaned forward, all devastating grin again. "And I'm pretty sure I could make you melt."

We left the restaurant after that, with me feeling incredibly flustered and unable to converse with Josh. Despite his talk, he'd paid for my dinner and escorted me back to the agency, then left—probably to give Carol a ride home.

I worked for a few more hours, pretending everything was normal, when Ryder eventually slunk back to her desk, every blond hair in place, her clothes neat. She said nothing about her transformation. I said nothing about it, either. If she wanted to talk, I was here.

Ryder never wanted to talk about it, and I understood.

When dawn crept over the horizon, Bath and Beau came into the office. They both looked alert and happy, whereas Ryder and I were dragging, as always, at the end of our shift. They greeted us, then headed on to Bath's office, their heads together as they talked. As soon as they got to the office, the door shut and Bathsheba's laughter trilled out.

Ryder smiled, even as it turned into a yawn. "It's nice to see people in love, isn't it?"

I shrugged. "If you're a hopeless romantic, I guess."

She made a face at me. "We work at a dating agency. We *should* be hopeless romantics."

She had a point.

Ten minutes after eight—as usual—Sara came into the office, an enormous cup of Starbucks in her hand and her mouth looking like she'd just been making out in the car. Which she probably had. "Good morning," she said cheerfully. "You two look fresh as daisies."

"Don't make me growl at you," Ryder teased with another yawn.

"She probably likes that," I said slyly and began to shut down my computer.

Sara only grinned, running a hand through her chin-length, shaggy red hair. "Did you guys get far on Bath's project?"

"Not too far," I admitted. "I'll give it more of a go tonight."

She just made a noise of assent and flopped down at her desk, texting on her phone with her free hand. A few minutes later, Beau left Bathsheba's office and strolled out. Bath immediately headed for the coffee, and I noticed her mouth looked recently kissed, too.

I felt an envious pang. Maybe there was a hopeless romantic inside me, after all.

With the day shift now in the office, Ryder and I

left. I drove home to my small apartment and tossed my keys and purse on the table by the door. I took a shower, changed into my pajamas, put on soothing music, and drank a cup of chamomile tea. I was utterly exhausted.

Yet when I got into bed and tried to sleep, it wouldn't come. My mind kept racing, thinking about Josh. His hand at the small of my back. That lazy, flirty grin he tossed my way as if it hadn't been a dangerous thing. His concern and affection for Carol, who didn't have anyone to look out for her.

I've never met anyone as alone as you, Marie.

If I was, it was because it would hurt everyone less when I died.

I tossed and turned for a few hours, wanting to weep in frustration. I glanced at the Virgin Mary figure on my nightstand. It had been my mother's before she'd passed on, and her mother's before her. I touched the figure. *Please. Let me sleep. Let this all be a bad case of anxiety.*

But I couldn't sleep. It was like my body no longer knew how.

Eventually, I got up and grabbed a jigsaw puzzle box. It was either that, or cry. I turned the TV on in the background and shook the pieces out on the table. My mother had loved puzzles and had done them when she'd been unable to sleep at night. Now I was following the same patterns she had followed.

The thought made me want to weep even more.

———

I twisted my hands in my lap, my feet swinging nervously under the examination table, the paper runner crinkling with every swing of my foot.

When the doctor entered the room, he wore a puzzled look. "Back so soon, Marie? Is everything okay?"

"Everything's fine," I lied. "I just wanted to talk about my medication."

The doctor flipped open my chart. "You've lost six pounds since you last came in."

I shrugged. "Just watching my weight."

He eyed me. "You were here last Tuesday."

"Stomach bug. I'm better now. That's not why I'm here, anyhow. I wanted to talk to you about the sleeping pills you prescribed."

"Are they upsetting your stomach?" he asked, folding his hands around the clipboard and studying me.

"Actually, I wanted to see if you had something stronger. Or if it's okay to double the medication from time to time."

Like every night.

The puzzled frown grew. "I already have you on the strongest dose, Marie."

"Oh, okay. I just thought I'd check."

He put down the clipboard and moved to my side, bringing out his scope to check my pupils. "You look tired. Are the pills not working?"

"Not really," I confessed. "Maybe a different pill? Something I haven't tried yet?"

"In the last few months, you've tried everything

I can recommend. If it's not helping, there might be other factors we need to look at."

"I'm sure it's nothing." I didn't want to become his science project or guinea pig once he found out exactly what I had. That was why I switched doctors constantly. "I've just been under a lot of stress lately, and I'm working nights, so I'm sure that's not helping things."

He ignored my excuses, checking my pupils and continuing to examine me. When he was done prodding, checking my ears, nose, throat, and my pulse, he stroked his chin, frowning. "Marie, I'd like to send you for more tests."

My heart sank. "All I really want are some stronger pills."

"If the pills aren't working now, a stronger dose isn't going to do anything for you. I think there's a larger problem at hand, and I'd like to run some blood work. There are some rare illnesses that can cause insomnia, and I'd like to rule them out."

Yeah, I was familiar with those diseases. I gave him a tight nod. "Sure. Whatever you say."

"We can schedule for you to run down to the blood center today, if you like, and once the results are in, we can discuss where to go with this. Again, it may be nothing, but I want to rule out every possible scenario so we can get down to a cure."

He patted my knee. "Just see Betty at the front desk on the way out and tell her that I'm sending you to the lab for more tests. I'll update your chart."

I grabbed my purse, thanked the doctor, and slid out of the room. He paused to talk to a nurse, then headed down the hall to see another patient. I glanced at the front desk, then turned and walked out the front door.

I wasn't going to go for more blood tests. I already knew what was wrong, and I didn't want a doctor poking and prodding me for the next six months in an attempt to find a cure, when the only one that I knew of involved fangs and neck-biting.

Still . . . My stomach knotted, I pulled out the card of the Alliance doctor and dialed.

"Little Paradise Family Clinic," a woman announced. "How can I help you?"

"I need to see the doctor. Today, if possible," I told her. "I'm having trouble sleeping and wanted to see if he could recommend something."

She typed for a moment, then paused. "The doctor has an opening at four today."

"Four sounds great. Thanks."

Chapter Six

*Y*ou look like hell," Sara told me bluntly as I entered the office Saturday night.

The office was only closed on Sundays, and Ryder and I alternated on the overnight shift on Saturdays. It wasn't so bad, since it was only a half shift until midnight.

"Thanks," I murmured, not even having the energy for a sarcastic comment. In the last three days, I'd gotten probably a half hour of sleep. My repeated catnaps and sleeping pills had only made things worse. I existed in a half-awake stupor, and my entire body felt as if it had been run over by a truck. This was just the early stages of the disease, though. It would get much worse from here on out.

"You sure you're okay?" she asked, moving over to my desk, looking worried. "Is something going on?"

"Just not sleeping well," I told her. Understatement of the century.

"Is something bothering you? Is it money?" She bit her lip, clearly concerned about me. "Family problems? I'm not trying to pry, honest I'm not. I just want to help. You look like you're going through a rough patch."

I gave her a wan smile. "I'm fine. Seriously. I just need some caffeine and I'll be good."

She reached out and squeezed my hand. "I'm here if you want to talk."

"Thanks, Sara, I appreciate it." *But I can't tell you anything, because you'd tell your sister.*

The bell clanged and a shadow loomed in the doorway of the agency, blocking out the setting sun—the massive form of Ramsey Bjorn, resident were-bear, scowling monster of a man, and tiny Sara's mate.

She gave my hand another comforting squeeze, then bounded over to him, flinging herself into his arms. "Hey Huggy Bear," she said. "Did you miss me?"

"Yes," he said gruffly.

She gave him an enthusiastic kiss in response and whispered something into his ear that made the man flush red. When he caught me staring, he scowled in my direction.

I hastily booted up my computer.

"We're out of here," Sara told me, sliding down from Ramsey's arms. "It's Xbox night at our place, so if you need me, just let it keep ringing. We'll hear it over the noise eventually."

"Will do," I said. "So, are all the Russells there when you guys play?"

Because a certain Joshua Russell hadn't shown

up in two days after promising to help me with my vampire situation, and it was ticking me off.

"All of them," she said cheerfully. "I'd invite you, but . . ."

"Work, I know." I wasn't all that interested in video games anyhow.

She brightened. "Maybe next weekend, when it's Ryder's turn to do the night shift?"

"Maybe," I agreed. If Josh kept avoiding me, I'd hunt him down.

They left, Ramsey's big hand resting on the back of Sara's neck and her arm looped around his waist. I watched them go, wondering how that worked for them—Ramsey was so enormous and strong, and Sara was small and fragile.

I blushed at the mental image. *Not my business.*

I buried myself in work, pulling out the stack of folders of inactive clients. I'd give Josh two more days, and then it was back to hunting down vampires in the hopes that they'd want to date me.

Right now, I see three things that are the problem.

That had bothered me more than anything. I wanted to know what those three things were so I could fix them and move on to the next stage of my plan.

I called clients for hours, leaving voice mails when the clients were unavailable. Voice mail was tricky. I had to make sure not to give away discreet information; no mentions of paranormals or shifting, and certainly not vampires. Nothing that could be used against someone. My message was bland.

Hi, it's Marie from Midnight Liaisons. If you're not currently seeing anyone, we'd love to set you up with just the right person. Give me a call back and let's talk about updating your profile.

I then gave the date and time. It was a late hour for most humans, but shifters and vampires and even fae ran all hours of the night, and a late call wasn't so odd. That was why the agency had a night shift, after all.

When I was a third of the way through the stack, the doorbell clanged. I glanced at the clock. Eleven thirty. I peered over my monitor, looking for a face.

A large drive-thru coffee cup appeared from around the side of my monitor, held in a big hand. Josh took a step forward. "I'd have brought you flowers, but you said you had an allergy."

I looked at it, then looked at him, then turned back to my computer. "I'm busy."

"You get off work in a half hour, don't you?"

"Yes, and then I'm going home."

He ignored my stiff tone and sat down across from me. "Coffee's not a great apology gift, I know. Next time I'll bring chocolates."

He had my attention now. "Apology gift?"

He set the coffee cup down on my desk. "Remember that I said all my clients were totally paranoid? Well, one was paranoid with good reason. Someone tried to take him out. I stopped 'em, and I haven't left his side in two days. He's hired a second shift, which has finally given me some time off."

I noticed the jagged scratch that went up his

tanned arm, then noticed a similar one running down one cheek and under his ear. He had circles under his eyes, too. I pushed the coffee toward him. "You take it. You look tired."

He gave me the slow, sensual smile that made me think we were sharing a moment. The one that sent shivers up my spine. He bowed his head over the cup as if I'd given him a gift, then he lifted it to his lips and drank.

I suddenly thought of that moment in the diner when he'd deliberately turned my cup and placed his mouth on the exact spot that I'd drank from. Heat crept through my belly, and I glanced away before he could notice my blush. My face felt hot with . . . embarrassment? Awareness? "There are things such as phones and voice mail," I reminded him. "And texts."

"Now you sound like my last girlfriend," he teased.

I raised an eyebrow.

"It was just a joke. Sorry. Next time I'll call when all hell breaks loose. If you want to kick in our vampire plan, we can start tonight."

I perked up at that, more than ready to get things moving. "I'm ready whenever. Say the word."

"Good. We'll go to your place after you get off work."

"Uh-uh."

He put down the coffee and raised his hands in the air. "Just a wardrobe check. Very innocent."

"I don't believe you have an innocent bone in your body," I told him.

He grinned. "You might be right."

———————

"No Xbox for you tonight?" I asked him as I stepped out of my car in the parking lot of my apartment complex. Josh had followed me here and was exiting his vehicle at the same time I'd left mine. "I thought it was tradition."

"It is," he said, taking the stairs behind me. "But I had other plans tonight."

And those other plans obviously included me. I wasn't sure if I was flattered or concerned. Probably both. I unlocked my front door and placed my keys on the small table next to the door, then flipped on the light. "Come on in."

I moved to the side as he entered, watching his reaction. If he was expecting stuffed animals and some knitting, he was in for a disappointment. I had a large flat-screen TV on the back wall, sleek floor lamps, and track lighting. A small white couch and a low table in the living room. My kitchen was always neat, my floors spotless. The only concession to a mess were the puzzle pieces laid out on my dining room table, but even those were neatly piled. I knew my bathroom was clean, the marble gleaming, and my bedroom was tidy, the bed made.

When one didn't sleep, one had plenty of time for housekeeping.

"Nice place," he said, glancing over at me as I shut the door. "It's not what I expected. I thought you'd be a slob. You know, so guarded on the outside and a wild woman on the inside. That's usually how it goes."

Was that why he was so interested in me? He was in for a huge disappointment, then. "So, you wanted to check out my wardrobe?" I moved toward the bedroom and went inside.

He followed close behind me and stepped to the side, surveying my room with a knowing smile. Josh's gaze flicked over my bookshelf (dusted), my neat queen bed (made) with perfectly arranged throw pillows, and the organized stack of magazines on the bedside. "Bed made, too? Man. You are something else."

He sat down on the bed and lay back, lacing his fingers behind his head and lounging amid my throw pillows. That casual, confident smile was on his face, and it unnerved me to see him relaxing. On my bed.

Like he belonged there.

"Make yourself at home," I said.

He winked at me and adjusted one of the pillows behind his head. "This is a prime spot for viewing."

"Viewing? You expect me to *model* for you?"

He shrugged. "How else am I supposed to tell you if you look soft or not? We're going for soft, and sexy and come-hither. With vampires you need to look fragile and helpless, not strong and independent."

"Fragile . . . and . . . helpless . . ." I repeated slowly, a bit dumbfounded.

Strong and independent? Was that how he saw me?

"They're predators. Women are their prey. If

you were out hunting for a woman, would you want a scowly, aloof one or a nice, soft, sweet one?"

And I guessed I was a scowly one. I sighed and headed into my walk-in closet, clicking on the light and glancing at my neatly arranged things. "I'm not much of a clotheshorse."

"That's fine. Show me your sexiest date outfit," he said from the bed.

I didn't have a sexy date outfit. I eyed my clothing and chewed on my lip, thinking. Then I pulled a sweater off a hanger, paired it with a dark skirt, and stepped out of the closet, holding it up to me.

"Try it on," he said.

I narrowed my eyes. "Not while you're lying on the bed."

"I'll be a perfect gentleman," he told me with a roguish grin that was anything but gentlemanly. He adjusted his baseball cap, tilting the brim back a little before cocking his head to the side. "If you don't trust me not to look, you can shut the closet door. I won't get up. Not when I'm so comfy right here."

I hesitated a moment longer. Did I really want to change in front of Joshua Russell, of all people?

But . . . I needed a vampire. And a small, irritating part of me wanted to impress him, to show him I could be attractive, too. So I entered the closet, shut the door, and took off my clothes. Then I pulled on the sweater and skirt and stepped out. "How's this?"

He sat up in the bed.

For a moment, my heart raced. Was he . . . pleased with my appearance?

"That is just terrible," he said.

I scowled.

Josh slid off the bed and moved to my side, examining me. "Where are your heels?"

"I don't have any high heels."

He looked surprised. "How can you expect to catch a man if you don't have fuck-me pumps? You wear those, and he's automatically imagining them digging into his back. Trust me on this."

"You're something else, you know that?"

"I may be something else, but I'm something that gets a lot of dates," he pointed out. "Tomorrow, buy some shoes. Tall heels. Think sexy." He turned me for a full view of my outfit. "This is all wrong, Marie."

"What's wrong with my clothes?" I asked curiously.

"Nothing, if you're looking to get a job as a church secretary. We need sensual, remember? Think sexy and loose and wild." He studied me for a moment, then reached up and tugged a lock of my curling dark hair, dragging it down to brush against the nape of my neck. "Like you normally wear it."

I pulled away, feeling a little self-conscious and flustered. He thought my hair was sexy and wild? "When do I ever wear my hair up?"

"When you're working."

I thought for a moment. I sometimes twisted my hair and shoved a pencil through it while I was working. He thought that was sexy? Even stranger, he remembered that I did that?

Josh moved past me and began to rake through the hangers.

I remained behind him, fingering my hair thoughtfully.

He eventually pulled out a sweater I hated; the tags still dangled from the sleeve. It was a long, navy blue tunic with a wide belt. It was meant to be worn with leggings and a big necklace. The problem was I had no leggings. He pulled the belt off the sweater and held it out to me. "Here. Put this on."

"I'm going to return that—"

He yanked the tags off and dropped it in my hands. "Put it on."

"I can't wear this," I told him. "I didn't realize when I'd bought it that it's off the shoulder, and I don't have a strapless bra."

Josh's eyes gleamed intensely, and for a moment he looked just like the cat he was. "So go braless."

"I don't have any leggings to go with it."

"You don't need leggings. Wear it as a dress."

I sighed and took it from him, heading back to the closet to change. I pulled off the other outfit, then hesitated. Braless in front of a big, delicious man suddenly seemed like a big deal, and I remembered how his eyes had gleamed at the thought. My skin prickled in awareness, and I knew that he was standing outside the closet, waiting for me to emerge, my breasts loose and my legs bare.

Sexy and wild, like you normally wear it. And he'd touched my hair.

A flush rose over my body and I had to fight it

down, force my breathing to calm. I was just worked up because I had a man in my bedroom, nothing more. Josh simply wanted to help me find a vampire to date.

I stripped out of my bra and tugged the dark sweater over my head, noticing that it seemed to cling to my curves as it slithered over me. The open neckline was asymmetrical and hung over one shoulder, exposing it and an expanse of my neck. Smart. I knew before I even stepped out of the closet that this was a good idea.

When I stepped out of the closet, his eyes had that catlike gleam again that made me want to shiver. He gave me another long, sweeping look that made my skin prickle. "Much better," he said, his voice husky.

My skin prickled in response and I felt my nipples grow hard. I crossed my arms over my chest, hoping he wouldn't notice.

He didn't. He was too busy pacing around me, and I got the weird sensation that he was embracing his predator side. Had I . . . brought that out in him?

Behind me, Josh leaned close, and I stiffened. I thought he was going to sniff me, oddly enough. But he only grabbed a handful of my thick, curly hair. "Up," he said softly. "It's gorgeous up. Do you have a clip?"

"On the nightstand," I told him, flustered at the compliment to my hair.

Two seconds later, he had the clip in hand and

was pushing it into the knot of hair at the back of my head. I could practically feel his breath on my neck, and I shivered.

"You have a great neck for vampires," he said softly and ran a finger down the back of my neck. "Nice and long and white."

"Gee, thanks," I told him, willing my body not to tremble. He was incredibly aware of my appearance, and I was growing all too aware of his presence, which I liked too much. His attention made my stomach flutter. "Do I pass muster?"

"I'm not sure," he said after a long moment, and I glanced over my bare shoulder at him. He rubbed his jaw thoughtfully, then looked at my behind. "Are you wearing granny panties?"

I gasped. "You do not ask a girl about her panties!"

"Granny panties," he said, "are toxic to sexiness. Both for you and for him. If you have a thong, wear one. It'll make you move sensually and make you more aware of what you're wearing underneath and how it feels. Go for something sexy in the fabric," he said, and my nipples went tight again at his husky, sensual tone.

"Sexy fabric?" I repeated, almost hypnotized by the sound of his voice. It was like something one would say to a lover.

"Mmm," he said in agreement. "Something that will tease and tickle at your skin. Lace . . . satin . . . something like that. You know why?"

"No," I said softly, my breasts aching and tight. "Why?"

He swatted my ass. "Badonkadonk."

Tabarnak. I was going to kill him with my own two hands. I pushed him away. "You are a jackass. Get out of my bedroom."

He grinned, all boyish charm again. "Not until you promise to wear that on your next date. Braless. You've got mighty pretty breasts."

I clutched the sweater neck tight. "Get. Out."

"Promise."

"Fine," I said. "I promise. Now get out so I can change back."

He did, grinning at me the whole time.

When I emerged a few minutes later, my hair was down again and I was wearing my ugliest, most worn-out pajamas. And a bra. Sending a very clear message seemed like a good idea.

Josh said nothing, but his eyebrow went up and that smile curved his mouth again. "Nice pajamas."

"Thank you," I said frostily.

He said nothing else about it, then leaned over my dining room table and casually turned a puzzle piece, trying to fit it into the half-finished locked-together pieces on the table. "I see you're into puzzles. This one's a hard one."

"I like them hard."

He glanced back at me and gave me a knowing grin.

I sighed. "Do you make *everything* innuendo?"

"Yes," he said firmly. "It's more fun that way. So why puzzles?"

"I do them when I can't sleep." I'd started that five-thousand-piece puzzle last night, and it was nearly done.

"Do you do a lot of them?"

I thought of my closet full of boxes of completed puzzles. "Now and then. So was there anything else you wanted, or are you done tormenting me?"

Josh shook his head. "It's not torment, my beautiful Marie. It's assistance. You're looking at this all wrong. Don't think of it as suffering. Think of me as your sherpa of sexy."

Did that make me Mount Everest? Some unattainable peak he felt the need to climb?

Now *I* was making everything innuendo. I forced myself to focus. "What now, then, oh sherpa?"

His face lit up with enthusiasm. "Now we go through the database and I give you the dirt on all the vampires."

Oooh, now we were getting to the good stuff! I grabbed my laptop off my desk and went to the couch, setting the laptop on the low table.

Josh slid onto the couch next to me, his thigh rubbing against mine. On purpose? Either way, I was hyperaware of it, even if he wasn't. Maybe he was totally casual with his personal space, too, and I wasn't used to it.

Or he just thought I was scowly and aloof, and this was all in my head.

I pulled up the Midnight Liaisons website.

Two hours later, we were down to only a few options. We'd made notecards on each of the available vampires in the database and arranged them on the table to get a better look. Then, one by one, Josh had plucked the cards off the table, whittling down my options.

This one was cruel to his last girlfriend. This one was a bit of a playboy. This one was newly turned and wouldn't be interested in humans. This one lost his blood partner a few years ago and probably wouldn't be looking for a serious relationship.

As Josh ticked off the reasons why they would be bad choices and handed me the cards, I kept a few of them. The playboy. The widow. Both of those sounded like likely prospects to me.

"This one is not a good idea," Josh said, picking another card off the table and handing it to me. "He's a kinky fuck. Men and women together, and he'll just watch."

I took the card with a frown. "How do you know this?"

"I got an invitation once."

I raised my eyebrows at him.

"I didn't go. I'm not into that sort of thing. I am a one-woman-at-a-time sort of guy." He leaned in, as if confessing a secret. "I like to devote all my attention to one woman. Make her feel sexy. Needed. Touch her body and bring every nerve ending to attention. Make her feel like she's the only thing in the universe in that moment."

My breath caught in my throat.

His gaze slid to my mouth before he looked away again. "Can't do that in a group."

"Guess not," I said weakly. The room sure felt awfully warm. Distracted, I placed the card at the bottom of the stack I was holding.

He watched, then reached over and snatched the two cards I'd earmarked. "What's this?"

"Nothing," I said defensively, reaching for them. "Give those back."

He looked at the first card, then at me. "You want to date the fanged Don Juan? Are you serious?"

"If he's not discerning about his dates, I have greater odds of getting him to go out with me."

"Marie, I thought you were looking for a guy with fangs. This makes it sound like you're looking for *any* guy." He gave me an odd look. "Is there something you're not telling me?"

"No," I said and reached for the card again.

He held it over his head, out of my reach.

As if that'd stop me. I climbed onto his lap and ripped the card from his hand, then shot him a triumphant look.

Suddenly his arm went around my waist, pinning me against him. My face was just an inch away from his, and his gaze was focused on me, his eyes intense. I became very aware that my breasts were pressed to his chest, and my legs were now straddling his. It was very . . . intimate.

"If I'd known that was all it took to get you to climb all over me, Marie," he said in a husky voice, "I'd have done that hours ago."

The words were playful, but I remained frozen by that soft, sultry tone in his voice. His gaze held mine pinned, and I noticed how beautiful his eyes were, how long his lashes. I thought of earlier, with him behind me, his hand knotted in my hair, his eyes flashing to cat.

And I suddenly didn't want to move.

"How good are you at kissing?" Josh asked me, his gaze dropping to my mouth.

"Kissing?" I repeated.

"Vampires have an oral fixation," he said, his hand stroking down my back in a move that made my entire body shiver in response. "Do you need to brush up on your kissing?"

I hadn't kissed anyone in over ten years. "I . . . I don't know," I admitted. "Are you . . . offering?"

"We can kiss and I'll tell you how you're doing, if you like." That hand continued to stroke my back, drugging me in an almost hypnotic way. His voice was low and soft, as if he was afraid I was going to bolt, and his gaze gleamed golden-green, reflecting like a cat's. "I can show you a few techniques. You can get comfortable with the thought of kissing someone with fangs in their mouth. See what it's like to taste them."

My gaze dropped to his mouth, imagining his lips on mine. My pulse beat slowly, awareness tingling through me. He wanted to kiss me and was just using this as a pretense. Yet . . . it didn't seem like a bad idea.

Perhaps I was crazy.

Or perhaps I really just wanted to kiss him. Perhaps that hand on my back was driving me insane, that low, soothing voice, smoothing away all my inhibitions.

And if he was right that vampires liked to kiss, I did need to brush up.

"All right," I said, suddenly feeling shy. I closed my eyes and waited.

Josh rumbled a laugh, and I felt it all through my chest. His other hand stole to my nape. "You don't want to watch my technique?"

Oh. Oops. I opened my eyes just as his mouth brushed lightly against mine.

All rational thought vanished. I stared at him, dumbfounded, as he closed his eyes and his lips played over mine. Oh, that was . . . erotic. I gasped against his mouth, feeling desire surge through my body. I watched, fascinated, as he tilted his mouth ever so slightly against mine and his tongue stroked between my lips, demanding entrance.

And then my eyes closed and I fell into the kiss, wrapped up in the sensation of his soft lips against mine, the harsh rasp of stubble against my cheek, the warm, solid thrust of his tongue that moved in a slow, delicious rhythm that made my pulse pound. His tongue slid against mine, coaxing and rubbing, before stroking deep again. Possessive and sweet and playful all at once. As if he had all the time in the world to kiss me.

His hand slid to my ass and he pulled me tighter against him.

I yelped and pushed at his chest, not sure where to look. Anywhere but at him. I pried his hand off my ass and slid away down the couch.

"Thanks, I think," I said softly. My mouth felt swollen and slick.

"You were right," he said. "Your technique needs some work."

I gaped at him. "I can't believe you just said that!"

A hint of a teasing smile played at his mouth and my gaze locked there, fascinated by his lips. I felt the absurd urge to lean down and lick them.

"We should probably practice more, until you're comfortable with it," those gorgeous lips said.

Then the reality of what he was saying sank in, and I grabbed a throw pillow and smacked him with it. "You just did that to kiss me!"

"Hey," he said, raising his hands to ward off my blow, a grin on his face. "You were the one crawling into my lap."

"Good night," I said pointedly.

"Suit yourself," he said, rising from the couch. At the door, he turned back to face me. "Just call me if you need me. I'm off for the next four days, then I'm on for the next eight. We can work on prepping you for your first date with a vampire, if you like. And we can practice more."

I shut the door in his face.

And then I leaned against it, ignoring his chuckle from the other side, and touched my mouth with wondering fingers. That kiss . . .

If I could have fallen asleep, I'd have dreamed about a kiss like that. To think that it had come from

him, the man who was supposed to have been helping me prepare for snagging a vampire. The man
who had repeatedly offered a one-night stand. No
strings attached, because strings weren't allowed
between human and Alliance. I had scoffed at the
offer every time. Sleep with Josh, just for the sheer
pleasure of it?

Before that kiss, I'd have never entertained such
a thought.

Yet now it was all I could think about. One night.
In Josh's arms. Kissing. Making love.

Part of me wondered if I should seize the opportunity while I could.

I was still thinking about that kiss when I went in to
work on Monday night. Maybe I could get Josh to
turn me?

Beau would be furious, but he couldn't stay mad
at his brother, and Josh seemed to like spending
time with me. He wouldn't have to marry me, after
all; just change me. Enough to give me a second
lease on life.

"Bad news," Sara said as I entered the office. Her
face looked drawn and unhappy.

My heart clenched. "What kind of bad news?"

"Remember that were-tiger who changed the
human girl? It just got worse."

"What happened?"

"Johnny decided he wasn't in love after all.
Dumped her. So much for true love, huh?"

My jaw dropped. "They broke up?"

"Oh, it gets even worse," Sara said bitterly. "She wanted to leave and go home. Naturally, the clan wouldn't let her. One of the males challenged another for her. It started a fight, and then the next thing we know, both males are hospitalized and the entire tiger clan is furious. The other clans are freaking out, the girl is freaking out, and Johnny just wants to run away. Vic's about to lose his shit. The other clans are flat-out refusing to have anything to do with the Alliance until those two are exiled and made an example of. Beau's putting them on a plane to Greenland this morning."

"Greenland?" I sat down heavily.

"Yeah," she said unhappily. "Some town just south of the Arctic Circle line, until things get ironed out. I don't know that things will, though. People are really furious." She swiped a finger under her eye, and I realized she was crying. "Poor girl."

I said nothing. I knew Sara had been turned against her will, and it had worked out for her . . . eventually. She'd apparently had a very stressful time of it for years and years. And the wolf pack was to blame for a lot of it.

My thoughts automatically went to Sara's wolf side. Maybe I could find a wolf to turn me . . .

And then I thought about Sara's predicament and scratched that idea. A wolf pack wasn't about to turn me and then let me waltz away. They'd lay claims, and from the stories Ryder had told me, several of them liked to lay claim at once. No, thank you.

"Everyone's going nuts about all the changes," she said sadly. "First my coming out as a human-turned-werewolf, which got the packs all riled up, and now this girl being turned into a cat. I feel sorry for the next guy that tries to turn a girl, because he's going to have a lynch mob after him."

I swallowed, thinking of Josh's kiss. "What do you mean?"

"If a human so much as breathes in a supernatural's direction now, every single alpha in the state of Texas is going to flip his lid and come gunning for them. No one wants to be the straw that breaks the camel's back." Sara shook her head. "Some supes give me dirty looks at meetings. I can only imagine what that poor tiger girl is going through. I wouldn't be surprised if the next person who turns a human ends up a smear on the pavement."

Smear on the pavement? I thought of Josh's laughing eyes. Those long lashes. That warm smile.

Guess I was back to vampires.

Sigh.

We were sitting on my couch, going over some of the vampire notes before my next date, when Josh looked over at me. "We should practice your kissing again."

"I beg your pardon?"

"Your kissing," Josh enunciated, as if I'd been deaf and not just surprised by his words. "I said it needed work and that I'd help you, remember?"

I gave him a wary look. If it had been anyone else, I'd have thought he was doing it to mess with me. That he was feeding me the world's corniest line because he wanted to kiss me and thought this would be an easy way to get what he wanted.

Except that this was Josh Russell who was offering. The playboy of the Paranormal Alliance. A man who could get any woman he wanted—and did, quite frequently. He had no need to play flirty little games with someone like me.

So it had to be legit.

I dug my nails into my palms to fight the blush that threatened to reveal how unsettled I was by his offer. When we'd kissed before, it had shaken me to my core and had made me want things that I wasn't supposed to want. Things that weren't part of my ironclad plans.

But now my entire body clenched with how much I wanted that. Flustered, I slid a bit closer to him on the couch. "You really think practice is necessary?"

"Absolutely." His gaze was totally confident and relaxed. "For one, I think you should work on your expressions."

"What's wrong with them?"

"Vampires are predators, right? So you need to think like prey. The last time I kissed you, your reaction wasn't very pleasing to the male ego."

"It could be because I was kissing you," I said, my light tone taking the bite out of my words.

"Ouch. I'm wounded, Marie." He clutched a hand to his chest in mock injury, then moved a fraction closer to me. "I'm serious. After a guy kisses you, you need to go all soft and sweet in his arms.

He'll think he's turned you into a pile of mush, and that'll please his ego. Especially a vampire's, since they seem to have bigger ones than most. Stroke it a little and you'll be sitting pretty."

My mouth quirked in amusement at the thought of faking softness after someone kissed me. Exactly how did one pretend to be soft? Picture marshmallows and let my posture slump? Poke my lips out in some sexy version of the duck face? What?

While I contemplated this, Josh moved his hands to my hips and tugged me forward. Suddenly I was pulled against his larger form. My hands automatically went up defensively, and I ended up resting my palms on his chest. His nice, firm chest.

I resisted the urge to flex my fingers against it.

Josh's face leaned in close to mine, and I could smell his breath, minty and sweet. He tilted his head slightly, as if moving in to kiss me.

My entire body tensed, waiting for the brush of his lips on mine, and I closed my eyes.

Nothing happened.

I opened them again.

He was giving me that same expectant look. "Kiss me, Marie."

"Why should I kiss you? I'm the one that has to be all melted at the thought of your lips touching mine."

"Soft. Not melted." He grinned at my grumpiness. "And if you kiss me, I'll show you what I mean, and then you can try it yourself."

"This feels like a scam," I muttered in protest, but I leaned in obediently and lightly brushed my lips over his closed mouth. Then I pulled back and watched him expectantly.

He laughed in my face.

I scowled. "What's so funny?"

"You think that was a real kiss?"

"We're pretending here, remember?"

He shook his head. "I'm almost offended at how bad that kiss was. Clearly we need to practice more than just your reaction." Josh turned to face me fully. "Here, let me show you how to do it." When I didn't move, he added, "Relax."

I gave a deliberate full-body wiggle and rolled my neck to show him that I was relaxed. "Hit me with it."

I shouldn't have been startled when his hand moved forward to lightly cup my neck. I mean, I was staring right at him, watching him lean in, his eyes so heavily lidded that they looked closed, his mouth angling for mine. But the brush of his fingers against my nape sent shivers down my spine and pleasure cascading through my body.

One thing was for sure—I loved Josh's touch.

And then in the next moment, his lips were on mine. Soft, gentle, ever so slightly gliding over my own. Prickles of awareness rushed through me, setting all my nerve endings alight with sensation. He tilted his head just a little and the delicate brush of his lips over mine changed, adding just a hint of pressure. It felt almost as if he'd been touching me all over my body, and my nipples grew hard.

This felt . . . dangerous. I had this crazy attraction to Josh that I couldn't afford to nurture, and kissing—this soft, caressing tease of a lesson—was exactly what I didn't need in my life right now.

I parted my lips to protest—and his tongue slid into my mouth.

I moaned, unable to help myself. His lips had parted, changed the intensity of the kiss, and the hand on the back of my neck was more urgent. He'd pulled me against him at some point and I'd gone willingly, my nipples brushing against his hard chest as his tongue dove into my mouth over and over with a sweet, hypnotic pattern of strokes that made heat curl deep inside me. I was lost in that kiss, in the power of his mouth slanting over mine.

His tongue stroked against mine, encouraging my responses, and I whimpered against his mouth, my fingers curling in his shirt to anchor him to me. Again, his tongue licked against my own, and my body wanted to follow that delicious movement. It made my mind go to deep, dark, dangerous places— like the thought of that wonderful tongue flicking my nipples into stiff little peaks. Or between my legs—

Josh pulled away, breaking the kiss and my erotic daydreams.

My eyes opened—when had I closed them?— and I stared at him in funny confusion. Why had he stopped? I wanted to ask, but the only syllable that fell out of my mouth was a soft "Whuh?"

His thumb stroked over the wet lower curve of my lip. "Like that," he said in a soft, husky voice. "Just like that, sweet Marie."

"Just like what?"

"You." He leaned in and pressed another feather-light, openmouthed kiss on my parted lips. "Soft. Gorgeous. Full of need. When someone kisses you, that's how you need to look back at him. Like he could pull you into his lap and make you his in the next moment."

I pulled away from Josh slowly—and a bit reluctantly. His words were destroying the delicious, erotic fog over my thoughts. I didn't want to kiss someone else. I wanted more of Josh, his expert tongue and amazing lips. His hard body pressing me onto the couch and covering me.

I certainly didn't want to think about kissing vampires at the moment. "So . . . that was good?"

"Pretty good," he said, and there was a husky note in his voice. His gaze seemed to go back to my mouth once more. "Did you want to practice again?"

"Can we?" Oh man, my voice sounded so breathy.

"Of course." He tugged at the curls on my nape and tilted my head back just a little.

I barely managed to swallow the gasp building in my throat before his mouth descended on mine again. He kissed the hell out of me—thoroughly, thoroughly kissed—and his tongue swept into my mouth again, driving all rational thought out of my head. There was only Josh and that powerful, endless kiss.

By the time he pulled away again, my thoughts were mush. My lips felt full and a little tender from his kiss, and my nipples—and my sex—ached with need. He could have definitely tossed me down on the couch and had his way with me.

As if sensing what I was thinking, he leaned in once more. I parted my lips in anticipation of his kiss—

And wasn't prepared for the sensual slicking of his tongue over my parted lips in a blatant move that left me breathless.

"That's how you kiss someone, Marie," he said in a husky voice as he broke the kiss and re-treated back to his end of the couch. "Did you take notes?"

"Buh?" I asked, still all foggy with need and in-credibly eloquent.

"You're getting better with your reactions," he said casually, as if we'd just been describing the weather. "Just let me know if you need more prac-tice."

"More practice?" I echoed, and then reality crashed over me.

That's all this was, of course. Just practice. I pulled away from Josh and scooted back on the couch, giv-ing myself space. "I'm good for now."

"Suit yourself," he said casually.

But he licked his lips, as if savoring my taste, and it sent another pulse of heat through my body.

———

"You ready for this?" Josh said, fixing the neck of my sweaterdress so it hung over one shoulder, exposing my neck, collarbones, and my upper arm.

I batted his hand away. "I will be just as soon as you leave, Henry Higgins."

"Who?" he asked.

"Never mind. Just go. Please," I said urgently, eyeing the empty table that I was supposed to be sitting at. Josh had been hovering behind a shield of plants at a two-seater table in another section and had come over to let me know that he was there. It seemed that my "coach" wanted to supervise my date. He said it was to give me pointers. I was starting to think it was because he wanted to keep an eye on me.

From what I could tell, Josh didn't trust vampires. And the more I found out about them, the less I liked. They were secretive and apparently untrustworthy. No one in the Alliance liked them much, and they didn't even seem to like other vampires much. Vampires were loners. Suspicious loners. It seemed to be a rather cutthroat community compared to the supernatural clans, which were more like a big family.

But I wasn't a girl with a lot of choices. I had vampires, or I had nothing. So I picked vampires.

Josh nodded in approval. "You look stunning tonight, Marie."

I was surprised by that compliment. "Really?"

"I want to lick you all over. But I'll leave that for your date."

I felt my cheeks heat. "Gee, thanks. I'm going to go sit down now."

He winked at me and grinned.

When I turned to leave, he swatted me on the ass.

The man was impossible, I thought as I went back to my table. It was going to be hard to concentrate on my date with a massive were-cougar male hovering nearby.

Lonnie Smith showed up a short time later. He didn't look several hundred years old, which his bio had listed. I'd never met him in person; whereas most supes liked to come in to the agency themselves, vampires were a reclusive lot and didn't venture out unless they had to. Getting one to show up for a date was a trick in itself.

He wore a black turtleneck with several gold chains looped around his neck and a black leather coat over it. His black hair was slicked back, and he looked like something from a bad '70s movie. Maybe vampires had a hard time keeping up with fashion.

I extended my hand for him to shake and gave him a quick smile of greeting. "Lonnie? Hi, I'm Minnie."

"Minnie, my angel," he said in a low, rumbling voice. He clasped my hand in his and held it tight. "You look more beautiful than in your picture. I am very pleased."

Though he held my hand a bit longer than was comfortable, I resisted the urge to pull it away. "Thank you. I'm glad you're pleased."

"Oh, very," he said, still holding on to my hand and sitting down in the chair next to mine.

I had no choice but to sit down as well. So he

was a little touchy-feely. I could deal with that, I guessed. After all, being turned had to involve a certain level of intimacy, didn't it?

He began to rub my hand. "So tell me about you, Minnie. What do you like?"

I adjusted my glasses with my other hand, noticing that his gaze kept straying to my bare neck. True to Josh's orders, I'd worn my hair twisted up in a loose knot, and it seemed to be getting Lonnie's attention. This date was already turning out much better than my last one.

"Me? Well . . ." I paused, thinking. I couldn't really give away too much, but I didn't want to sound boring. Unfortunately, all the things I liked were pretty boring. "I'm kind of a homebody."

"Me, too," he said with a close-lipped smile. "What kinds of things do you like to do at home?"

"Well, I like to curl up and watch a good movie. And puzzles. I like puzzles."

"Puzzles?" Lonnie looked as if I'd just said the most unappealing thing in the world. Oh, no. I was losing his attention.

"What do you like to do?" I asked quickly.

He gave me a half smile. "Not puzzles."

I cast around for something else to say. I never realized small talk was so hard, especially when your date wasn't exactly helping things along. "Do you like sports? Running? Tennis?"

"I'm a vampire. Unless it happens at night or indoors, I can't do it."

"Oh, of course," I said quickly, feeling flustered. "Maybe table . . . tennis? I like table tennis."

He glanced at the door. Shit, I was losing him.

"And sex," I added desperately. "I *love* sex."

His eyes flared with interest, his attention moving back to me. The grin returned to his face. "You don't say?"

God help me, but I was desperate and didn't want him to end this date. "Oh yes, all the time. I totally need it."

He leaned down and examined my hand, then pulled it to his mouth, kissing the back of it delicately. "You smell incredible. What's your blood type again?"

"O positive."

"My favorite flavor," he said with another close-lipped smile before leaning in to kiss my hand again.

I let him, pleased that the date had turned around. "So what about you?" I asked. "What do you like to do at home?"

"I like," he began slowly, then nipped at one of my fingers. "Reading."

"Oh?" I asked. "What sorts of things?"

"My favorite is *The Perfumed Garden*." And he nipped at another one of my fingers. "Though I am also fond of *The Story of O* and *Lolita*."

I knew of *Lolita*, but not the other two. Classics? Or maybe he was a poet at heart? Not really my thing, but kind of sweet. "Those sound nice. I haven't read them."

"I'd love to go through a few passages with you," he said and rubbed a hand down my arm.

"Sure," I said. "Maybe next time we get together, you can bring me one to borrow."

His eyes narrowed, and I could practically hear his breath hiss. "That sounds incredible."

Wow, this guy was really into those books. I began to feel a little uneasy about that and decided to turn the subject. "So what else are you into?"

"Frottage."

I frowned. "I . . . see." What was that? I was pretty sure that it was dirty, but I wasn't sure how dirty. I decided to play stupid, smiling widely. "I'm a big fan of *fromage* myself."

He studied me a moment, then laughed as if I'd said something hilarious. "You have quite a clever tongue."

"Thank you." Why did everything this man was saying sound dirtier than it was? Was I just taking things the wrong way? I continued to smile at him as if we'd connected at some deeper level.

At least he wasn't looking at the door anymore.

"I do have a particular favorite," he said, leaning in and running a finger down my bare shoulder.

"Do tell."

"Have you heard of 'the shocker'?"

"Is that a TV show?" I asked politely.

"All right," Josh said, appearing from behind the wall. "That fucking does it." He grabbed my date by the collar and hauled him into the air.

"Josh!" I got to my feet. "What are you doing?"

Lonnie clawed at his throat, glancing over at me with alarm.

"I'm ending this date," Josh said. "This asshole is done with you."

"Butt out," I snapped at him. "It's my date."

"You're done," he repeated, setting Lonnie on his feet and leaning into his face. "Get out of here."

"Now see here," Lonnie began.

Josh's eyes began to gleam like a cat's and he leaned in, so close that only I could hear it. "Beat it, buddy. She's human."

The vampire's eyes widened and he looked over at me, then back at Josh. And then he took off, weaving between tables as he exited the restaurant.

Outrage slammed through me and I turned to Josh, fists clenched. "What the hell do you think you're doing?"

"Saving you from a bad situation," he told me, grabbing my hand and beginning to pull me toward the front door. "We need to talk. Somewhere private."

I bit my lip—it was either that or start screaming at him. I was so angry that I couldn't see straight as Josh dragged me out of the restaurant. So the vampire had been a little fresh. Who cared? I needed to be turned. And about two minutes ago, I'd had a vampire practically eating out of the palm of my hand until my do-gooder "coach" had decided to change the rules on me.

As soon as we got to the parking lot, I jerked my arm from his grasp. "I thought you said you were helping me date vampires!"

"I am," he told me between gritted teeth and steered me away from the crowd. "Just not that one."

"What was wrong with that one? He liked me!"

"Yeah, because you told him you like puzzles and knitting and oh yeah, sex. Way to break the ice."

"I didn't tell him I liked knitting," I said. "And he looked like he was bored! He was staring at the door! I had to keep his interest somehow."

Josh glared back at me, walking quickly to the far edge of the parking lot and dragging me along behind him. He halted so abruptly when we were at his car that I almost ran into his back. Then he turned and pulled me against his car, his arms grasping mine. He looked furious and oddly possessive. His jaw was clenched, his mouth turned down into a frown. And he was staring at my mouth. He looked like he was inches away from kissing me. A lot.

And that made my breath quicken.

"Do you even know what 'the shocker' is, Marie?"

"I'm guessing it's not a game show," I snapped back at him.

He held his hand up and tucked his fourth finger back against his thumb. Then he tilted his hand and showed me the gesture. "This is the shocker."

I stared at the pairing of his first two fingers and the pinky, not recognizing the gesture. If it weren't for the fact that his ring finger was tucked in, it'd almost look like a Vulcan hand gesture. "Is that supposed to mean something?"

"You're really sheltered, aren't you?" Josh stared at me, then shook his head. He did the gesture again and explained, "The saying is 'Two in the pink, one in the stink.'"

I stared at his hand. Two in the pink . . . ? And then I blushed, hard, slapping his hand away. "Oh. Ew."

"Yeah. Not exactly first-date material. Which, I might add, you set yourself up for."

"I'm guessing frottage is pretty dirty, too, then."

"You'd be guessing right," he said, a hard edge in his voice. "Jesus, Marie. How is it that a smart, pretty girl like you can be so clueless when it comes to men?"

I stared at him, wounded. "I just wanted him to like me."

"And would you have slept with him just to get him to like you?"

I hesitated. If he wanted the honest-to-God truth, I didn't have that answer. I'd thought about it, and I wasn't averse to using my body to get a vampire's interest. If sleeping with someone bought me fifty extra years of life? I'd do it in a heartbeat.

"I don't believe you, Marie." Josh stared at me as if he didn't know me. "What is going on in that brain of yours?"

I shook my head and got my keys out of my purse. "I'm going home."

I expected him to protest, but he only stared at me.

I got in my car and left.

I dated another vampire the next night, and I didn't tell Josh. I didn't want him sabotaging my personal business.

As soon as I got there, though, I realized I'd made a mistake. This one? Flat-out scared me. He arrived with a bodyguard walking two feet behind him. The bodyguard stood behind the table at all times, and he jumped at the slightest noise.

We dined at an Italian restaurant, though my date ate and drank nothing. It made me uncomfortable, and I had a hard time eating my meal as well. We made small talk, and I didn't throw down the sex-bomb. I'd learned my lesson.

The entire time we talked, the vampire watched me.

At first, I didn't think too much of it. He had a direct stare, but I attributed it to his watchfulness and the presence of the bodyguard. But as the night went on, I began to grow more and more uneasy at his tightly controlled motions and the dead, emotionless expression on his face. Even when he smiled, it didn't reach his cold, cold eyes.

I felt like prey.

For the first time since working at the dating agency, I was uncomfortable in the presence of a supernatural. And I began to see what Josh had been warning me about.

This man didn't want a date. He wanted a diversion. At best, he wanted an easy meal. At worst, he wanted someone he could easily bury in the backyard.

I suffered through two hours of the date before calling it done. Even then, I felt his gaze watching me as I left. We were only two blocks from the dating agency, but I didn't trust him enough to make the walk alone. I called a taxi and hid in the restroom until it arrived.

Another lesson learned.

When I got back to the agency, Josh was there, waiting in my seat.

He was chatting with Ryder but got to his feet when I entered the door. A sexy smile curved his mouth at the sight of me, and he pulled out an enormous box of chocolates with a big ribbon on the top. He held the chocolates out toward me and pulled out my seat, inviting me to sit down. "Peace offering?"

I glanced at the chocolates, then back at his too-innocent face. "Are you going to interrupt one of my dates again?"

"It depends," he said easily. "Is another man going to offer to give you the shocker?"

"Do *what*?" Ryder's wide blue eyes turned to me. "Did he just say what I think he said? Did someone try to give you a shocker?"

"No," I hissed, yanking the chocolates out of Josh's hand and dropping them on the desk. "Can we please change the subject? I'm still mad at you, Josh. What you did is unforgivable."

Josh looked nonplussed. "So I should have left you there and let that guy manhandle you? Say disgusting things to you? Perhaps let him demonstrate his moves on you?"

"Yes," I snapped. "You should have. Are we dating? No, we're not. Therefore, not your business."

Josh's face grew hard. "Well, then, I'm sorry

if I took up your time, Marie. It won't happen again."

My chest began to have this funny ache, but I said nothing when he stormed out the front door, making the bell clang loudly against the glass.

Ryder stared at it. "I think that's the first time I've ever seen Josh mad."

It was the first time for me, too. I'd pushed him too far. Instead of being indignant about the whole thing, I just felt . . . awful. Like I'd screwed up. He'd only been trying to help me. He'd been protecting me, been a friend. And I'd been nasty to him. He'd come to apologize and I'd chased him away again.

I chased everyone away.

Suddenly weary to the core, I laid my head on my desk and felt like crying.

"Do you want to talk about it?" Ryder asked softly.

"No."

"Do you have someone else you want to talk about it with?"

I had only one other friend besides my coworkers. And he'd just stormed out the door because I'd been awful to him. I sat up and pressed my face in my hands. "Why am I so bad with people, Ryder?"

"It's a gift," she said lightly.

"Thanks."

"I don't know Josh as well as you," she said thoughtfully, toying with the glittery ruler on her desk. "But unless I miss my guess, it's hard to get him angry, and it's probably harder to keep him angry. Maybe you should . . . gee, I don't know, try apologizing?"

I stared at the box of chocolates on my desk. I'd turned down his flowers and his coffee, and yet he'd kept trying. He was determined to break through my icy shell and get to the real me inside, the one I hid away from everyone. Why? Was it the challenge of trying to score with me? Was he fascinated because I turned him down? Or was Josh simply being the nice white knight to me like he was to Carol?

Either way, after tonight, I doubted he was going to flirt with me ever again.

Maybe it was the exhaustion, or my disease, but I was tired of pushing everyone away. "Ryder—"

"Red Bull run? Sounds great," she said. "Pick one up for me, will ya?"

"You're the best."

She grinned. "I know."

I hurried out to the parking lot, thinking for a moment. I could text him . . . or I could swing by the diner and see if this was one of Carol's nights.

Sure enough, I caught Josh as he was tucking Carol into the passenger side of his car. I threw mine into park and jumped out, racing over to his side. "Josh, can we talk?"

He gave me a cool look as he calmly closed Carol's door, then turned away from me. "I'm pretty sure we've both said enough tonight."

"I think there's more to be said," I added quickly.

"I don't." He began to walk around the other side of the car.

"Josh," I began.

He didn't turn around.

"Josh," I said again, louder, trying to get his attention.

He opened his car door, as if he was about to drive away.

"Will you please pay attention to me?" I snapped. "I'm trying to apologize to you."

He paused, then leaned against the side of the car. His eyes flashed like a cougar's, and I knew he was still angry about my words earlier.

Merde.

"Doesn't sound much like an apology so far," he told me.

"That's because you're not making this easy," I said, stalking toward him. I moved directly in front of him, and when his gaze grew even more direct, I dropped my eyes. "And I'm not good at apologizing."

I felt his hand go to my waist, and a shiver ripped through me.

"Nor am I good at letting people in," I admitted. "I'm sorry. Please don't be mad at me. I can't stand the thought of you being mad at me."

His hand reached up and brushed my cheek. "Marie," he said, so softly I could barely hear it. "I don't know what's going on in that gorgeous head of yours. I don't know why you're determined to visit every vampire in this territory and see if he wants to sleep with you. I can't begin to imagine what this is." His beautiful eyes studied me. "Some sort of personal challenge?"

"Something like that," I told him. Seemed safest.

His thumb stroked across my lower lip. "What do you have to prove? I know that you are beautiful. And sexy. And you drive me crazy. You know that, too."

My eyes widened.

"And if you want a one-night stand with a supernatural," he said, leaning in so close that his breath brushed against my cheek, "I'll break out my fangs, lick you for hours, and then ride you so hard that you'll be bowlegged the next day."

And he kissed me. Hot. Wet. Possessive. His mouth swooped over mine and his tongue thrust against mine in a move that was a decided claim. And then he pulled away, leaving me dazed and wanting.

"So you think about that," he whispered.

He got in the car, buckled his seat belt, and drove away with Carol.

I thought about his hard, possessive kiss. Josh was so laid-back and easygoing, yet he'd grown fierce on vampire Lonnie when he'd felt I'd been threatened. He'd grown even more possessive when he'd kissed me. He constantly touched me and complimented me. I felt branded. Claimed by him.

This . . . was going to be a problem.

And yet I toyed with the idea of taking what Josh was promising. Not as a solution to my problem—if he turned me, it'd be a death sentence, like Sara said. It would destroy the Russell clan if one of the cougars turned a human when they'd banned the act for others. No one would trust them, and the Alliance would crumble.

So I still needed a vampire.

But I could have just a quick fling, like he'd offered. Get this wild attraction out of our blood, since he didn't do long term and I couldn't do long term. We could make wild, passionate love with no strings attached.

And then he could go back to just being Josh, and I could go back to finding a vampire to turn me.

Did I want a one-night stand? I wasn't a virgin. I'd given that up back in high school, despite being gawky and insecure. My boyfriend then had been equally gawky and insecure, and a few rounds of sex had done nothing for his confidence or mine. After my mother's death, I'd deliberately had very few friends. I didn't date. I didn't do casual sex.

I didn't do casual *anything*, I realized. Maybe it was time to change that.

I thought of the vampire I'd had dinner with tonight and I shuddered, getting back into my car. Josh was sexy and alive and inviting. That man had been a cold killer. A night of hot were-cougar sex might be the only opportunity I had for pleasurable sex ever again.

The rest of that evening at work crawled by. Ryder and I answered phones, updated files, and went through a backlog of email. The usual stuff, except that I was working at half speed. I was finding it hard to focus, and I kept rubbing my eyes and seeing the letters on the screen blur anyhow.

"Girl, you need to go home and get a good night's sleep," Ryder told me, sounding cheerful and buzzed despite the early hour. She sipped another cup of coffee and straightened her stack of folders. "You look wiped."

I shook my head and squinted, trying to focus my gaze. "I'm good." It wasn't as if I'd be able to sleep anyhow.

My phone rang and I picked it up, fighting the wave of anxiety crashing through me. My screen was still blurry, my vision skewed. "Hello?"

"*Ma petite puce*, it's me. Got a minute?"

Oh, Lord. Little flea—my nickname from when I was a child. "Of course, Dad. What's up?"

"Well, I was realizing it's been a few weeks since we've gotten together," he said, all smiles in his voice.

My vision finally cleared, and I breathed a sigh of relief. "It has been a few," I agreed. "I thought you were busy with work?"

"I am, but I have this next week off," he said. "Posey and I are going to Vegas again!"

I forced a smile so he'd hear it in my voice. "That sounds great, Dad. You'll have to have a drink on me."

"We want you to come with us! It'll be fun, just the three of us. We can hit all the casinos. You haven't seen someone play blackjack until you've seen Posey play."

I grimaced at the thought. "I don't think I can get off work, Dad."

"Oh, call in sick. How often do you get to spend time with your dear old dad?"

Not often enough. But I looked at the box of chocolates on my desk. Thought about the fierce kiss Josh had given me in the parking lot. Thought about the next vampire date, booked two days from now. "I wish I could. Maybe you guys can swing by after the trip and tell me about it?"

We chatted for a bit longer, my father extolling the virtues of Posey and me listening patiently as I nibbled on a chocolate. They were delicious—the expensive kind, and Ryder had swooped up a handful, unable to resist as well. I nodded and made the appropriate responses as my father talked about the adventures on his latest flight. The weather had been bad on his last trip; he'd been stranded for two days in Manila. And did I know that he'd tried balut for the first time last week?

When Bathsheba entered the office, I decided to end the call. "I'm sorry, Dad, but my shift's about to end. Call me when you're back from Vegas and we'll meet up, okay?"

"Sounds good. I'll put a few chips down in your honor."

I smiled. "You do that. Love you, Dad; have fun."

Bath paused by my desk, eyeing the half-eaten box of chocolates and scattered cans of Red Bull on my desk. "Long night? You look wiped."

I was getting really damn tired of everyone telling me that I looked awful. But I knew she didn't mean anything by it, so I simply gave her a faint smile and held the box up. "Chocolate?"

As she plucked one from the box, my vision wavered and went blurry again. Anxiety clenched my stomach as strange lights flashed before my eyes.

Was my disease getting worse? The next step was hallucinations—which meant it was progressing, and fast. I rubbed my eyes and silently willed the sliding colors to go away.

When I opened them again, the colors were gone. Relieved, I reached for my computer mouse . . . and halted.

It looked like a giant cockroach.

I held in a screech and abruptly got up from my chair. Ryder glanced up at me, and I gave her a shaky smile. "I think I need a soda." I hurried away from my desk, hoping that by the time I returned, my mind would stop playing tricks on me.

It was going to be a long night.

Chapter Seven

I was just sitting down to one of my puzzles when the phone rang.

"Hello?"

"Hey. You asleep?" It was Josh.

Oh, if he only knew the answer to that question. "I'm not tired," I lied. "Why?"

"I have to run some errands today and I was wondering if you wanted to come along."

I tapped a puzzle piece on the table, thinking. Was this a trick question? My suspicious mind automatically wondered what he was up to. "Exactly why would I want to come along with you to run errands? Are you bored?"

"Nah. I just like spending time with you."

"You do?" I blurted out, surprised. Josh . . . liked to spend time with me? Immediately I wondered if it was just another flirty come-on and felt stupid. Of course it was.

"I do," he responded cheerfully. "Plus, I have a surprise for you if you spend the day with me. It'll mean an all-nighter for you, but I can handle it if you can handle it."

I couldn't resist the smile tugging at my mouth despite myself. "I'm used to all-nighters," I told him. "But tell me the surprise first."

"Nope. It's a secret. I'll tell you if you spend the day with me."

"Is this bribery?"

He laughed. "Of course it is. It's the only way I can get you out of your pajamas and into my arms, so I'll use it."

I blushed and put down the puzzle piece. "I'm not falling into your arms."

"I'll settle for spending some time together, then. Come on. What do you say?"

I hesitated.

"Remember, big surprise at the end of the day," he teased. "Well worth the missing hours of sleep."

"I'm getting dressed," I said, standing up and heading to my bedroom, curious despite myself. "Are you coming by to pick me up, then?"

"I'll be there in ten minutes."

"Only ten minutes? I thought you lived farther away."

"I do. I'm already on my way there."

Figured. "And what would you have done if I'd said no?"

His chuckle was warm. "I knew you wouldn't say no. You find me irresistible."

"*Batarde.* I do not." I hung up before he could come back with something suitable. I couldn't stop smiling, though. Okay, Josh irritated me, but it was a fun kind of irritation. He was incorrigible and flirty as hell, but I enjoyed his antics.

I'd barely finished dressing when I heard a knock at the door. Sure enough, Josh was ready and waiting, all grins. He didn't look the least bit tired, even though I knew he'd been up all night, just like me. He held out a cup of coffee as I opened the door. "Ready to go?"

I nodded and locked the door, pocketing my phone. "Thanks for the coffee."

"Thanks for being my company," he said cheerfully. "It's the least I could do."

"So where are we headed?" I asked as we trotted down the stairs and back out to the parking lot.

"We're going by Carol's place first. She promised to make me breakfast."

I gave him a cross look as we got into the car. "We're doing all this so you can get a free breakfast?"

"Not exactly. Free breakfast is just a perk."

We were quiet as Josh pulled onto the highway and began heading south. I sipped my coffee, content with watching Josh and the road. The neighborhoods got progressively worse and worse the longer we were in the car, and by the time we pulled into an apartment complex, I was ready to lock my doors and not get out of the car. "Carol lives here?"

"Rent's cheap, and she doesn't make a lot of money," Josh said. "Come on. She'll be thrilled to see you."

I followed him through the parking lot, trying my best not to be judgmental. The building could have used a good coat of paint, and the long carport stretched out in front of the building looked as if it was on its last legs. Graffiti covered a nearby Dumpster, and as we walked to Carol's first-floor apartment, I noticed dirty window-unit air conditioners hanging out of nearby windows. Classy. One of her neighbors had foil in the window. Double classy.

There was an enormous box on Carol's doorstep, and Josh immediately moved to it. "Can you hit the doorbell? I'm going to start moving this for her."

I did as I was told, and a moment later, Carol opened the door, giving Josh and me a beaming, wrinkled smile. "Josh, my love. You brought a friend today. Come on in!"

"This the entertainment center you ordered, Carol?" Josh hefted it, his voice strained as he carried the massive box into the house. "Or did you order a box of bricks?"

"Silly boy," Carol said, tittering. "Have you eaten breakfast yet?"

"Of course not," Josh said, moving into the living room of the tiny apartment and setting the entertainment center box against the door. "I knew you'd fix me up something delicious. That's how I talked Marie here into coming over."

She beamed a smile over at me. "Why don't I make some coffee?"

"Coffee sounds great," I told her, reaching down at the cat rubbing on my jeans leg. When she left the room, I looked over at Josh, who'd pulled out a pocketknife and was slitting open the sides of the box. "Is that what you came over for? To put together an entertainment center for her?"

Josh nodded, peeling tape back from the box. "Her last one broke a few days ago. I told her to buy one and I'd put it together."

Carol returned to the room, a fresh cup of coffee in hand. There were layers to Josh that I was just beginning to discover, and every time I thought I had him pegged, he surprised me.

Carol was a much better cook than the one at the diner. Her coffee was great, and her pancakes amazing. As she loaded me with breakfast food, Josh took bites between working on the furniture. It was clear that she was pleased that she had company, and I began to warm up to our visit. After a while, she pulled out some photo albums and showed me pictures of her family, all deceased.

I was starting to realize why Josh visited Carol so much, and my estimation of him grew. He worked hard on the entertainment center, screwing and bolting together the wood as if it had been no big deal, and looking pleased to do so.

Hours later, when it was all put together and we'd gone through all of Carol's pancakes, Josh set up her TV and programmed it for her.

"That's wonderful, Josh. You're such a good boy." She reached up and ruffled his hair, as if he'd been a child. "Do you think you could stop by Lula's place after you go? Her toilet won't stop running and she said her water bill was ten dollars more last month. She's quite concerned."

"You know I will," he said easily.

We said our good-byes to Carol, petted her cats one more time, and left. Josh immediately went next door and knocked.

"Lula?" I asked.

"Yep," he said. "Do you mind?"

"Not at all," I said honestly. At this point, I was more curious about how many people Josh stopped to help than anything else. I eyed the foil in the window and felt bad for internally mocking it when we'd first arrived. Was she trying to lower her power bill? A few dollars wasn't much here and there, but maybe she didn't have the money.

Lula was a wizened old woman with thick, outdated glasses and a floral muumuu. Her hands were twisted from arthritis, and she gave Josh a toothless smile. "There you are. Are you here to fix my toilet?"

"That I am, Miss Lula," Josh said cheerfully. "Why don't you show it to me?"

As she shuffled inside, I followed Josh, noting the dark interior of the apartment and the spotless floors and counters. Miss Lula was old, but she wasn't feeble. It was clear she was pleased to see Josh, talking a mile a minute and gesturing at her toilet as if it had been the biggest problem in the world. He listened politely, then set to working on it.

My estimation of Josh grew more. He was patient and kind—kinder than I was—and unfailingly nice. This didn't mesh with my mental vision of the careless, wild playboy that I'd always thought he was.

After a few minutes, Josh replaced the tank lid. "I need to get my toolbox, Lula. Can we come back in an hour?"

"Of course, of course," she said with a wave of her small hands. "I'll make you sandwiches for lunch. Does that sound nice?"

"You know it does," he told her. "We'll be back very shortly."

We piled back into Josh's car, and I gave him a curious look. "Where now?"

"To my place—the Russell place. I need to borrow some tools. That okay, or are you too tired to go on?"

"I'm fine," I told him truthfully. "And I want to come back."

The drive out to the Russell house was long but pleasant. Josh and I bickered over radio stations, and it turned into a game—find an obnoxious song on the radio and see if you could annoy the other person. It was childish, but it made me laugh, and the time with Josh passed so pleasantly that I couldn't remember why I'd ever been irritated with him.

When we finally parked in the driveway, I was surprised to see that a few cars were already there. "Someone home?"

He laughed. "I live with my brothers and cousins. Someone is always home."

Good point.

The Russell house was a two-story monster of a

house out in the country. It was spare on furnishings, which wasn't surprising, considering the fact that only men lived there. The place was clean and neat.

"I need to go find the toolbox," Josh told me. "It's in the garage. Just wait here a minute."

"Can I see your room?" I was suddenly wildly curious to see what kind of digs Josh had.

"Why, Marie," he said with amusement. "You want to see my bed?"

"Just curious is all," I said lightly, ignoring his innuendo.

"Go right ahead. Last room at the back of the hall upstairs. I'll just be a minute."

I waited for him to disappear, then headed up the stairs to his room. The door was shut, and I pushed it open slowly, feeling very much like an invader.

His room was messy in typical guy fashion. His clothes hamper was overflowing with laundry. The bed was covered with dark plaid blankets, tossed into a ball. Pillows were strewn all over the mattress, and magazines lay scattered in a nearby chair. I picked one up. Science magazine. The one underneath it was about cars, and the one below that was travel. Okay, that told me nothing about the man. I glanced over at his dresser. A few photos were stuck along the edge of the mirror, and a scatter of small objects decorated the surface.

I gravitated to the photos, mostly a montage of shots of Josh and his brothers on vacation. There was a photo of Beau, much younger, hanging off Josh's shoulders, both of them in swim trunks. And there was an older man who resembled Josh—his father? I'd heard Beau mention once that his father was deceased. Poor Josh. I knew what it was like to lose a parent.

An answering-machine light flickered, and I checked the display, curious. Thirty-one messages. Good Lord. If his messages were anything like the ones he got at the dating agency, they were all from women. My fingers hovered over the playback button, and I fought the urge to listen to them. That would be a major invasion of privacy.

"Whatcha doing?"

I whirled around, my face hot, to face one of the twins. I didn't know if it was Everett or Ellis. They looked exactly alike to me. "Um, hi."

He took a bite out of an apple, giving me an interested look. "Checking things out?"

"Um, no. I was just, uh, looking around. Josh is getting a toolbox." I stepped away from the answering machine, feeling guilty. "We're about to head back out."

"Mmmhmm." He took another bite of apple, still watching me. After a moment, he said, "He keeps it full on purpose."

"Huh?"

"The answering machine." He nodded at it. "Keeps it full on purpose. If it's full, no one can leave him a message. He prefers that. The girls don't leave him alone otherwise."

Oh. That was interesting. "I see."

"You were wondering about it, admit it."

I would admit no such thing. "You know, they might leave him alone if he'd actually pick up the phone. It's what normal people would do."

He snorted, as if I'd said something funny.

"You tellin' all my secrets, Ellis?" Josh appeared, clapping his cousin on the shoulder. "Maybe you should learn to keep your mouth shut."

Oh, hell. Now I was really caught red-handed.

"Eh," Ellis said, unafraid. He took another leisurely bite of apple. "I figured if you let her up in your bedroom unattended, she's probably pretty special."

"Probably," Josh agreed with a drawl.

"So he doesn't normally let women hang around in his bedroom?" I asked Ellis, unable to stop myself.

He only grinned, and I felt silly for asking.

"Come on, Marie." Josh nodded at the door. "We need to get a move on if we're going to fix Lula's toilet for her. We have to be done by five."

"Why?" I was curious despite myself. "What happens at five?"

"We have to leave for our date."

"Date?" I sputtered. "Are we going on a date?"

"We're going on a double date," he told me with a grin. "A pair of newly turned vampires. I figured you'd want to ask them some questions."

Ellis gave me a speculative look. "What kind of questions?"

Excitement flared through me. "None of your business. Josh, do you mean it?"

He nodded at me, looking pleased with himself.

I sucked in a breath in excitement. "You're the best, you know that?"

"Yeah," he said with a grin. "I know."

My palms were sweaty with excitement. I slid them up and down the legs of my jeans to dry them and tried not to look overeager.

Josh, meanwhile, sat next to me in the booth, his legs sprawled under the table as if he'd had not a care in the world. His beer was coated with condensation, however, and the large plate of food in front of him sat untouched, a sure sign that Josh wasn't nearly as relaxed as his manner suggested.

The restaurant was crowded despite the late hour, but dimly lit. Josh and I occupied a booth near the back, close enough to the bathroom that I looked up every time someone came near our table.

Here I was, dying to date a vampire—no pun intended—and I couldn't get them to go out with me. Yet all Josh had to do was snap his fingers and they'd come running to do him a favor.

I'd have resented it if I hadn't been so utterly thankful that he'd set this up. "You're the best, Josh," I told him again.

"I know," he replied, not looking at me. His gaze was rooted to the door. "You can thank me later."

I lightly smacked his arm, just imagining what that thanking would involve. "So they know about . . . me?"

He shot me a look at that, and I nearly melted at the heat in his gaze. God, Josh was sexy when he was riled up, and he was definitely riled up at the moment. "They know what I told them."

"Which is . . ."

"That you're dating a vampire, so you want to know what vampire society is like from reliable, unbiased sources."

That sounded about right. What surprised me was Josh's reluctance about the meeting.

I nudged him with my elbow. "You okay?"

"Fine," he said in a flat voice.

"You don't sound fine. You sound grumpy."

He glanced over at me, his mouth pulled into an unhappy line, arms crossed over his chest. "You know I'm not a big fan of all this vampire business."

"I know you're not. I appreciate the effort, though."

His gaze softened and he leaned in closer to me, as if he was about to kiss me. I tilted my face up toward his.

Josh's nostrils flared and he sniffed the air, then slid back into his seat again, moving away from me. "They're here."

My heart leapt in my chest. I immediately craned my neck, trying to see around Josh to the restaurant floor. "I don't see anyone."

"You'll recognize them when you see them," Josh said, placing a hand on my shoulder as I leaned over his lap. "Sit down."

I did, forcing myself to be patient. I could have contacted a vampire or two myself through the agency, but they tended to be suspicious and, because I was human, reluctant to open up. The fact that two were willing to come and sit down with me and talk was flat-out amazing . . . and I owed it all to Josh.

I squeezed his arm happily at the sight of the couple approaching the table. I recognized the tall, lanky man with the wild tuft of hair and the short, curvy woman at his side. "Valjean! Ruby! Hi there!"

Valjean had been my client for about a half a minute before he'd shacked up with Ruby, and he'd been on my dating list for vampires. Ruby had only used the agency a few times herself, but I was familiar with her, since her sister, Jayde, was one of our more notorious clients.

I glanced over at Josh. "You didn't tell me it was going to be them."

"They're both fairly new to the vampire world," he said with an easy shrug of his shoulders, leaning forward. "Thought it might be good for you to get their perspective."

"Pleasure to see the two of you again," Valjean said in a courteous voice, smoothing a hand down the front of his coat. He gestured for Ruby to slide into the booth and she did, her glittering gaze focused on me in a look that wasn't exactly friendly.

Oh, dear. Was she feeling territorial? I knew from dealing with her sister that were-jaguars tended to be a bit . . . demanding. And given the fact that Ruby was the other vampire, I wondered how it affected her nature. My suspicions were confirmed when Valjean slid into the booth next to her and she immediately latched onto his arm, her lips tightly pursed, as if she wanted to bare her teeth at me.

As if sensing the mood at the table, Josh casually threw an arm over my shoulders and tugged me close, as if I'd been his date. Ruby immediately relaxed, her smile growing a bit more genuine. I realized in that moment that it wasn't territory that was freaking Ruby out—it was Valjean. She was worried I'd try to snag him from her or something, and she was staking her claim early.

I would have been amused by it, except that a picture flashed in my mind of Josh going out with another woman, and I felt a distinct flash of rage. My fingers curled into my jeans and I bit the inside of my cheek to blot the thought from my mind.

"Thank you both for coming," Josh said. "I appreciate you taking a bit of time out of your schedules to answer Marie's questions."

"We're visiting Ruby's family," Valjean said easily. "Then it's back off to Rome for us. I promised Ruby a sightseeing tour for her birthday."

A flash of a smile crossed Ruby's face, and I peered at her teeth. No sign of fangs. Of course not. Why did I think these new vampires would be different from any other vampire I'd seen or dated? The fangs were retractable. For feeding, they extended several inches, like snake fangs. Any other time, they remained hidden and looked like nothing more than sharp incisors.

"Rome sounds nice," I said conversationally, not sure if I should jump right in with the vampire questions or if that would be rude. "Have either of you been before?"

"I visited when I was first turned," Valjean said, steering the conversation to the subject I wanted to hear about the most. "I—"

"What was it like?" I blurted, wanting to keep the subject on vampires and turning. I felt desperate to get some answers. "Did it hurt?"

Not that it mattered. I was pretty sure it hurt less than dying. But now that it felt within my grasp, I was . . . curious.

"I don't remember." Valjean grimaced apologetically. "I was drunk and passed out when I was turned."

"And I was dying from being shot in the back, so I'm no better with that answer," Ruby offered. "All I remembered was that Michael put his mouth on my neck and the world was getting foggy."

"Michael?" I asked curiously.

To my surprise, Valjean blushed bright red. Ruby gave him an amused, affectionate glance. "His vampire name is Valjean. Real name is Michael. Now that we're together, we're trying to switch to new names, but we keep forgetting to use them from time to time."

"New names?" I asked politely. "Is that a thing with vampires?"

"It is. It's best, since you're essentially making a break from your old life. Most vampires change names every twenty years or so, in order to not arouse suspicion from the locals." Valjean's mouth gave a wry twist. "Vampire society has a lot of rules."

"So you were dying, Ruby? Did you not want to be turned?"

"I hadn't asked her," Valjean said. "I thought maybe, after a few years together, I'd broach the question before she started to get all middle-aged and saggy—"

Ruby gave a mock gasp and curled her fingers into menacing claws. At least, they would have been menacing if her eyes hadn't been gleaming with amusement. "Don't make me come over there," she purred.

My face flushed. This sounded less like teasing and more like foreplay. "So you didn't have a chance to ask her?" I repeated, steering the conversation back on track. Josh's hand rubbed between my shoulders, a comforting, subtle presence.

"There was no time," Valjean said. "I took a risk and hoped that she wouldn't be too mad at me."

"Furious," Ruby said in that soft, rumbling purr that was anything but angry.

Valjean flushed red again and Ruby looked pleased.

"There are lots of rules with vampires, you say?" I encouraged. These two were cute and all, but they weren't giving me much that I didn't already know.

They exchanged a look, then Ruby shook her head. "Can't talk about it to non-vampires. We'll get in trouble."

"Trouble with who?"

After a moment, Valjean said, "Other vampires."

"Let me guess. Another vampire rule?"

"Bingo." Ruby grinned again, and I noticed that her canines were a bit elongated. "It's kind of like the first rule of Fight Club and all that."

"Gotcha. But what about family?" I asked, thinking of my father. I couldn't exactly leave him behind. I was all the family he had left in the world.

"If your family is Alliance, it's not a big deal," Ruby said. "Since the secret is more or less out. Non-Alliance, however, are expected to remain out of the loop."

I swallowed hard. So either way, my father was going to lose his daughter. "I see."

Josh pulled me closer to him, as if sensing my distress. "What else should Marie know about dating a vampire?"

"Or turning," I added quickly, ignoring Josh's frown.

"Lots of things change when you turn," Ruby began, pausing when the waiter arrived with glasses of water for her and Valjean. When he left, she delicately pushed the glass to one side, rejecting it. "I don't know about Valjean, but my appetites have changed slightly. Shifters like a heavy meat diet, but I find that I can't stomach any of that now. As a vampire, you don't need food or drink, just blood. And you have to drink often."

"Exactly how often?"

"Two to three times a day, just like human meals," Valjean said easily. He picked up his glass and took a sip of the water, as if determined to prove a point. "And eventually your stomach resettles and you can tolerate most drinks. Ruby is new, so it still turns her stomach."

Valjean offered Ruby his glass of water. She wrinkled her nose at him and pressed fingers to her lips, as if holding back bile.

"What about sunlight?"

"Killer," Ruby said flatly. "You sleep through it most of the time, but if you get stuck out in it, you're hosed."

This was sounding more and more depressing. I felt a flare of anxiety but forced it aside. This was my best option, and I was going to run with it. "So what are the perks of being a vampire, then? You've mentioned some of the unpleasant things, but there has to be a plus side, right?"

Josh gave me another suspicious frown.

Valjean and Ruby exchanged a look. He grasped her hand and pulled it to his lips, kissing the back of it in an achingly tender motion. "You get to spend eternity with the one you love. That's worth everything, don't you think?"

Except I wasn't in this for love, just survival. I couldn't picture any of the vampires I'd met so far affectionately kissing my hand like Valjean had Ruby's, or tenderly pulling me to his side and teasing me like Josh did.

Did I want eternity with a cold man I didn't love? I looked over at Josh, whose normally laughing eyes were somber, his mouth drawn into that

thin line again. Or did I want what little time I had
left with a man I was beginning to like a lot but
couldn't have?

A few weeks ago, my answer would have been
instantaneous: I wanted eternity.

But now I wasn't so sure. All I could think about
was some stranger kissing my hand, like Valjean
had kissed Ruby's . . . and how much it would hurt
Josh.

My stomach flipped a little. "Eternity sounds
great to me," I said in a fake enthusiastic voice.

"It beats dying," Ruby said dryly.

That it did. Time to change the subject. "So,
vampire dating pointers . . . ?"

Chapter Eight

"No more callouts," Bath told me the next day as I came in to work. "We're putting a temporary hiatus on the inactive-client roundup."

"Why's that?" I asked, glancing at the stack of folders on my desk. I'd barely made it through a third of them. "Is something wrong?"

"Everyone's all riled up over the situation with the tiger clan," she said, crossing her arms under her breasts and leaning on the side of my desk. "Beau has another meeting with the heads of the clans tonight to try and smooth things over. They're trying to shut our agency down."

"Shut us . . . down? Why would they do that?"

She chewed on her lip for a moment before answering. "I don't know if shutting us down is the right word, as much as . . . installing new management."

"Because we're human?" I guessed.

"Bingo," she said with a sigh. "Many feel that it's better if a supernatural service actually has supernatural staff."

"What about Sara?" I pointed out.

"They consider her to be 'not enough' supernatural presence. Sure, she's a shifter, but she was human, and she's a werewolf, and that's two strikes against her." Bath sounded tired. "Beau's refusing to shut us down, but right now it's best if we lay low."

"I see," I said, trying not to panic. If we were shut down, I wouldn't have access to the Alliance database to find my vampire. "So we'd be unemployed just because we're human? That's totally unfair."

"And it doesn't help that people are starting crazy rumors, too."

Uh-oh. "Crazy rumors?"

"That we're setting them up with humans and trying to pass them off as shifters. Two months ago, everyone wanted a human. Now everyone just wants to keep things separate. Long story short, no more callouts for now. If they want our services, we'll let them come to us."

"Gotcha," I said, feeling sick. I had a sneaking suspicion that someone had leaked that they'd either seen me on a date, or one of my dates had let it slip that I was human. Damn it. I needed to talk to Josh. This was going to put a massive kink in my plans.

I texted him. *Where are you tonight?*

Busy for the next few nights, beautiful, he sent back immediately. *You won't forget me, will you?*

So I won't see you for a few days? I have a date

tonight. *I thought you were going to be my wingman. And by wingman, I mean hover unseen like an overprotective older brother.*

The next text came back right away. *Jesus, Marie. Way to kill a guy's boner. Don't ever call me your brother again.*

And then, *So who's the date with?*

Some vampire named Andre. He was on your "maybe" list, remember?

His next text came almost ten minutes later, and I spent the entire time tapping my fingers impatiently. *I don't know.*

Why? What's wrong with him?

Sorry. Busy. Gimme a few. Busting a few heads right now.

He came back a few minutes later with *Nothing's exactly wrong with him, other than he's a vampire. I've worked for him before. He's quiet. Doesn't say much. Very polite.*

This didn't sound like a problem to me. *So what's the issue?*

The issue is that I'm working for the next several nights and I can't be there to protect you.

You don't have to be there.

In fact, it might be best if he wasn't. His getting possessive wasn't going to help me, yet I enjoyed it far too much.

And that was a problem.

His next text came a few minutes later. *Just . . . go someplace really public and be careful. And text me when you're done to let me know how it goes.*

I promise, I sent back. *Who knows, maybe this one won't be a dud.*

I hope he is. You'll have no choice but to fall into my arms.

That made me smile.

I decided to follow Josh's advice about the venue. Someplace public. Someplace noisy and crowded. And someplace close enough to the office that I could sprint back at a moment's notice. In other words, Greek food at Konstantine's.

I was more conservative in my clothing, too. I wore a bra with the tight pink boatneck sweater, and an equally black tight skirt that gave me an overtly feminine flair without saying, *Please suck on my neck right now.* I'd borrowed the clothes from Ryder, and I wore high heels. After all, I wanted to seem interested.

I fidgeted at the table, waiting for my date to arrive. Was I going to get stood up again? I checked my watch. He was ten minutes late—not a good sign. To my horror, I started to have another vision-blurring spell. They were hallucinations, I knew. Last time I'd gone to sleep, I'd spent half the time staring at walls that had seeped blood. Willing my brain to stop sending me the horrible visions, I'd known that it was just another stage in my slow decline, but that hadn't made things any easier. The hallucinations would keep coming, and eventually I wouldn't be able to tell reality from fiction.

Worst of all, there was no one I could talk to about it. My burdens were mine alone, and sometimes it felt crushing. But I'd made the choice to handle this on my own—a choice I just regretted in weak moments.

Maybe I could tell Josh. Sure, he was reckless and flirty and needed his ego reined in, but . . . I liked him. I felt safe with him. Maybe because we'd been spending so much time together. I pulled out my phone and started a text to him, then stopped.

If I told him, he'd stop flirting with me. Sick wasn't sexy. A dying girl wouldn't pique his interest. If I told him the truth, our flirty friendship would disappear.

I put my phone away.

"Minnie?"

I looked up at the sound of the male voice and stared. The man in front of me was gorgeous. Tall and athletically slim, he had short, straight blond hair that was slicked back from a widow's peak, pale skin, and bright blue eyes. He was smiling at me, and I noticed that his canines were only slightly longer than they should have been.

"I'm Andre."

"Oh, wow," I said, unable to hide my smile. I stood up and extended my hand. "Hi. I'm Minnie."

"Wow?" he asked with a grin.

I was charmed by that toothy smile. Everything was out in the open with him—he didn't hide his fangs under a close-lipped smirk like the last guy.

It made me feel like I could trust him. "You just look . . . better than I expected," I said honestly.

"The vampire thing?" he asked delicately, though the grin remained on his face.

Oh, I must have offended him. "No," I said quickly. "The dating service thing. I seem to strike out a lot."

"I can't imagine why," he said, moving behind my chair to push it in for me. "You look just fine to me."

"Thank you," I murmured, and sat down. He moved back to the other side of the table and sat down across from me. As one of the waiters zoomed past, Andre raised a hand to call him over. Cuff links glinted, and I studied his clothing. He was wearing a dark gray suit jacket over a lighter dress shirt. Nice togs.

For some reason I thought of Josh's endless T-shirts and jeans, then I shook the thought away. Thinking about him on my date wasn't going to help me with anything.

"A bottle of red wine, please." Andre glanced over at me, the polite smile remaining in place. "If that's all right."

"Wine's fine," I agreed. Heck, I was just happy that my date was going to drink instead of stare at my neck all night. When the waiter left, I clasped my hands in my lap to stop their nervous twitching. "So, Andre, what do you do?"

He blinked at me, puzzled.

Merde. I must have said something wrong. "I'm sorry. Old money?"

"Oh," he said with a slow laugh. "Yes. Sorry. I didn't understand the question at first. It's not really done in my circles."

"I'm sorry," I said, wishing I could crawl under the table. Embarrassment made my cheeks hot. "I didn't realize."

"Guess it's a big deal with were-otters?" He gave me an assessing look.

"Overprotective parents," I lied with a smile.

"I can only imagine," Andre said easily, glancing up at the waiter as he placed two wineglasses on the table. We waited in companionable silence as the waiter popped the cork and began to pour. When he'd left again, Andre picked up his glass and raised it to me. "Toast?"

I raised my glass and looked at him expectantly.

"To the start of something delicious," Andre said.

Now that was something I could get behind. I clinked my glass to his and took a drink.

"Shall we order?" Andre said, picking up his menu.

I glanced down at mine and sucked in a small breath. The letters on the menu blurred and bled off the page, my eyes doing that weird thing again. I closed them for a minute, and then gave Andre what I hoped was a helpless, feminine smile. "Will you order for me?"

He looked pleased. "But of course."

Dinner went well. Better than well. Andre was cultured and polite, and very amusing. For every topic we touched upon, he had an interesting story to tell. I learned that he was four hundred years old, owned a nearby art gallery that he'd purchased some fifty years ago, and loved classical music. He hated modern music, television, and cell phones, but he adored modern cars, especially sports cars.

I did my best to keep the conversation focused on him, all the better to not have to make up an elaborate story about my fictional self. Andre seemed more than happy to talk about himself. The date went on for hours as we chatted, and we slowly went through the bottle of wine. Inside my purse, my phone buzzed over and over with texts, but I ignored it.

My date was going *great*. Hell, *yes*, I thought, smiling at Andre over my glass. I had this one in the bag.

"So, Minnie." Andre tilted his wineglass and smiled at me. "I have to ask. You're young. You're very pretty. And female shifters are in quite a lot of demand, I hear. What made you decide to look . . . elsewhere?"

Basically, *Why are you dating a vampire?*

I thought for a minute, remembering Josh's words. Vampires were predators. They liked the chase. I needed to give him something to hook his interest without scaring him off.

I bit my lip, and his attention immediately fell to my mouth. Ah. Vampires. Biting fetish. I'd keep that in mind for later. I bit my lip for a bit longer, then gave him what I hoped passed for a shy smile.

"Most of the men in my clan are rather young, and the older ones are domineering. I like men with experience, but I don't like the brutish alpha attitudes."

He smiled and gave the barest of nods. "Culture can be hard to find, sometimes. It's a good thing we've met, then."

Oddly enough, that made me think of Josh, with his baseball cap and his sly, knowing grin. He was the opposite of cultured, but he was utterly delicious.

I pushed the thought away. "I can honestly say that I am incredibly pleased to meet you, Andre."

His smile deepened. "The feeling is mutual."

I snuck back to the agency an hour later, slightly tipsy and giddy with how well my date had gone. Things were looking up. Way, way up.

"How'd it go?" Ryder asked as soon as I walked through the door.

"Like a charm!" I told her.

And then I blacked out.

"Marie? Marie!" A warm hand patted my cheek frantically. "Wake up, girl."

I put a hand up and batted the patting one away. Then I cracked my eyes open and stared into Ryder's concerned face, and the office ceiling above her. What was I doing on the floor? My body throbbed in places that shouldn't have been injured, but I couldn't remember falling.

"Mmm. What happened?"

She sat back on her haunches and shook her head. "How about you tell me?"

I sat up, wincing, and rubbed my forehead. "I must have fainted."

"Did you drink too much?" Ryder's gaze was obviously concerned. "Do you want me to call an ambulance?"

I waved it off. "No, no. I'm fine." *The ambulance can't do anything for me.*

She looked at me dubiously.

"I'm serious. I'm fine." To prove it, I got to my feet, wobbly in the high heels.

Ryder helped me up, and I moved toward my desk. As soon as I sat down she leaned over me, brushing lint and dirt off the sweater I'd borrowed. "You sure you're okay?"

I gave her a wry smile. "It's nothing that a good night's sleep wouldn't cure." I raised a pinky into the air and looked at her. "Pinky swear that this goes on the list of dirty secrets known only to you and me?"

She sighed but hooked her pinky in mine. "Pinky swear. I just worry about you, Marie."

"I know you do. But I need this to stay a secret, Ryder. It's important."

She sighed heavily. "It'll stay under the pinky rules. Just be careful with yourself."

And that was why Ryder was my best friend.

She insisted on getting me a drink of water, then

she went back to her desk. I clicked over to my Minnie profile to log my date—a requirement of all participants in the Midnight Liaisons dating service—and noticed that I already had a message.

From Andre.

I clicked on it, feeling a flutter of excitement in my breast.

Beautiful Minnie. It was an utter pleasure to meet you this evening. I feel incredibly lucky that I had the opportunity to go out with you, and would love to make lightning strike twice. I'd love to see you again. Say, Friday? You pick the venue. All my devotion, Andre.

If I could have stood up, I would have done a touchdown dance. I might not die after all!

Despite my pounding headache, I was so excited that I could barely concentrate on work. I quickly accepted Andre's request for a second date. After that, I threw myself into updating files and answering emails, logging information and keeping busy. All the while, my brain was racing a mile a minute.

This could really happen. I was one step closer to getting someone to turn me!

By the time the morning shift got to the office, I was so wired with excitement that I bounded to my car and sped all the way home.

I pulled into my parking space and raced up the stairs, only to stop short in surprise. Josh was sitting on my second-floor stoop, his baseball cap pulled low. He stood at the sight of me, his eyes feral and glinting in the early morning sunlight.

"Where have you been?" His intense gaze ran over me, as if checking me over and reassuring himself. "I've texted you for the last several hours and you haven't responded. Is everything okay?"

Even Josh's concern couldn't harsh my buzz. I quickly unlocked my front door and sauntered inside. "I was on a date with an amazing vampire, and everything is great."

He followed me in, frowning. "Amazing . . . vampire?"

"Andre, remember? He was on the list."

"He was a 'maybe,' Marie. I'm not sure that I like him as your pick. There's something about him that's untrustworthy."

I waved his concerns away, shutting the door. "Andre's one of the better ones. He's good-looking, friendly, polite, and he wants to see me again!" I punctuated the last with a giddy little hop and grinned at him. "Isn't that awesome?"

He stared at me as if fascinated.

I stilled, giving him a blank look. "What? What is it?"

"You." The awed expression remained on his face. "I think that's the first time I've ever seen you smile, Marie."

I grinned up at him. I hadn't had a lot to smile about lately, but right now? The world had potential, and I was thrilled to be in it.

Josh's hand went to my waist and he stepped

forward. He kept staring down at me, and my smile began to slide away, my pulse quickening. Was something wrong? But then he tilted his head toward me, slowly, his eyes going hazy with desire, and I realized he was going to kiss me. Those lips that I'd been fantasizing about for days moved closer to mine.

I should have turned him away. Should have thrown on the brakes and stepped out of his grasp. There was Andre, the vampire with potential, to think about. My future of living a full, healthy undead life.

But Josh was here, in my arms, his strong arms wrapped around my waist, his gorgeous face tilted close to mine. He looked completely and utterly delicious, and so ready to kiss me.

I tilted my face to his.

"You sure you want me to kiss you, Marie?" Josh said softly, his mouth so close that I felt his lips whisper over my own, a merciless tease.

"If I didn't, you'd be sitting on the front step right now," I told him, looking up into his eyes. They were still gleaming like a cat's, and it was even more noticeable now that we were inside my dark apartment. I was fascinated by the way they reflected the light.

"Good," he said, the sound half a growl. Then his mouth descended on mine.

I whimpered at the fierce possessiveness of his kiss. This wasn't the coaxing tease that he'd given me before. This was a brand of ownership, and I was totally unprepared for the intensity of it. His mouth swooped over mine, hard, hot, his tongue sliding into my mouth in a slow rhythm that left no doubt in my mind what he intended.

Josh was kissing the hell out of me, and it wasn't because he was excited for me that I'd found a vampire. He was kissing the hell out of me because he wanted to claim me for his own.

Surely not.

But then he was kissing me harder, dazing me with the intensity—and deliciousness—of his kiss. He sucked at my lower lip and bit it in a sensual invitation. "You're so beautiful," he told me softly, and his hand stroked up my back, pulling me tight against him.

I moaned at the feel of that big, warm body against mine. My hands went around his neck, my face tilting up for another kiss. Why stop now?

He seemed happy to oblige, but this time it was a light, teasing kiss intended to coax my mouth open and leave me wanting.

"You're mine," he whispered against my mouth just before he stroked his tongue into my mouth again.

My internal brakes squealed to a halt.

Chapter Nine

I shoved at his chest. "Excuse me?"

Josh didn't respond, and I pushed his jaw away when he leaned in to nibble on my neck. "Joshua Russell!"

He finally leaned back. "What?"

"I am not *yours*."

A devastating, confident grin spread over his face. "Then quit kissing me back, Marie." When he leaned in to kiss me again, I averted my face. He drew back, looking puzzled. "Why is it not okay for me to kiss you?"

"Because you're declaring ownership like some sort of Neanderthal. I'm not *yours*. I am *mine*. If you still want that one-night stand you keep mentioning, I'm totally game for that. Just not anything else."

He stared at me as if I'd grown another head.

"What?" I asked. "You're the big ladies' man. You said yourself that you don't date more than once. Can't I do the same?"

Josh's eyes were flashing cat in that way that told

me he was completely irritated. "So you want a one-night stand?"

"Sure." My heart thudded at the very thought of spending the night with Josh. No strings attached. Just him and me, in bed together, doing lovely, dirty things to each other. "I'm fine with that."

"And then you're going to turn right back around and go out with that vampire again, right?"

When he put it that way . . . "Right."

"And you think I'm not going to have a problem with this?"

I put my hands on my hips. "Why not? You're a serial dater. I'm surprised you don't have ten women lined up in the wings, just waiting for you to crook your finger and they'll come running. You just snap your fingers and panties go flying."

"I haven't dated anyone in weeks, Marie. Not since I started helping you out. Does that tell you anything?"

I forced myself not to play through the possibilities. "All it tells me is that you're going through a dry spell."

He hissed, and to my shock, it sounded just like . . . a cat. I watched his eyes go completely feral, his nostrils flaring. His eyes glinted with the low light and I gasped, realizing that they were changing to were-cougar eyes. Josh was losing his grip on his humanity. His hands went to my shoulders, and I felt his claws prick against my shirt, digging into the fabric just enough to let me know that they were there.

He smiled, and I watched his canines elongate. "Is this what turns you on, then, Marie? You want to see some crazy supernatural shit in bed? I don't understand this fetish, but if that's what it takes to make you look at me, I'll give you what you need."

He thought I was a freak with a vampire fetish? That . . . hurt. I gave him my iciest look. "Get your hands off me."

He flung himself away, pacing into my living room. His movements were quick, jerky, as if he was working hard to control himself. He wouldn't look at me.

I felt . . . awkward. Unhappy. I was losing his friendship, which wasn't what I wanted. Not at all. How was I supposed to fix this situation? How could I? Why had I let him get close in the first place? "I'm sorry, Josh. You just don't understand."

He laughed, but there was no amusement in his voice. "I don't *understand*? I've been hitting on you for weeks, Marie. I know it's hard to get it through your thick skull, but I *like* you. I like your personality. I think you're beautiful. I live for one of those rare smiles. I love it when you chop people down to size with that tongue of yours. I don't even mind when it's me. Every time you speak French, I get instantly hard. And all you want are . . . vampires?"

He turned around, and I saw frustration in his face. "So tell me, Marie. What does a vampire have that I don't? Because I'm seriously interested, but it seems that all you're looking for is a cheap thrill.

Is it that they have bigger fangs? Is it the undead thing? What?"

I said nothing.

He swore. "I'm sorry—I'm done here. I can't win this one, and you won't talk to me, so have a nice life, Marie Bellavance. I'm sure you'll find just the right vampire, since only a vampire will do."

He opened the door.

Panic flared in my chest. He was going to walk away. Forever. If he left now, it was for keeps. "Josh—I'm dying."

He slowly turned. He stared at me. After a long, tense moment, he said, "What did you just say?"

I felt naked, laid open in a way that I was un-used to. Josh was the first one I'd shared this with. "I'm . . . dying." To my horror, my voice broke a little on the last word. "I probably have six months to a year before . . . the end."

Which wouldn't be pretty. And I'd be a mess long before then, completely out of my mind and unable to function.

He quietly shut the door and leaned against it, staring at me as if unable to grasp what I was telling him. "I . . . Marie, I didn't know."

"Well, of course you didn't," I told him, forcing my tone to be light and wry, as if my world hadn't been falling apart right then. "I haven't told anyone except you."

"Is it cancer?"

I wish. The thought came immediately, and I began to laugh hysterically, because the thought was absurd. God, that was fucked-up.

"No," I said. "It's not cancer. It's something called fatal familial insomnia."

"I don't know what that is."

"It's very rare. My mother had it. Died from it ten years ago. I inherited the gene. It's not supposed to kick in until I'm forty or so, but it hit early."

He shook his head, moving closer, and reached out toward me. "Marie—"

I moved away before he could touch me, hugging my arms to my chest, feeling sick. Admitting it to another person meant that it existed. It meant really, *really* acknowledging it. I was flat-out panicking, and I felt the absurd urge to cry.

He followed me as I walked away. "Do you . . . do you want to talk about it?"

Another hysterical laugh bubbled in my throat. "No, I don't want to talk about it. I just . . ." I sighed, staring at my blank walls. I suddenly felt exhausted. "I want to take a freaking nap."

"Fatal . . . insomnia," Josh repeated. "And that means you can't sleep?"

I pushed forward, suddenly desperate to show him what it meant to not sleep. To have someone else *get it*. I opened my closet door. Hundreds of boxes were crammed in there, neatly stacked on shelves that I'd built to hold them all. "I do puzzles when I can't sleep. I've done every single one of these," I told him. "Some, even twice."

He said nothing, simply looked at the puzzles, then back to me.

"And here," I said, racing across the apartment to my small bathroom. I went to the counter and threw open the medicine cabinet. I grabbed boxes of over-the-counter sleep aids, prescription bottles, and shoved them all at him. "I tried taking all of these. None of them work. *Nothing* works. I close my eyes, but I can't sleep. Maybe ten minutes, if I'm lucky, but after that, nothing. My brain can't shut off, and I'm so tired that I could just collapse. Except when I collapse, I still can't sleep."

He remained silent, his eyes dark as he watched me.

"Do you know what it's like?" My hands clenched into fists as my frustration and helplessness built inside me. I wanted to scream, but I forced my voice to be calm. "Imagine being hungry all the time, yet you can't eat. You just can't. For no good reason at all. I go through that every single fucking night. And it's going to kill me.

"There are four stages of the disease. When I was eighteen, my mother stopped sleeping. Then she started getting panic attacks, kind of like I'm having right now," I said, feeling my pulse flutter wildly in my chest.

"Marie—"

"I need to get all of this out while I can." I took a deep breath, forcing myself to calm a little. "It starts with the inability to sleep. Next you have panic attacks. Then paranoia. Then, you start to hallucinate. The insomnia continues to get worse, and toward the end you become completely out of your mind from the lack of sleep. And then you die. It's horrible, Josh. Absolutely horrible. My mother . . . she was beautiful. French-Canadian. Long, dark, curly hair and the happiest smile. I miss her every day," I said softly.

"What about a doctor?"

I shook my head. "They can't help. I've tried pills of every kind. I've tried therapy. Hypnosis. I've seen specialists. They all want to run tests on me, and if they discover the cause, then the experimental treatments will begin. I'll spend the next six months being monitored and drugged and poked and prodded, and none of it will do a bit of good, because no one knows how to fix it. I'm better off spending those six months actually doing something about my disease."

"And this is why you want a vampire," he said quietly.

I nodded. "I thought of it a few weeks ago. That I could get someone to turn me. Sara said that diseases skate right off shifters. And vampires, well, they're already undead. I have all these resources in the agency, right? So why not use them?"

He reached for my hands and tugged them into his own. "Why not a shifter, then? I can change you."

"No, you can't," I said quietly. "You're Beau's brother. He's trying to hold the Alliance together with the force of his will alone. Everyone's freaking out over that tiger clan incident. They exiled that tiger couple, and exile is permanent. For a shifter, I imagine it's close to death. You're no longer to your family—I won't have you living in exile just to turn me. Not when there's a perfectly good vampire around—they don't have to follow all of the Alliance rules."

"But vampires don't turn just whoever they want and then walk away. There's commitment involved."

"I know. I just have to take that chance. Maybe I'll be lucky and find a nice vampire to spend eternity with."

Josh gave me a flat, emotionless look. "So I'm off the table because I can't turn you. But I'm perfectly fine for a one-night stand?"

I bit my lip. "I shouldn't want to sleep with you, but I do."

"Damn, Marie," he said, yanking his cap off and raking his hand through his hair. "I don't know what to say."

I twisted my fingers. "I know it's complicated."

He gave a short, bitter laugh. "Yeah, I'll say. Call me crazy, but it doesn't sit quite right with me to sleep with you and then turn you over to the next vampire in the hopes that he's the one for you."

It didn't sound right to me, either, but I didn't know what else to do. "You said yourself that you weren't big on commitment. I'm the ultimate in noncommitment relationships."

"That is *not* a selling point."

"You could always wait until I'm turned," I said softly. "Maybe we could always give . . . you and me . . . a try after I'm turned."

He shook his head. "Marie, if a vampire turns you, he's going to want you to be his blood partner.

That's a mate for life. It's taken very seriously. If you get turned, you're off-limits. Jesus," he swore. "This is a hell of a plan."

So I could have hot Josh and an early tombstone, or I could have a cold vampire and eternity. "I'm not changing my mind," I said quietly. "Not when I'm this close to getting someone to turn me."

Not when I was hallucinating at least once a day now. My disease was accelerating at a rapid pace.

He stared at me for so long that I felt uncomfortable. "Marie . . . I need time to think about all of this. I don't know that I can keep helping you. I just . . . I don't know."

I was guessing that the one-night stand was off the table now, too. I felt a flash of bitterness at that, but I wasn't surprised. Finding out that someone was dying totally changed the dynamic. It was hard to nail and bail on a dying girl, after all.

"I'm telling you this because you're my friend, Josh," I said. "Not because I want more than you've already given me."

He put his hands on my shoulders and kissed my forehead. And then sighed. "I have to go. I need some time to think about all of this."

I didn't try to stop him. Either he'd see things my way, or I'd lost a friend. I didn't have options this late in the game, and if he didn't understand that, then I was better off without him.

Strange how that wasn't sitting so well in my gut, though.

———

Josh didn't call me that day. I knew it was hard for him to absorb all at once. I'd been living with it for ten years, and it was still hard for me.

But I was exhausted, mentally and physically. It was as if telling Josh had sucked all the energy out of my body. Normally I held it together pretty well, but by the time I got to work that evening, I was running on empty. I'd doubled my daily vitamins and sucked down an espresso on the way to the office, but I still felt tired as hell.

Which was why it took a moment for it to register when I sat down and noticed that Savannah Russell sat at Ryder's desk, and Ellis Russell sat at Sara's. I stared at them, frowned, and checked the calendar on my computer. I had the right day.

Oh, no. A sick feeling landed in the pit of my stomach. I rubbed my eyes. Was this a hallucination? Oh, God. It seemed so real. Anxiety fluttered through me, and I felt my jaw clenching in the onset of a panic attack. This was bad—

"There you are," Sara said cheerfully, sticking her head out of Bathsheba's small office. "Come here for a second."

I walked carefully to the small office at the back. I was surprised to see Ryder inside, sitting across from Bathsheba.

"Good, everyone's here now," Bath said with a smile.

"What's going on?" I asked.

"Girl's night out. It's time for a little team bonding. How do you feel about heading out to a bar and getting our drink on?"

I hesitated. I was exhausted, and with the cocktail of (rather useless) medications I was taking, I wasn't supposed to really drink. "Who's going to man the phones?"

Sara laughed. "Jeez, you are totally a zombie before you get a few cups of coffee in you. Didn't you see Ellis and Savannah out there?"

So they were real? Oh, thank God. My knees felt weak with relief. I put on a big smile. "So where are we going?"

I stared at the tight, gleaming butt cheeks ten feet away and turned to glare at Ryder. "Who thought a strip bar was a good idea?"

Ryder sipped a margarita and pointed at Bathsheba. Bathsheba turned bright red and pointed at Sara.

I turned to my left. Grinning and shaking her ass to the thumping music, small, innocent Sara waved a five at a nearby dancer.

I stared at my watered-down hurricane. "I think I need to have what she's having."

"I think we all do," Ryder said with a grin.

The wild, thumping beat made my eardrums want to explode. A new guy danced out onstage, dressed as a cowboy. Naturally. He wore a sparkling silver vest with lots of fringe and pants that I was sure were about two minutes away from being flung into someone's face. Women crowded all around us in the club, shoving forward to look at the dancers, laughing and drinking.

"I thought it'd be fun to get out and unwind," Bathsheba yelled as he began to dance. "I didn't get a bachelorette party, and Sara thought this would be a good substitute. I never see you guys anymore, now that Beau and I got married."

I was pretty sure it was more due to everyone's life going to hell all at the same time, what with my disease, Sara's coming out as a werewolf, and Ryder's secret transformation into . . . whatever Ryder was.

"I think the timing has just been off for everyone," I told Bath.

She looked relieved, and I immediately felt bad. I'd been a bridesmaid in her wedding a few weeks ago; I'd even caught the damned bouquet. Before she'd gotten married we'd chatted regularly, and while I wasn't exactly the most open of friends, I considered her one.

It seemed like I'd been shutting everyone out lately.

"Heeeere," Sara slurred, and shoved a five into my hand. "You're supposed to be enjoying the dancers, silly. Go and enjoy that one."

As if he could smell the money, the dancer ripped his pants off and grinned in my direction. *Tabarnak.* I got up, folded the money neatly in half, and patiently waited amongst the shoving women until he wiggled his G-string in my direction. I tucked it in, then retreated to my seat.

Ryder high-fived me.

"Why aren't you up there shoving money into his pants?" I asked.

"Because I like to watch," she told me with a feminine leer.

Sara wobbled past me and slapped a few ones into her sister's hand. "Your turn!"

"Oh, I don't know—" Bath began.

Sara rolled her eyes and tugged on her sister's arm. "No take-backs."

I watched in amusement as Sara dragged Bath-sheba, protesting all the way, to the stage. As Sara bounced and danced to the beat, Bath stood as stiff as a totem pole. She quickly shoved her money at the dancer, then dragged her sister away.

Our boss wasn't half the fun-loving drunk that her sister was.

Bath deposited Sara in the chair next to me. "I'm heading to the bar to get more drinks. Watch her for me, or she's going to run out of money."

Sure enough, Sara had pulled out her wallet and was digging out a few more dollars.

Ryder just grinned. "That's kind of the point, isn't it?"

Yeah, but Sara had an enormous, rather posses-sive boyfriend. I placed a hand over Sara's, stop-ping her.

Sara snarled at me, wolflike.

"Save it for the next dancer," I told her. "I heard

he's really hot." I hadn't heard any such thing, but she was too tipsy to figure that out.

She nodded, leaving her money on the table and sucking the last bit of alcohol out of her glass.

"Well, this was unexpected," Ryder told me, leaning in to yell in my ear as the bass line thumped again. "Seems like alcohol makes one sister a wild woman and the other one even more of a prude."

"I heard that," Sara said on the other side of me.

Ryder just grinned and got up to tuck a dollar into the overflowing G-string of the man gyrating onstage.

I watched him dance, mentally comparing his body to Joshua's. The man onstage was a big, muscled slab of meat. Josh was muscular, but he was leaner. He had big shoulders but didn't carry his weight like a bodybuilder. The dancer turned, flexing rock-hard buns, and Sara whooped at the display.

Those were indeed tight buns. I wondered how tight Josh's ass was in comparison. The man onstage was tanned a rather dark orange, which was unattractive. He was also greased up, and his long hair was pulled into a slicked-down ponytail. It made me appreciate Josh's clean, if short, hair.

The dancer rocked his hips, thrusting repeatedly, and the crowd went wild. My fantasizing of Josh took an abruptly dirty turn and I shook my head to clear it, reaching for my almost-untouched drink.

"Sooo," Sara said, leaning over my shoulder.

I glanced over at her.

She nodded at my drink. "You gonna drink that?"

"I was," I said in a dry voice, but I handed it to her anyhow. "You're having fun."

She shrugged, taking my straw in hand and raising it to her mouth. Then she sniffed and gave me a perplexed look. Before I could ask, she leaned in and sniffed me. "Why do you smell like Josh?"

A hot, humiliated blush crossed my face. Thank goodness the strip club was dark. "I'm pretty sure I don't."

"I may be drunk, Marie Bellavance," she said with a wag of her finger at me, "but my nose isn't. And it definitely smells a horny were-cougar on you."

How was that possible? I raised my shirt to my nose and sniffed it. I didn't smell anything.

Sara smacked my shoulder. "Not your clothes, dummy. You. Your skin. You normally smell like a medicine cabinet. Now you smell like a medicine cabinet and Beau's brother." And she waggled her eyebrows at me. "So gimme the dirt."

I didn't know which part made me more mortified—the fact that I smelled like a medicine cabinet, or the fact that she'd picked up on my strange situation with Josh. It wasn't even friends with benefits. All we'd done was argue with each other and share a few kisses.

A few really hot, really wet kisses.

"It's nothing," I told her. "No dirt."

Her eyebrows shot up, and she grabbed my drink. "You going to love him and leave him?"

"Something like that."

"Ooo," Sara said with a grin. "High five." She raised her hand in the air and completely missed mine.

"Yeah, I think I'll take that back now," I told her, pulling my drink out of her hand.

She leaned over my chair, throwing her arm around my shoulders and eyeing the drink. I had the sneaking suspicion that if I looked away, she'd grab it again. "Can I give you a word of advice?"

"Oh, please do." Nothing better than advice from drunk people.

"Josh is a nice guy. Really nice. Big soft spot for women." She poked at my breastbone as if to demonstrate where that soft spot might be. "But he's not what you'd call a 'commitment' kind of guy."

She made drunken air quotes just as Ryder sat down again, hands empty of money.

"I know he's not," I told her. "But thank you."

She nodded sagely, then brightened at the sight of Ryder's half-full cup. "You going to drink that?"

"Get your own," Ryder said, holding her cup protectively.

Bath returned from the bar with new drinks and began to pass them out. As she did, I glanced up at the stage. A new man had danced out, and my heart skipped a beat at the baseball cap he wore. A moment later, I relaxed, seeing the baseball uniform he wore and the tattoos going up his arm. Not Josh. Not even close.

You going to love him and leave him?

That was what I was going to do, wasn't it? Have sex with him and then turn around and seek a vampire to turn me? And if the vampire wanted a blood mate, I wouldn't say no.

So what did that make me? I wasn't sure I wanted to be a player. And Josh wasn't sure if he wanted to be played, judging by the lack of a return phone call.

Why did everything have to be so damn complicated?

One of the dancers sauntered past, wearing a wreath of bills around his waist and not much else. Sara whistled sharply, drawing his attention, and pulled out a twenty. "Lap dance!"

"Oh, no," Bath said.

But Sara eyed us and then pointed at Ryder, who also shook her head, eyes widening.

The dancer zoomed to Ryder's side and began to gyrate, shaking his pelvis. Bath looked mortified. Sara bounced up and down with giddy excitement.

Ryder looked . . . terrified? Confident, self-possessed Ryder?

The dancer grabbed her hand and placed it on his pectoral, shining with baby oil. And he gave Ryder a lascivious look, grinding up against her.

She shut to her feet and bolted for the ladies' room.

The dancer staggered backward, almost knocked over by her hasty exit, and Bathsheba looked shocked.

"What's with her?" Sara asked.

The terrified look on Ryder's face was so unlike her. And then I thought of the . . . thing . . . that I'd seen Ryder turn into. I plucked the twenty out of Sara's hand and stuck it in the dancer's G-string. "She probably drank too much and had to throw up," I told them, and pulled out another twenty from my pocket. "How about you give me a lap dance next?" I said to the dancer.

Sara whooped in response, and the dancer grabbed my free hand, rubbing it on his oiled stomach.

Ryder *totally* owed me for this.

We left the club a few hours later, flat broke and way past tipsy. Well, the other three were tipsy. I'd sipped the same drink all night, letting Sara chug the rest of mine. Alcohol never sat well with the anti-anxiety medication I was on to suppress the panic attacks.

Our designated driver met us outside, and at the sight of him, drunk-but-still-kicking Sara whooped and scrambled for her last dollar. She folded it in half and waved it under the surly were-bear's nose, gyrating at him.

"Dance for me, baby," she cooed. "I'll give you some money."

"No," Ramsey said in a flat voice.

Sara just laughed uproariously and danced away, wobbling.

Ramsey snatched her from midair and swung

her over his shoulder like a caveman. Sara laughed and squealed, kicking her feet.

I could have sworn that Ramsey's mouth twitched in a hint of a smile.

"Oh, boy," Ryder said at my side. "I hope he doesn't keep swinging her around like that or she's going to puke. I might puke just from watching it."

I snorted. Bath tottered across the parking lot behind the wildly laughing Sara and big, burly Ramsey, and I took up the rear, beside Ryder. When the others were far enough ahead, I tugged at her arm and whispered, "You okay?"

Her face tightened and she nodded. "I just . . . I can't . . . I can't process touch. Not well."

I immediately pulled my hand away. "I'm so sorry."

She rolled her eyes at me. "Not yours, dummy. Men. I . . ." She exhaled a long, deep breath. "Never mind. This is on the secret list."

I linked my pinky to hers and nodded, then we followed the others to the car.

Chapter Ten

*W*ell, this was awkward.

I smiled tightly at Andre as he poured me another glass of red wine and I tried to ignore the scowling bodyguard standing right behind him.

Why did my date suddenly need protecting? Who was he afraid of? Was I in danger?

And most of all, out of the entire Russell Security team, why did it have to be Josh? He loomed over our date like a ghastly third wheel.

So very, very awkward.

I downed my wine quickly. Maybe if I got drunk, this wouldn't be so bad.

"You're very thirsty tonight," Andre said, his tone holding affection and amusement. "Long day?"

I nodded and held my glass out for a refill. The truth was, every day was a long day lately. I hadn't been handling the insomnia well this week. I'd also been stressed about how things were going with Josh, so I'd fretted and checked my phone for messages a hundred times an hour.

But he hadn't texted.

Part of me had expected it. Still . . . I had thought we were friends. Feeling abandoned, I'd even cried a little. I'd trusted him and he'd run.

And now *he* was glaring at *me*? He could go jump off a cliff, for all I cared.

"You seem distracted," Andre observed, extending his hand across the table.

I put my hand in his, which was unnervingly cool against mine. "I'm sorry." I couldn't even come up with an explanation that would put his mind to rest.

"Is this a bad time for you? Should we cancel our date tonight?" He gave me a concerned look, his other cool hand moving on top of mine. It was like being hugged by clay.

I squeezed his hand to reassure him. "I'm just a little . . . distracted by your bodyguard. I thought this date would be more private."

"Is that all that's bothering you?"

Joshua shifted on his feet, frowning fiercely at me, arms crossed over his chest.

"I just worry that you're in danger." I had Andre's full attention, and he was smiling at me again, so I tilted my head, exposing my neck a bit. "Are you sure you're okay?"

"My dear, I am perfectly fine," he said, his voice husky. "It's simply a precaution. If he's bothering you, I'll see if the waiter can find him a nearby table so we can . . . talk privately."

"That sounds lovely." It was hard to be into Andre when the much hotter and far more alive Joshua was looming over him.

I needed to want the *vampire*, not the were-cougar.

Andre turned and flicked his fingers at Josh, indicating that he should scram.

Josh gave a curt nod, and he retreated to a nearby table and sat with a thump, his gaze still on us.

"Better?" Andre asked.

I nodded. "Thank you."

"I want you to be comfortable around me," he said, his voice low and soothing, almost caressing. "I know it's hard for some of your kind to relax around a vampire, but I assure you that I'm a man, just like every other man."

He's a predator. He wants to chase his prey. I gave him a slow, sensual smile and tossed my hair. "Just like *every* other man?"

His gaze grew hot with desire. "Not quite. There are a few . . . subtle . . . differences."

A hot blush crossed my cheeks. "You don't say."

"Am I your first?" he asked softly. When my eyes widened, he chuckled and lifted my hand to kiss it. "Your first vampire, I meant."

I wasn't sure that was what he'd meant, and I kept my tone flirtatious. "If I say no, will you hold it against me?"

Just then, my cell phone buzzed. Text message. I pulled my hands away and fished out my phone.

Do not go there, Josh had sent. *Not with this guy.*

I clicked my phone off, gritting my teeth. "Sorry. I thought it might have been *important,* but it's not." Since Josh had super shifter hearing, maybe he'd get the hint.

But Andre's flirty chuckle returned and he laid his hand back down on the table once more. Guess I'd have to put mine in his. I did, forcing away the disquiet I felt when touching his skin. It was only because Josh was so close. If he hadn't been, I wouldn't have been nearly as bothered.

Even if I was, I'd learn to like it. I could hold a clammy hand or two in exchange for eternity.

"Another man?" Andre asked as his fingers curled over mine.

"I don't know if I should tell you," I said coyly, startled at how seductive I sounded. Go, me. "It's not as if we're exclusive, are we?"

He pressed another light kiss to my fingertips. "Perhaps we should be?"

Yes! Inside, I did a touchdown dance. Outwardly, I gave him a hint of a smile. "I'll think about it."

That's right, predator. Come catch this prey.

Exclusive. With a vampire. That was one step away from having him turn me, right?

"So tell me, Minnie . . . do you like sports cars?"

"Don't know a thing about them," I confessed. "But I'd love to learn."

"Would you like to see mine?" His eyes gleamed, and his wide, white smile suddenly looked a little . . . toothy?

Was this some sort of euphemism? *Hey, baby, let me show you my Audi? Check out what's under my hood?*

But I was all-in when it came to this, right? And Andre was definitely interested, even though I was holding him at arm's length. We hadn't even kissed, and we'd had two awesome dates.

Sooner or later, he'd want to put those lips on me. I thought of his cool, almost clammy hands and shuddered at the thought of his lips feeling the same. What the hell was wrong with me? It was just body temperature.

I looked at Josh, two tables away, and glared at him. He was a big, good-looking distraction that I didn't need.

"Why don't you show me what you've got under the hood?" I found myself saying.

We drove around for about an hour, with the top down on his Audi TT sports car. Josh's car tailed us from a discreet distance, just barely staying in sight. Andre drove out to a secluded spot, put the car in park, and put an arm over my shoulders.

I let him pull me close. I even let him kiss me. It was . . . strange. I was wildly aware of the tongue slowly thrusting into my mouth and how different the body temperature was. Andre's fingers rested lightly on my cheek, brushing over my skin as he kissed me.

And then, something changed. Boy howdy. It was like every nerve ending jolted awake. Suddenly Andre's kiss was the most erotic, intense thing I'd ever felt. My pulse began to pound, and I whimpered a little when he nipped at my lip.

If I didn't climb on top of him in the next two

minutes, I was going to die of desire. I had to have this man between my legs so badly that I ached.

Someone knocked on the car door, and we broke apart. I tilted my head back, drugged by Andre's kiss, and saw Joshua's scowling face.

"We've had another call, Mr. Jurov. I think you should wrap up the evening."

Andre bit out a curse in another language, then looked at me with regret. "I am afraid we will have to do this some other night, Minnie."

"Yes," I said in a daze.

Andre dropped me back at the restaurant, and I barely wobbled back to work an hour before the shifts were scheduled to change. I still felt flushed, overheated. Oversexed. I was pretty sure that my panties were wet. From one kiss? That was so . . . *weird*. I hadn't been into it, and then bam! Instant turn-on. I couldn't shake the feeling that it was a little odd, so I checked my reflection in the compact in my purse. My pupils were enormously dilated.

So strange.

By the time I got home the fog had worn off, leaving me just perplexed. It was good that I liked Andre's kisses, right? Still, I wished that Josh hadn't been sitting in the parking lot, watching.

Was he mad when Andre held my hand? Jealous?

Or was he understanding, now that he knew why I was pursuing vampires with such determination?

I changed out of my work clothes and into flannel pajamas, sliding my feet into my slippers. Then I sat down at my puzzle and picked up a piece, my brain still on my date.

Andre wanted to be exclusive, which was incredibly encouraging. We'd made out in his car and probably would have gone further if there hadn't been an interruption. Ten bucks said that the interruption had all been Josh's idea.

Why did he care? I'd poured my heart out to him, and he'd flat-out ignored me for two days.

I should have been excited as hell that things were moving with the vampire.

Instead I just felt . . . confused.

My doorbell rang.

It was eight thirty in the morning; who in the hell was at my door at this hour? This was theoretically bedtime for me. I padded to the door and peered in the keyhole.

Josh stood there, big hands propped against the door frame. His face was angled away, the baseball cap masking his expression.

Uh-oh. I paused on my side of the door, thinking.

"I can hear you there, Marie. And I can smell you. You smell good, by the way."

I blushed.

"You can't hide from a shifter. Might as well open up and let me in."

Damn. I opened the door and looked at him, taking in his clean-shaven face, the sexy mouth pressed into a firm line. The tense shoulders. He didn't seem happy. Well, that made two of us.

I tilted my head. "What are you doing here?"

"We need to talk," he said, and he didn't look very pleased at the thought.

"I thought you didn't have anything to say to me."

He adjusted his baseball cap, a sure sign he was annoyed. "Can you just invite me in, already?"

I moved to the side, my face a careful mask. Inside, I churned with a mixture of irritation and hurt and . . . if I was being honest with myself, pleasure at seeing Josh again. "So what brings you over? Just get off work? I'm surprised the boss didn't keep you late. You know, just in case more of those ill-timed calls came in."

He tugged his cap off, then raked a hand through his hair, trying to judge my expression. "You mad?"

Caught red-handed. "I'm just trying to figure out your game here. It seems remarkably coincidental that you're bodyguarding the guy that I'm seeing."

"Not coincidental at all," Josh said, coming closer, "considering that a friend of mine made up the threat as a favor to me. Andre called in an extra guard for the night, just in case."

I stepped back, glaring at him. "You faked a threat just so you could shadow him on his date with me?"

"No. We just told him there was a threat. We let vampire paranoia do the rest." He looked rather smug.

"I don't believe you," I said with disgust. "Is that going to happen on my next date, too? Because I don't know if you've thought about this, Josh, but if he's going to turn me, he's going to want to do more than hold my hand."

That familiar scowl darkened Josh's handsome face. Was that possessiveness I saw in his eyes? I stalked across the room to put some distance between us and sat on the small love seat that was at a right angle to my couch. If he was going to talk to me he'd have to sit on the couch, because the love seat couldn't sit more than one comfortably.

No sooner had I thought it than he was sliding next to me, his hips pushing against mine, his thigh pressed to my own. He turned his big body toward me and leaned in.

"Are you going to let him kiss you again?" There was that gleam of possessive cougar in his eyes again.

"Josh," I said softly, "I need him to turn me. You know that."

"Let me talk to Beau," he said, his voice dropping. "We can tell him that I want to turn you."

I eyed him, wary. "And then what? You go into exile with me? Because I'm pretty sure neither of us will like Greenland."

"That won't happen," he said confidently.

"Don't lie to me, Josh."

"Fine," he bit out, looming over me, all delicious and sexy. "Here's the truth. I don't like it when he kisses you. I don't like it when he touches your hand and you smile at him. It makes me so fucking crazy that I want to drag him away from you. I want to pull you into my arms and kiss you the way you should be kissed. By a man, not by some undead guy."

That was a lot of honesty. My breathing was faster, more shallow. He was so close that I could smell the warmth of his skin, and it was doing crazy things to me inside.

"So yes, I hate it when he touches you. I couldn't stop myself from interrupting. And I'm not sorry. The only reason he's still in one piece at the moment is because this is what you need, and I am trying"—he ground his teeth, then gritted out—"to be understanding."

That was . . . sweet.

"I didn't enjoy kissing him," I told him.

Josh scowled. "Oh, come on, Marie. Every girl enjoys vampire kisses. Their saliva is an aphrodisiac."

"It's . . . *what*?" That explained how I'd been completely uninterested, and then it was like a switch flipped and bam, insta-lust. "Aphrodisiac?"

That sounded . . . appalling. He'd deliberately *drugged* me with his kiss?

Josh looked surprised. "You didn't know?"

"Well, that explains a lot. I guess there are some rather large gaps in my supernatural education."

I felt violated. Andre had taken me to a quiet, secluded spot knowing how I'd react to his kiss. And if Josh hadn't stopped it, I was pretty sure there would've been full-on sex. I shuddered.

"Now you see why it bothers me to see you with

him?" His fingers stroked a curl of my hair, brushed it behind my ear in a tender caress.

A *very* tender caress for a man who had ignored me for the past two days. I shoved at his chest. "You don't get to be jealous. I poured my heart out to you and told you my secret, and you ignored me for two days."

I couldn't help the note of hurt that had crept into my voice. I only hoped he hadn't noticed it. Mr. Playboy didn't get to hurt my feelings. I was ice. That was how things were safest.

But he just kept stroking my hair, then lightly grazed the shell of my ear with his fingers. "Give a guy a break, Marie," he said softly. "You just told me that the girl I'm crazy about is dying. And the only way to stop her from dying is to let her sleep with another man and have him turn her into a vampire. And there's nothing I can do about it, because I understand it. But that doesn't make me feel any less helpless."

My gaze went to his mouth, so firm and strong. His gaze was direct, and I resisted the urge to reach out and brush my fingers over those impossibly long lashes. So unfair for a man to have lashes like that. They made his eyes soft. Sultry. Delicious. His gaze sent shivers through my body. "You're crazy about me?"

"Must be my hero complex," he said softly. "I wish I could leave you alone and make this vampire thing easier for you. But it's driving me nuts. All of it. You in his arms. The thought of you dying.

The thought of walking away and just leaving all this to play out. I'm stuck no matter which way I turn, Marie." His fingers trailed across my cheek, and his thumb slid to my mouth, brushing over the curve of my lower lip. "So I'd rather be stuck here with you."

His touch felt incredible. He was here, with me. And I realized that this was his way of supporting me.

I bit at the tip of his finger when he brushed it over my lip, then released it. "So what are you going to do?" I whispered.

"Well," he said, and his weight pressed over me on the love seat, his mouth moving ever closer to mine. He plucked my glasses off, then tossed them onto the nearby couch. His hand moved back to me, cupping my cheek and tilting my face toward his. I felt hot and flushed, in a clearer, purer way than when the vampire had touched me. This time, I felt the heat pulsing through my body, felt that delicious excitement at his touch. "Right now, I'm fighting the urge to throw you down on this love seat and fuck the hell out of you."

That sounded way too tempting. "Why are you fighting it?"

He groaned and leaned in, pressing his mouth to my neck. "Marie, I can't be with you without . . . putting some sort of claim on you. If you and I do this, I'm not going to be able to walk away like you want me to."

"I don't want you to walk away," I said, and bit his lower lip, unable to help myself. "I never said that."

"I don't know what the solution is, but we'll figure something out," he said and nipped at my neck. The bite was flutteringly light, just a tease.

"Let's just take it one day at a time," I told him. "And today, I want my hands all over you."

"Good, because mine are about to be all over you."

"Then do it," I dared him. "Or are you chicken?"

"Fighting words," he said. His mouth was hot on my skin and incredibly distracting, and I loved it. He buried his head against my neck, and I felt his tongue swipe over my collarbone.

I gasped at the sensation that jolted through me.

He pulled up, eyeing me. "Everything okay?"

"I hope you're not going to ask that every time I make a noise," I told him, smoothing my hands down his chest in appreciation of the muscles there.

He undid the first button of my ugly flannel pajamas and exposed a bit more of my skin, then pressed his mouth there. "For someone so cranky, you sure do taste good."

I smacked his chest, and his chuckle at the hollow of my throat sent a shiver through my body. I immediately lost track of all teasing thoughts, especially when he nipped lightly at my skin. Small, soft little bites, just the barest scrape of teeth against flesh. It gave me goose bumps, and I moaned when he gave my neck a long swipe with his tongue in response.

"Sorry," he said, and his voice sounded rough with need. "Couldn't resist."

"Do it all you like," I said dreamily. It felt amazing.

"You shouldn't tell me that," he growled, then licked my collarbone again.

"Then maybe I shouldn't tell you how wet it makes me," I whispered.

He bit me. I gasped in shock as I felt his teeth dig into my skin, the sting traveling up my neck. "Josh?"

He licked the spot carefully. "Sorry. Just had to do it. You were just begging for it."

"I was not begging for anything," I told him, running my hands along his back. I loved touching him after weeks of imagining how he'd feel.

"Really? Because all I'm hearing is 'Josh, I need you to lick my breasts,'" he told me in a husky voice, kissing lightly along my jaw.

I sucked in a breath, my nipples going hard.

"Liked that, did you?" he said with a chuckle. Then he leaned down and undid the next button of my pajamas with his teeth. I watched, dazed, as his mouth moved to the curve of my breast and began to gently kiss it. "Can I undo the rest of them?"

"You're asking permission?" I said, unable to stop looking at his mouth on the valley between my breasts.

"I need to know that you want this, too, Marie." He looked up, and I saw his dark eyes reflecting with the were-cougar side of him. "You've got to encourage a man a bit, Marie."

"What happened to all that talk about foreplay?"

I was finding it hard to breathe. It was like all the air had left my lungs at the sight of his dark head over my chest.

He grinned. "Just talk, baby."

I snorted at that.

He gave me a wounded look. "You're killing my ego here, Marie."

"It might need a nice, healthy deflating," I told him, and then to take the sting out of my words, I ran a finger along his chest. "But I wouldn't mind if you were shirtless."

"I'll go skins if you go skins," he said with a grin. Josh crawled off me and stood up, then offered me his hand.

I placed mine in it slowly, feeling a little out of my element as he pulled me to my feet. Okay, a lot out of my element. All my expertise in flirting and being sexy was ten years rusty. And here I was in ratty pajamas, with dark circles under my eyes.

Then he tugged his shirt over his head, and my mouth went dry.

Josh was . . . gorgeous. In the future, I needed to see him naked at least once a day. Maybe more. I couldn't resist reaching out to touch him. Taut, strong shoulders that framed a lean, tapering torso and a flat stomach. He had a sprinkle of hair on his pectorals and a line of it down his belly. Elegant. Delicious. His biceps were hard and strong, and I couldn't help squeezing them as I ran my hands over him.

He remained perfectly still as I explored him,

touching him the way I'd wanted to so many times before. I brushed my fingers over those pectorals, so well defined and hard, and jumped as a low rumble started in his chest under my fingers.

"Sorry," he said, putting his hand over mine and trapping it against his chest again. "Should have warned you. We purr."

Sure enough, a deep rumble just like a cat's purring came from his chest as his hand held mine over his heart. "I didn't realize your cat was so . . . close to the surface."

"Don't worry, I'm house trained."

"Very cute." I stared at that delicious skin, entranced, and ran my fingernails down it, raking them over the lean muscle.

He groaned, pulling me against him for another hot, quick kiss. "Your turn."

I pulled out of his arms and felt my cheeks heating with shyness. Would my inexperience show? I hoped not. I finished unbuttoning the pajama top, keeping the fabric together until the last minute. Then I shrugged my shoulders and let it drop to the floor. I closed my eyes, waiting for his response.

"Beautiful," he said, his warm hands moving back around my waist and pulling me against him for another hot, openmouthed kiss. We were naked chest to naked chest, and dear God, the sensation was sinful. Hopefully when his tongue was stroking into my mouth so sensually, like I was something delicious to be enjoyed for hours. One of his big hands stroked down my spine and I whimpered, pressing my breasts closer against his chest. I loved his warmth, his big body. I wanted to feel him all over me.

His hand slid to my ass and tugged me closer as the kiss deepened, became more possessive. My pulse heated, pounding through my body in excitement. His mouth slowly pulled away from mine, and he stared down at me with hot eyes. "You want the bed or right here? Because we should probably go there now."

"Bed," I said softly, my fingers twined in the silky hair at his nape.

He picked me up, kissing me as he carried me to my bedroom, then laid me on the bed and crawled on top of me. I wrapped my pajama-clad legs around his waist as he leaned in for another kiss, his chest hair tickling against my nipples.

And then he thrust against the juncture of my thighs, and I moaned. Oh, wow. Even through his jeans, that felt really, really good.

He swallowed my moan with another hot kiss, thrusting again, rocking against my core. My mind went blank with pleasure as he slid his hands to my waist and kissed my neck again, then down my collarbones.

When he leaned over and took the tip of one breast into his mouth, I dug my fingernails into his skin. "Joshua!"

He was purring again, nuzzling against my nipple, and he licked and sucked the sensitive tip, rolling it against his tongue. I felt the purr vibrating through his body, and it was doing crazy things to the way he felt against me. My sex felt hot and slick with need, my thighs clenching around him involuntarily. "Please . . ."

"Please make love to my other breast?" He blew across my sensitive skin, and my entire body prickled in response. "If you insist." And his mouth latched onto my other breast. His thumb went to the nipple he'd just abandoned, teasing the peak as he licked and nibbled on the other.

I writhed under him, my back arching. I didn't want the sweet, intense torture to ever stop. I wanted more, desperately. My fingernails dug into his skin and my hips began to rise instinctively. "Please," I breathed again, because I loved the consequences and wanted to see what he'd do next.

"Please," he whispered huskily. "Put my mouth on you?"

I inhaled sharply, and nodded.

His fingers tugged the waistband of my pajamas and slid them down my legs. "I've been thinking about how you'd look for weeks. It's been driving me crazy. I can't wait to see all of you."

I held my breath as his gaze moved over my body. His hand followed his gaze, skimming up my leg, then my thigh, the dark curls at the junction of my sex.

"Lovely," he whispered, and leaned in to press a kiss to my belly

That simple movement set my body aflame. I reached for him, dragging him back on top of me and kissing. He slid between my thighs and I parted them, letting him rock his weight against me again. His jeans rubbed against my sex in a raw way that sent shivers through my body. His kisses were deep and drugging, and I utterly loved the taste of him. I could kiss him for hours on end.

He slowly pulled away. "I need to take my pants off before they geld me."

I giggled, and he grinned. "Do you want me to use a condom?" he asked.

"Shouldn't you automatically do that?"

He shook his head. "Shifters don't get diseases, and I can only make someone pregnant if she's in heat."

I propped up on my elbows, thinking. "What about me? Can you make me pregnant?"

He shook his head. "Not unless you've got shifter blood in you. It won't take."

I grabbed the front of his jeans, tugging him toward me on the bed. "Then we're good."

He grinned and dropped his hands to my hair, smoothing it away from my face. "You gonna do the honors?"

Finish undressing him? The thought was . . . titillating. I looked up at him, feeling a bit anxious, but the hot look in his eyes reassured me. He was into this as much as I was. I carefully undid the button and lowered the zipper, shoving the jeans down his legs and revealing red briefs that left almost nothing to my imagination. "Oh . . ."

"Pretty impressive, huh?" he said with a teasing grin.

"Actually, it's smaller than I thought," I teased back.

"Oh, really?" he said with a challenging tone in his voice. "Then quit staring."

"I can't," I admitted and brushed my fingers over him through the fabric he was tenting.

He groaned, his fingers tangling in my curly hair. "God, Marie. I want your hands on me so badly."

"I can do that," I said softly, tugging at the waist of his briefs and pulling them down. He quickly wriggled out of them and then was naked in front of me.

Naked, and gorgeous. And hugely erect. His cock was long and thick, the crown tipped with a bead of moisture. I brushed a finger over that bead and was rewarded with his deep groan in response. My fingers moved hesitantly over the length of him, just testing. Fluttering. That was . . . exciting. I wrapped my hands around his length and bent to take the head into my mouth.

His breath exploded. "Oh, God, Marie. That's so good."

Encouraged, I swirled my tongue around the crown, then sucked it again. I wanted to please him, to make him as crazy for me as I was for him. My grip tightened on his cock and I sucked harder.

He thrust into my mouth, then pulled away. "You can put your mouth on me next time," he whispered, giving me another hot kiss. "Right now I want you pinned under me, screaming my name."

That visual stole the breath from my lungs.

He raised up over me, staring down at me with incredible tenderness, his hands spreading my hair around my head in a halo. "I always wanted to see you like this. Beautiful and soft."

"And naked in your arms?" I guessed.

"Naked in my arms," he agreed, then leaned in and kissed my shoulder. "With your breasts in my face, your nipples calling to my mouth," he continued, and followed that statement with his lips grazing over the tips of my breasts.

I gave a low, shuddering cry.

"Naked in my arms, with your thighs over my shoulders," he said softly, moving down my body and lightly running his mouth down my belly. His thumbs moved to my sex, and he ran one down the wet seam.

"Josh," I moaned, unable to do anything but breathe his name. "Please. I want you inside me."

He ignored my pleas, parting the lips of my sex and licking me in a long, slow motion that set me to shuddering and whimpering.

"You taste so sweet, Marie," he whispered, and I felt that wild purr start up again. "Slick and wet and so good. I could spend hours here."

I moaned at the thought. I wouldn't be able to survive hours. I'd expire, happy and content and boneless. When he licked again I squirmed under him, feeling that ache deep in my core rising and helpless to do anything about it. My hips rose in response to his next lick, and I cried his name out again.

"Need you," he breathed. "Next time, I'll spend hours there."

"Whatever," I said, twisting under him, desperate with need. "Please. I *need* you, Joshua."

He surged back over me, pushed my quivering legs wide, and settled on top of me, propping his body up on his elbows. Then he leaned in to kiss me again. The man loved kissing more than I'd thought possible.

He lifted one of my legs, anchoring it around his waist. His hand slid between us as he positioned himself, and I felt the head of his cock nudging at my entrance. I tensed a little, anticipating his slow slide into my body.

It had been so long that I wasn't prepared for his thrust as he sank in to the hilt, and I yelped.

He stiffened, the hot, glazed look in his eyes turning to horror. "Marie . . . baby? You okay?"

I squirmed, digging my fingernails into his flesh. He was so big. "I'm good. Just give me a minute. It's been a while."

He stared at me. "How long has it been?"

"A few . . . years. Maybe . . . a decade."

He swore, trying to pull off me. "Fuck, Marie. I'm sorry. I didn't know. I would have—"

I silenced him with a kiss, wrapping my legs around him. The last thing I wanted was to be treated like some delicate flower. "Shhh. Can we just go on with this?"

He kissed me back, almost grudgingly. "Tell me when you stop hurting."

I took his lower lip in my mouth and sucked on it, eliciting a groan from him. His hips jerked against mine, resulting in a little dig of his cock buried deep inside me. And it felt . . . good. A little twingey, but I was adjusting. I rocked my hips a little against him. "Oh, yeah. It's definitely stopped hurting. Give me more, Josh."

Strain creased his forehead. "I'll go slow, but you have to tell me if you hurt." And he very slowly rocked his hips against my own in a smooth, circling motion. I followed his lead, once, twice, and then he began to pump into me slowly, his gaze intent on my face, watching my reactions.

"I'm not a virgin, so you don't have to be so—" My mouth parted as he stroked into me. "Oh . . ."

"Good oh or bad oh?" His voice sounded strained, his movements stilling.

My fingers clenched his ass. "*Good* oh. Keep doing that, Josh."

He began to pump into me, harder, faster. The twinges of discomfort were soon buried in an onslaught of sensation. I'd never felt anything like this before. Every nerve ending was alive and on fire, and my hips rose to meet his with every thrust, my movements clumsy in comparison to his, but I didn't care. I needed him, needed this.

Josh whispered against my neck as he rocked deep into me, each thrust jolting my body, his movements becoming rougher, jerkier. My body was tensing but I wasn't quite there yet, and my fingers dug into him harder as his hips pistoned against my own. "Josh . . . I need . . ."

"I know," he gasped, punctuating his words with another thrust. "I'm going to give it to you."

Watching my face, he slid his hand between us, searching. His fingers parted the lips of my sex and found my clit, and then he thrust again, rubbing against it.

If I thought I was on fire before, I was an inferno now. My entire body jolted like a live wire, and the pleasure I'd been chasing came closer. "Right there!"

He continued to thrust, his fingers teasing the bud with quick, rapid movements. Thrust, stroke, thrust, stroke, and my body kept tensing harder until I thought I would snap in two, my muscles locking so tight.

And then I went over the edge, my entire body clenching around him in a hard, rocking orgasm. I screamed his name as he thrust hard and wild into me. His teeth locked down on my collarbone, biting me as he came in his own quick, violent release.

He rocked over me a moment longer, kissing my mouth one last, slow time, and then rolled over to lie next to me. He exhaled a deep, gusty breath.

I echoed it, my body still quivering. "Damn," I said softly.

"A decade, huh?"

"Hush up, Josh."

He kissed my palm. "In all seriousness . . . are you okay?"

"I think I pulled a few muscles—but I've never been better."

———

Even exhausted and deliciously sated from love-making, I couldn't sleep. Next to me, his hand curled in my hair, leg thrown over mine, Josh slept, his chest rumbling in a purr. I closed my eyes and tried to will my body to sleep, but after an hour of tossing and turning, I gave up.

I carefully detangled myself without waking him and tiptoed down the hall for a quick shower. Then, after I toweled off, I headed for my puzzle.

Chapter Eleven

I was just putting away the completed puzzle when Josh wandered into the room, yawning and scratching his head. He looked so deliciously disheveled that it made my pulse race.

He moved to my side and glanced at the puzzle box. "Did I sleep for long?"

"Seven hours." I was envious.

He wrapped his arms around my waist and pulled me in for a kiss. I went reluctantly, feeling awkward. Wasn't this the part where he was supposed to tell me he'd call me sometime and then skate out? But he nibbled at my lips, and when I softened against him he began to languidly kiss me, his tongue sliding into my mouth with a slow promise. By the time he released me I was dazed, desire pulsing through my body.

His mouth inches from mine, he chuckled low. "You shouldn't have let me sleep so late. We could have had more time for . . . other things."

Heat flickered through me, especially when his hands slipped to my ass and began to knead it. I tried to focus my thoughts. "Do you have to work tonight?"

He nodded, molding my hips against his. "More vampire guarding. The usual."

And I had to work, too. Too bad we couldn't stay here all night and simply hold each other. A lovely thought. Josh certainly didn't seem ready to move. He kept caressing my backside and watching me with that possessive, intense gaze. I touched a hand to my hair. "I suppose I should start getting ready for work."

And he probably wanted to get going.

But he didn't seem to be in a hurry. He kissed me one more time and then released me. "Want to go out for breakfast?"

"It's dinnertime for everyone else."

Josh's smile was achingly sweet. "Not for you and me."

That made us sound like . . . something more. Did he always go out to breakfast with his dates afterward? I'd gotten the impression that he got away from them as quickly as he could. But the two of us were in that weird zone that was more than friends but less than a couple. Friends with benefits.

And friends could go out for breakfast.

"Sure," I said. "Give me fifteen minutes to get ready."

I wasn't surprised when Josh suggested the diner. I didn't even mind when he left me to go hunt down

Carol and pull her into a big bear hug. The elderly woman lit up at the sight of him, and I smiled in response.

I felt that way whenever I saw him, too. There was something so boyish and exuberant about Josh. He was open and flirty and pleasant to everyone—everything I was not. What on earth did he see in me?

Voyons, it was obvious: he had told me himself. He was a predator, and predators liked the chase. I'd been playing hard to get, and now I wasn't hard to get anymore.

I felt a twinge of anxiety. Was I going to be another one-night stand?

But that was what I wanted, right? So why was I even thinking these things?

Carol showed us to the same booth we'd had last time, gave me a knowing wink, then headed off for coffee. The evening was young and the restaurant was full. When I slid into the booth, Josh slid in beside me, just like last time.

Except this time I didn't pull away. And this time he put his arm around my shoulders, drawing me close and kissing my temple. Affectionate. Sweet. Loving. Like a real couple.

Which we couldn't be. Disconcerted, I grabbed the menu. "What are you getting?"

"The usual," he said.

I grinned, amused. "I think I'll go with something smaller this time."

I ordered a breakfast platter when Carol returned, and Josh spent a few minutes chatting with her about how she was doing, and her cats. His arm remained around my shoulders the entire time, and Carol didn't blink at the sight.

Did he bring many dates here? It didn't seem like a date spot. Was she used to seeing him with his arm around random females? The thought made me unhappy.

As soon as Carol walked away, my phone rang. I fished it out of my purse and winced at the name displayed. Dad. I'd been avoiding him ever since my insomnia had hit and I'd started pursuing my crazy plan. I felt a little bad about that, but he was so wrapped up in Posey that I didn't think he noticed. His calls were less frequent and tended to be about the exciting places they were going, and why didn't I join them.

"Hi, Daddy," I said, giving Josh a warning to be quiet.

"*Salut, ma petite puce,*" he boomed into the phone.

"How's it going, Dad? How's the trip to Vegas?"

"We're back early," he said. "You sound like you're in a restaurant! Hot date?"

"Not exactly. Just breakfast with a friend."

That friend slid his hand on the inside of my thigh and nipped at my shoulder. My entire body flushed in response.

"Friend, huh?" Josh murmured against my neck.

My dad was still chatting. "Have you been seeing this friend for long?"

"Not long," I said lamely. Thank God Josh couldn't hear the conversation . . . or could he? Shifters had good hearing. "So you enjoyed Vegas?"

"Vegas was great! But Posey spent all her money and we got bored. The show she wanted to see was cancelled, so we thought we'd come back and see you instead."

It was getting difficult for me to concentrate on the conversation, since Josh had his hand on my thigh. I could have sworn it was inching up even higher. Josh was watching me with an intense gaze, even as the food was set down. I gave him a faint smile, trying to concentrate on the call. "I'm working all week, Dad. I don't know if I can—"

"You get off at eight a.m. tomorrow, right? Posey and I'll bring you breakfast! It'll be grand. You know we'd love to see you."

I wanted to see my dad, too, but I wasn't sure about him coming over. I was worried he'd suspect something. "Gee, I don't know."

"Oh, come on," he said cheerfully. "Posey's been saving you some Avon samples, and she's dying to show them to you. And you should bring your friend so I can meet him."

This was rapidly getting worse. "Daddy—"

"What's the matter?" Josh murmured against my neck. "Don't want to be seen with me?"

I froze. "I just—"

"Come on, honey. I'm dying to see you again."

Josh pressed a kiss to my neck and then began to nibble at my free ear. His hand slid higher up my thigh, until he was practically cupping my sex under the table.

"Okay," I squeaked when his tongue flickered at my earlobe. Anything to get off the damn call. "Just call me in the morning, Dad."

"See you then," he said cheerfully. "Love you."

"Love you, too," I said, and hung up. As soon as I did, I squirmed away from Josh. "What are you *doing*?"

"Getting myself an invite to breakfast, looks like," he said with a grin.

"My dad thinks we're dating now," I hissed, annoyed.

He shrugged and picked a piece of bacon from my plate, ignoring his own platters of food. "I promise not to propose marriage, then."

"Josh, he doesn't know about my disease. I don't want him to know."

He stared at me, surprised. "You haven't told him?"

"I haven't told anyone but you." I shook my head, remembering Dad's ravaged face as he'd sat at my mother's bedside when she'd gotten sick. His devastation when she'd been so weak at the end, and his infinite, sad patience when she'd gone completely insane and failed to recognize him. He'd tenderly cared for her anyhow, and I'd seen how it had destroyed him, day by day.

"It took him years to recover from my mother's death. The only thing that got him out of his funk was Posey." And that was why I couldn't hate her. "I can't ruin his happiness just as he's found it again."

"Marie," he said slowly. "You need to tell your father. What if—"

"There's no what-ifs," I told him sharply. "None."

If that meant I was living in denial, so be it. It was the only way I could deal with this.

He frowned. "You don't think he'll guess something's wrong?"

I knew what he meant. My face was wan, the circles under my eyes enormous. I'd dropped at least ten pounds, and people constantly asked me if I was all right.

But I could chalk it up to the flu as long as I had a good distraction. I slipped my arm through Josh's. "We're going to be so sickeningly cute that he's not even going to think to ask."

And as if to prove he could be cute, Josh leaned in and kissed the tip of my nose.

And I melted. Just a little.

Minnie had a message waiting when I got in to work.

> *Tonight is not good for me, my dearest. Can we meet tomorrow? I'm counting the hours until I get to see your lovely face again.*

It was signed with AJ—Andre's initials. That was . . . sweet, I guessed. "My dearest" sounded a little stiff, but it also sounded affectionate. I'd take it. I sent him back an email that tomorrow night was fine.

Oddly, though, I wasn't looking forward to seeing Andre again. The entire relationship felt so . . . controlled. On both his part and mine. It was strange to be seeing a guy without his picking up the phone or sending messages to see how I was doing. We only interacted on our dates. Were all vampires like that?

It should have bothered me more, but I was distracted by Josh. Josh, with his cocky, confident grin that made my knees weak. Josh, who'd kissed the hell out of me in the parking lot outside Midnight Liaisons. I'd barely managed to stumble through the door, earning a suspicious glance from Ryder.

"Everything okay?"

"Just . . . fine," I said as I sat at my desk, dazed.

Sara had been waiting for a client to call back about an issue with his file, and she transferred the case to me, since she was leaving for the day. As she pointed at the screen, I noticed she kept glancing at my neck.

Did I have a hickey? I blushed at the thought and forced myself to concentrate on her instructions, taking notes. When she finally left, I fished a compact out of my purse.

There were no love bites. Nothing I could see. Huh. Maybe I'd imagined her interest.

The night crawled past. The phones were slower than usual, and I wasn't in a chatty mood. Ryder wasn't, either. I spent hours staring at my computer monitor, daydreaming.

I kept imagining Josh's big body over mine. The way he'd kissed my mouth and licked me all over.

The way he'd pushed into me so fiercely, so possessively.

And I remembered the tiny kiss he'd pressed to
my nose at breakfast.

It had felt . . . like being a real couple. Not a
hookup. This felt special. But maybe I was just
being sentimental. Maybe this was how Josh made
all his girlfriends feel. Maybe that was why so many
of them complained to the agency when he wouldn't
call them back.

On a whim, I pulled up his profile. There he was,
leaning against a wall, thumbs hooked into his belt
loops, pointing you-know-where. The pose showed
off just how muscular his arms were, how flat his
stomach. How cocky his grin. He looked like a guy
who knew he was hot.

Current status? Available.

That bugged me. It wasn't like I could claim
him, of course. But I wasn't sure I wanted him
claiming anyone else.

I looked at his profile history. He'd been a client for
the past four years and had dated dozens of women.
I scrolled down through the dates, uncomfortably
aware of just how much of a player he was. His last
date had been three weeks ago—a were-fox named
Hayami. She had sent messages to him through the
site, but they'd gone unanswered. In fact, his entire
inbox was full of personal messages from other females. Some he had a history with, and some were
brand-new.

I scrolled through the messages, feeling like a

snoop. But it wasn't really snooping, since I worked for the company. We told people we monitored their dates and their messages, so they knew it wasn't private.

Still, when I ran across the nude photos that one girl had sent Josh, I deleted them with a scowl.

I was still feeling a little out of sorts when he dropped by to pick me up the next morning. I stifled a yawn behind my hand as I slid into the car next to him. We'd only taken one car to dinner last night because that had seemed smartest. Now? I wish we'd taken two.

Josh looked tired. Slightly on edge and annoyed. But he leaned in to kiss me, and I studied him as he pulled onto the highway. "Everything okay?"

He glanced over at me. "Long night, that's all."

"More vampire problems?"

"Just one vampire being high maintenance and demanding." His mouth firmed. "Look, Marie, I hate to ask this . . ."

Oh, no. Here it was.

"But I don't think you should see Andre anymore. Even other vampires steer clear of him. There's something going on underneath that nice-guy exterior, but I don't know what it is. He's secretive."

Phew. I'd thought he was going to suggest that he and I not see each other anymore. "I thought you said all vampires were secretive."

He frowned. "They are."

"So what makes this one worse? Have you heard something?"

His jaw clenched a little. "No. But my instincts tell me he's hiding something. I just need to find out what."

I didn't know a thing about cat instincts. But I did know that Andre was my chance to live. I was willing to put up with a little weirdness for that.

"You can't ask me to stop seeing him," I told him softly.

His hands clenched on the steering wheel, and he sighed. "I know. I just want you to be careful." Josh glanced over at me, his eyes serious. "For me."

I put my hand on his thigh, feeling strangely possessive of him at the moment. "I'll be careful."

As soon as I got home, I took one look at my spotless apartment and realized I had a problem. My father knew me better than anyone, and he knew that I liked to clean when I was stressed. This would make him ask questions.

I immediately took off for the bedroom.

"Where are you going?" Josh asked.

"I need to dirty this place up," I told him breathlessly. "My father will know something's up when he sees I've been cleaning."

He scratched the back of his head as I raced around, trying to find something that would suitably "dirty" up the place. "I have a couple of dirty shirts in my car. You want me to grab them?"

I stopped to stare at him. "Why do you have dirty shirts?"

He shrugged, looking a bit uncomfortable. "Didn't get home a day or two."

"Do I even want to ask? But that's fine—grab a couple of your shirts. We can toss them on the floor." As soon as I said that, I cringed, mentally wanting to clean the place at the thought. I went to the kitchen as he headed out to his car and threw some leftovers onto a couple of plates, then dumped the leftovers into the garbage. I tossed the dirtied dishes in the sink and set a half-full glass of soda on the counter, hoping that it'd get flat fast. I opened a bag of chips and ate one, then scattered the crumbs on the counter, twisting the bag closed messily.

After that, I pulled out a puzzle and arranged it on the table so it looked as if I was still working on it. Josh returned to the apartment and held up his shirts. "Where do you want these?"

I stuffed them behind the couch, then threw a blanket on the love seat in a messy pile. There. I surveyed my handiwork and turned to Josh. "Does this room look lived-in?"

He grinned back at me. "Perfect."

I flopped down on the couch, suddenly too tired to do anything else.

"Why don't you rest? I'll go make the kitchen look a bit more lived in and make myself a snack."

As he left, I noticed he had one of my sleep tees tucked under his arm. What did he want with that? Interesting.

Before I could ask, there was a knock at the door and then the doorbell, just in case we hadn't heard them the first time.

"They're here," I called to Josh, dragging myself off the couch. I peeped through the peephole and grimaced at Posey's bright pink outfit.

I quelled my nervous breathing. With Josh here, there were bound to be questions. This would be the first date I'd ever introduced to my dad . . . and we weren't even dating. Josh was just a friend helping me out. My real date wouldn't rise until after dark, because he was undead.

That thought disturbed me.

I swung the door open and smiled brightly. "Hi, Dad, Posey."

"Marie-Pierre!" my father said. He leaned in to give me a kiss, then stepped into the apartment. "Baby, you're not going to believe what we got you in Vegas."

"Oh, I'll believe it," I said dryly and welcomed Posey in with an awkward hug. "Hi, Posey."

"Hello, Marie-Pierre," she cooed in a thick south Texas accent. The way she said my full name with her drawl made it sound *Pee-uh-air*, which I'm pretty sure was not what my mother had intended when she'd named me. "How are you doing, sweetie?" She examined my pale face, then brightened. "Look at you, so pale. The gothic look is so 2009, honey. I brought you some makeup samples. There's a new line I'm promoting, and I think it'll bring out the apples in those cheeks for you."

My father beamed. "Isn't she thoughtful?"

Oh, yes. Telling me that I looked like hell was so thoughtful of her. But my dad loved her, so I smiled brightly. "That's awesome. Thanks, Posey."

Josh hung at the back of the room, waiting to be introduced. I looked over at him and his easy, amused grin, and felt suddenly flustered. Dad was looking at me expectantly, and Posey had a lunatic grin on her overly made-up face.

"Well?" Dad said. "Introduce us to your friend, *ma petite puce*."

"Sure," I said, moving to Josh's side. "Dad, Posey, this is . . . my friend. Josh."

Josh casually put his arm over my shoulders, and I gritted my teeth.

"Marie . . . Pierre?" Josh asked, glancing over at me, and I could hear the chuckle in his voice.

"Her mother was French-Canadian," my father explained. "It's a family name. For some reason, Marie doesn't like it."

"I think it's lovely. And it is so nice to meet you, Josh," Posey said, sweeping forward to hug him in a cloud of perfume. "Marie-Pierre has told us so much about you."

"Has she now," he said, taking the hug with no hint of awkwardness, though his nostrils flared from her heavy scent.

My dad moved forward, extending his hand. "Good to meet you, son. Have you two been dating long?"

"We're not—" I began.

215

"Really keeping track of things," Josh said with an easy grin. "Taking it one day at a time."

"Nothing wrong with that," Dad said and gestured at Posey. "We brought donuts and coffee and orange juice. I hope that's okay?"

I smiled. "That sounds great. Thank you."

Posey unloaded makeup and skin-care samples on me while Josh and Dad set out the food. They cleaned the puzzle off my dining room table, and I could hear the two men chatting in low voices. Josh was already at ease around my father. I supposed that was a good thing, but it bothered me. If they fell in love with him, it would just make things more difficult.

"Breakfast is ready," Dad called cheerfully, saving me before Posey could start dabbing a wrinkle cream on my face.

As I moved forward, Dad threw his arm over my shoulders and hugged me close. "You look tired. You're not working too hard, are you?"

Josh stilled, watching me.

"Just been putting in some long hours," I told him with a faint smile. "I'll catch up on my sleep this weekend."

"Don't let them work you too hard. Those overnights are rough on the body." He turned to look at Josh. "I'm counting on you to keep an eye on her. She has a one-track mind."

"Oh, I know," Josh said, taking a sprinkle-covered donut from the box.

My dad chuckled.

———

I watched as Josh charmed Posey and my dad. He told them funny anecdotes about his security job, never mentioning that he bodyguarded vampires, of course. He told them about his big family, all brothers, and how Beau had raised him as a teenage boy when their father had passed away. How we'd met while I'd been at work, and how he'd talked me into going out with him.

My dad loved him, of course. It was impossible not to when Josh was on full-charm offensive. He made Posey blush with his obvious compliments, but she didn't mind those in the slightest. And they laughed and chatted as Josh devoured almost a dozen donuts on his own. They didn't seem to find that unusual.

After my dad and Posey left, Josh turned and grinned at me. "They're really nice. I like them."

I said nothing.

"I think they like me, too." He sounded almost smug about it.

"Of course they do," I said crankily. "You charmed their socks off."

He ignored my bad mood and cleared the plates off the table. "You should really tell your dad, you know. It's not right to keep a secret like that from someone."

I gritted my teeth. "It's for the best."

"No, it's not," he said, coming to my side. He put his hands around my waist, tugging me in close. "It's not okay. You're sick and you're hiding it from him."

"That's right," I snapped, jerking out of his grip. "And it's none of your business."

He looked at me in surprise. "What's wrong with you?"

"All of this," I told him, gesturing at my dirty apartment, the empty plates. His dirty shirts tossed over the couch. It bothered me, just as much as his ease sliding into my personal life did. "Just because you met my father doesn't mean you have the right to . . . to . . ." I struggled to find the right word for exactly who Josh was to me.

"To act like we're a couple?"

"Yes," I exploded. "We're not! We can't be!"

His eyes glinted, hard. "So what was last night about?"

I stared at him, surprised. "You, of all people, should know that it wasn't anything serious."

"'You, of all people'?" He raised an eyebrow, and I got the distinct feeling that I'd hurt him. "Is that some sort of jab at me?"

It was, and it wasn't nice of me. I deflected. "You know this thing between us can't be. Set up shop in Greenland permanently? Destroy the Alliance? Ruin your brother's life and Bathsheba's? Force the agency to close? No, thank you."

"How about you try trusting me?" Josh said with a growl.

"How about you trust *me* to decide what's best for me?" I fired back. "What's best for my father? You don't know us. You only think you know me. Just because we slept together once doesn't give you the right to decide my life now. I told you that this couldn't be anything. I never lied about that."

He glared at me. "You're making a mistake."

"Why? Because it doesn't fit your plans?"

"My plans—"

"—can change now that you've nailed me. Congratulations."

Josh's gaze darkened. "You think that's all I was after?" he said in a harsh voice. "That I just wanted to get a little tail?"

"You said yourself that you're a predator and you like to chase the prey. What else could it be?"

His mouth curved in a sneer. "What else when it comes to *me*, right? Is that what you wanted to say?"

I didn't reply. It was.

The realization dawned on his face, and I watched his expression harden. "You know what your problem is, Marie? You say that you don't want to hurt others, but I think that's not it. You don't trust anyone not to hurt *you*, so you just cut everyone out of your life."

"You have me all figured out." I gave a slow, mocking clap of my hands. "Way to go."

He shook his head and picked his cap off the counter. "You want me to go? Fine. I'm gone."

"Fine! Then go."

Josh gave me one last hard glare before slamming out my front door. I watched him go, arms crossed over my chest, feeling righteous in my indignation.

It was only after he'd gone that I wondered if he was right.

In pushing everyone away, was I protecting me . . . or them?

Chapter Twelve

*M*innie. It is good to see you again," Andre said, standing up as I approached the table. "You look beautiful, as always."

Such a thoughtful lie. I looked like hell and knew I did. No amount of makeup could cover up the hollows under my eyes, and I looked weak because I was too tired and sick to even contemplate eating. I just wanted a long damn nap. Maybe a good cry. Unfortunately, I had to sit here and romance a vampire. I gave him a smile, hoping it looked more enthusiastic than I felt.

It wasn't Andre's fault that he wasn't Josh, after all.

I'd taken care to look as good as I could. I'd worn a black cocktail dress that tied behind my neck and left a lot of shoulder and cleavage bare. I'd paired it with tall, open-toed heels and worn my hair twisted up, a few tendrils curling at my neck. When his glance went there, I knew that it didn't matter how big the circles under my eyes were. I might as well have waved a red flag in front of a bull.

He took my hand, and I felt that disconcerting

oddness of his cool flesh against my warm skin. He leaned in to kiss me and I panicked, averting my face so he kissed my cheek. "It's good to see you, too," I said, air-kissing his cheek in response.

He pulled away and gave me a scrutinizing look, but he didn't comment on my reluctance to kiss him on the lips.

It was stupid, I knew. But the thought of kissing him again made me uneasy. Josh wasn't here tonight to stop him if he drugged me again. I glanced around the crowded restaurant. "No bodyguards tonight?"

"Oh, I have one," Andre said easily, moving to pull my chair out for me. As I sat, he leaned in and whispered in my ear. "But I didn't think you liked the last one, so I changed things up a bit. I want you to feel easy in my presence, Minnie."

I smiled, not sure if I was relieved or saddened that Josh wasn't here. I hadn't seen him and he hadn't called, but why should he have called? I'd been horrible to him. "That was sweet of you to think of me, Andre. But he didn't make me nervous."

"Didn't he? You watched him all night."

My cheeks felt hot. Well, now. How to answer that? "Just wary, I suppose. Most men don't need a bodyguard for their dates."

"I am not most men," he said and gave me a disarming smile.

"No, you're not," I said boldly and gave him my most direct, intense smile. Time to kick things up a notch. "That's what I like about you."

"Is it?" he chuckled, as if amused by my response. "You'll be pleased with tonight's bodyguard, I think."

"Oh?" I scanned the wine menu. I'd need something strong soon. My stomach was churning and my head ached, a sure sign that I was going to start hallucinating. It made me anxious, and alcohol would help that.

"Yes," Andre said, distracting me. "I'm surprised you didn't notice him right away."

I glanced up. "Why?"

"Because he's one of the otter clan. Should be a cousin of yours." His dark eyes watched me intently.

Oh, shit. I scanned the restaurant again. It was small and elegant, but the tables were only half full. There was no one seated by himself, and no one that seemed like a bodyguard. Unease fluttered in my stomach.

"Is there a problem, *Minnie*?" Andre asked coolly.

I looked back at him and realized he was no longer giving me that charming smile. Damn it. The gig was up. He'd figured me out. Or he knew something was wrong. Either way, I was fucked.

Utter panic shot through me, and I felt the urge to burst into tears.

Instead, I took a deep, calming breath and laid it all out on the table. "I lied," I told him quietly. "I'm human and I'm looking for someone to turn me. That's why I looked you up."

"I see," he said mildly. "And your real name?"

"It's Marie."

He studied me, leaning back in his chair as if he'd been the king of the world, deciding what to do with one of his subjects. After a long, long pause, he said, "Marie is a better name than Minnie."

That . . . didn't sound like rejection. "I like to think so."

"Are you the Marie that works at the agency?"

"I am. That's how I found you. I am a member of the Alliance, if you want to see my ID."

He flicked a hand, as if brushing away a ridiculous thought. "So, tell me, Marie, what am I going to do with you?"

"I still want to date you," I told him quickly.

"Correction. You want to be turned."

I swallowed. Now I felt like a supplicant instead of the one in control of the date. And I felt like a whole lotta prey at the moment. But I needed to be turned. "Yes."

"I am four hundred years old, my dear girl," he said, and gone was the soft, laughing notes in his voice. In its place was utter boredom. Sheer jadedness. It struck me how well he'd been masking it all this time. "And in all that time, I have never turned someone to be my companion."

My heart seized painfully. No! I refused to give up. "You hadn't met me, though," I said boldly, taking a page from Josh's book. "I'd be honored to be your first."

"Would you?" he said, and I thought I saw a hint of amusement on his face.

Before I could say more, the waiter dropped by, all pleasantries and smooth rolling voice as he began to recite the evening's specials. Andre, who was all lazy smiles now, ordered an expensive bottle of wine for us and sent the waiter on his way.

"For someone who wishes for me to turn her, you were quick to avoid my kiss, darling Marie."

"You didn't tell me before that it was an aphrodisiac," I pointed out.

"No, I did not," he admitted, still amused.

"Then you'll understand why I avoided it tonight. I need my wits about me."

He inclined his head. "This I understand."

The waiter returned, opened the wine, and poured. When our glasses were set in front of us and the wine bottle left on the table, Andre picked up his glass and swirled it, admiring the dark red contents. "I'm not entirely sure of where we move next, Marie. I feel as if my trust has been betrayed, yet I enjoy your company. You are clearly not repulsed by mine, and I feel like we have more to offer each other. Yet . . . I do need trust. It is critical for a vampire."

This didn't sound like an immediate brush-off. Hope shot through me like adrenaline, and I leaned forward, wanting to grab the table and shake it in my giddiness. "You can absolutely trust me. I'm a very private person."

"That is good, but I need more than words."

And he swirled his wineglass again, looking at it thoughtfully, then back to my neck.

I sat back, all the excitement deflating from my body. Oh. That movement was rather obvious. "You want to . . . drink from me?"

"You do wish to be my companion, do you not?"

"I do. More than anything." It sounded desperate, but hell, I *was* desperate.

"Then prove it." His eyes were cunning as he stared across the table at me.

I didn't even hesitate. "All right. Let's do it."

He placed his wineglass on the table and got up from his chair. When I stood, he crooked his arm for me to place my hand through.

It was a gentlemanly gesture, at odds with this power play we were going through. I linked my arm through his, letting him lead me out a side door.

We went into the night, walked around to the side of the small building. I could still hear the music playing from the speakers attached to the door of the restaurant.

"This is acceptable," he said, maneuvering so we stood in the shadows of the building.

Here? It seemed too open. I supposed anyone that passed by would see a couple making out, however, not a vampire sucking someone's blood. "All right," I began—

Andre pushed me roughly against the brick wall, scraping my skin. But more alarming was the hand that went to the base of my throat, tilting my head back and exposing my neck. I struggled against his grip, and he arched an eyebrow.

"I thought you wanted this, Marie?"

"I did. I do." So why did being pinned against a wall fill me with so much panic? I forced myself to calm, stare him in the eyes. "I can handle this."

He grinned, and as I watched, his fangs elongated. I stared in appalled horror as they stretched out of his mouth, easily two or three inches long. That was . . . awful. A car passed by, the glare of the headlights moving over his face and making those awful teeth gleam. "This is what you want?"

I swallowed hard. If I said no, he'd never turn me. "It is."

"But not my kiss?" Despite the long length of his fangs, he seemed to have no trouble speaking, though he was slow and deliberate in the pronunciation of his words. "You refused that?"

"I don't want to be drugged," I told him. "I want to be fully aware . . . of everything."

He grinned at me. "As you wish."

When he leaned in, I felt a flare of alarm. I *didn't* want this.

I wanted Josh.

I didn't want to be a vampire. I didn't want this vampire. Underneath his polite exterior, there was something cold about Andre, and it had come out tonight.

Teeth sank into my neck. There was a hard pinch of pain, and then a rip of agony flashed through me. I yelped and stiffened, and Andre's hand covered my mouth.

It felt like I'd been skewered with two hot pokers, but even worse was the sucking that followed. I felt blood dribbling down my throat, against the fabric of my dress. He slurped at my neck, and drank. And drank. It seemed to go on forever, painful and messy.

Finally, his fangs pulled free from my neck with a nasty sucking sound. He stepped away and grinned as blood gushed down my neck.

"You'll want to apply pressure there," he said, wiping at the corners of his mouth. As I watched, his fangs receded. He pulled out a white handkerchief and handed it to me.

I pressed it against my neck. Blood was everywhere, down my neck, dribbling into my cleavage. I felt weak . . . and revolted.

I'd just let a vampire drink from me. It was the most violating thing I'd ever felt. Far worse than the kiss. With the drug of his saliva, the kiss had been tolerable. This was just . . . beyond revolting. I swallowed hard. "I . . . I think I'm still bleeding."

He adjusted his cuff links, then smoothed a hand over his hair, seemingly bored now that he'd fed. "Was it everything you expected?"

"No." Honesty had served me well thus far.

Andre grinned, and I was repulsed by the red tinge of his teeth. "Have I scared you away?"

"No. I still want you to turn me."

"We'll see," he said lightly. "I do have need of a blood partner."

My heart sped up with hope.

"I'm just not sure that you're the right woman for the job. It'll require a little more . . . time."

My stomach gave a sickening clench. I knew what he meant. Time and a few more feedings to decide if he wanted to cut me loose or keep me on. I swallowed hard. "Just call me, then. I'm available."

So much for letting the predator chase his prey.

But he gave me a thin smile. "Oh, I will." He leaned in and brushed a finger along the curve of my breast, wiping off a bead of blood. He lifted it to his mouth and grinned. "Delicious. Thank you for dinner, dear one. You look a mess, though. Perhaps we should call our date off early?"

I felt a little dizzy and used, standing there with the handkerchief pressed to my neck. "That sounds fine to me."

He leaned in and gave me a dry kiss on the cheek. Then he winked and walked away, whistling.

I picked up my purse from where I'd dropped it on the ground, and I nearly staggered, black spots dancing in front of my eyes. Andre had taken quite a bit of blood. I didn't know how much, and my neck was still bleeding. I kept the handkerchief pressed there and staggered back to the agency.

It was still bleeding a few minutes later, when I heavily sat down at my desk and stared at the dancing screen saver on my computer.

"Marie, are you okay?" Ryder scrambled up from her desk. "You're covered in blood!"

"I'm fine," I said. But there was a stupid wobble in my throat. I felt weak as hell, and there was blood everywhere. I wanted to go home and take a hot shower. And cry. Crying sounded good.

"Do you want to talk about it?"

I shook my head and raised my pinky.

She sighed and raised her pinky in response. "Can I get you anything?"

A shoulder to cry on, perhaps? I gave her a wan smile. "Do we have any Band-Aids?"

"I'm pretty sure we do," she said, hustling to the office bathroom. "Be right back."

I pressed the handkerchief against my neck harder, and I wasn't surprised when my desk wavered in front of my eyes and the walls of the office seethed, as if covered by spiders.

Great. Another hallucination. I closed my eyes and prayed tonight would be over soon.

By the time the day shift came in to work, I wore a pink sweater over my stained dress (the sweater borrowed from Ryder) and had my hair down over the Cookie Monster Band-Aids on my neck. I'd had a few glasses of water to help with the loss of blood, but I was still feeling incredibly weak. I didn't have the energy to type, much less answer the phone.

Ryder was a good friend. She'd routed all the calls to her own phone, gotten me a drink when I'd needed one, and insisted on my lying down on the couch in the file room. I'd rested for a few hours.

At one point, she'd suggested calling Josh to take me home, but I'd shot that idea down. If Josh had gotten one whiff of me covered in vampire scent, he'd have gone nuts.

And part of me had thought, longingly, that I'd have loved it if he'd gone nuts over me. For him to have pulled me into his arms and comforted me. Stroked my hair. Held me close. But no matter how badly I'd wanted Josh at that moment, I had to take my licks. I'd chased him away. I didn't get to call him back just because I was having a bad day. He'd made that quite clear.

Bath and Sara entered the office chatting, cups of coffee in hand. Sara looked concerned as she plopped her oversized purse in her chair. "You okay, Marie? You look like you're not feeling well."

"Just tired," I said automatically and forced a smile to my face. "Glad to see the day shift, though."

She paused in front of my desk as Bath continued on to her office. Her nostrils flared, and she studied me for a moment "You . . . sure you're okay? Your eyes are a little glassy."

I blinked rapidly. "Just tired and ready for a nap. That's all."

She nodded and seemed to sniff the air, then moved back to her desk again. "Get some sleep."

"Oh, I will," I said, hauling my tired body to my feet.

"Hey, Ryder, can I talk to you?" Bath said as I left.

"Sure," Ryder said, glancing meaningfully back at me.

I stuck my pinky out, indicating that she should keep her mouth shut. I hadn't come this far to be undone by my best friend's concerns.

———

It was the longest car drive home ever. I took the back roads, terrified to get on the highway, lest I pass out. Luckily, I made it into my apartment. I collapsed on the couch and slept for a few hours, though it wasn't very restful. I knew it was due to the loss of blood, not to any recovery.

The worst part was knowing that if my plan was going to work, I'd have to do this again. Repeatedly. I shuddered. I needed to scrub the skin under those cheery Band-Aids and wipe myself clean of his touch.

This was a nightmare.

I sat up and rubbed my face, composing myself, and forced myself to look at things rationally. I might only have to put up with Andre for a short period of time. It didn't sound like he was averse to the thought of turning me. I could use him until I got what I wanted, and then terminate the relationship. Surely vampires broke up every now and then, didn't they?

So why did it feel so very awful and mercenary? Andre wanted to use me, too—last night was proof of that.

My phone rang. I picked it up and stared at Josh's number, then let it go to voice mail.

If I talked to him right now, I might give in to self-pity. I might be ashamed of my choice and regret it. And I couldn't afford that.

I showered and had just changed into a T-shirt and yoga pants when the doorbell rang. I frowned and moved to the door, looking through the peephole. It was Josh, a brown grocery bag in hand.

"I heard that groan, Marie-Pierre," he said cheerfully. "You keep forgetting that shifters have great hearing."

I felt a nervous, excited little flutter in my belly at the sight of him. Pure hormones, I told myself. I shouldn't have been excited to see Josh. Not after we'd parted in such an ugly fashion.

I'd done my best to drive him away, yet here he was, back again. He was determined not to let me shut him out.

He wasn't going to let me be alone in this.

Tears flooded my eyes and I blinked them away quickly, then opened the door. "Hi," I said warily.

Josh looked mouthwatering. He'd exchanged his black security T-shirt for a dark blazer over a V-neck shirt, with jeans and a pair of sunglasses. He looked like a male model, so strikingly masculine that he took my breath away. His baseball cap was gone, his thick brown hair neatly combed.

I felt the oddest urge to drag my fingers through it and mess up that hair. It was too tidy and unruffled to be my Josh.

"Can I come in?" he asked, holding up the bag of groceries.

I nodded and moved aside. To my surprise, he leaned in and gave me a light kiss on the mouth, then continued on to the kitchen.

I shut the door behind him thoughtfully. "Where are you going, all dressed up?"

"Hot date," he announced, moving into the kitchen.

My heart clenched. *Criss.* I kept my voice light. "Oh?"

"Yeah," he said casually, clanging about in my kitchen. "I know this chick who digs French stuff."

Out of curiosity, I followed to see what he was doing. And stared as he set up a small FryDaddy on my counter.

"Well, French-Canadian cuisine," he amended, and grinned at me.

All my anxiety went out the door, and I felt like laughing. I went forward, peering over his shoulder as he pulled a bottle of oil out of the grocery bag. "What are you doing?"

"I am making you *poutine*," Josh said. "I'm going to make you some french fries, and then we're going to slather those tasty things in disgusting cheese curds and brown gravy."

I laughed and smacked him on the arm. "It's not disgusting. It's delicious."

"Says the woman named Marie-Pierre."

I chuckled as he prepared the fryer. "This is a lot of work, just to make me some *poutine*."

"I know it is. I had to go to four damn stores to find cheese curds. It's ridiculous." As he plugged in the fryer, he stepped away from it and toward me. "The good news is that I get to give you a proper greeting while that's heating up."

He reached for me, his fingers brushing over my tangled hair. He leaned in, that slight, roguish smile tugging at his mouth, then paused at the sight of the two Band-Aids on my neck. Some emotion flickered over his face, as if he was warring with himself. Then he leaned in a bit further and kissed me, ever so lightly, on the nose.

That was . . . disappointing.

I frowned as he stepped away. Did he not want to kiss me anymore? Just when I'd had my toes all curled in preparation?

He moved back to the grocery bag and paused, resting his fists on the counter. His clenched fists, I noticed. Oh. He was furious and trying not to show it. Furious at me, then?

I bit my lip, suddenly feeling anxious tears spring to my eyes. I didn't want things to go like this between us. "I'm sorry I was so awful to you yesterday."

"You're scared," he said to the bag of groceries, not looking in my direction, his shoulders and fists still tense and clenched. "Your natural reaction is to try and push me away. I wanted to show you that you can't push me out of your life. I want to be here for you."

They were good words. Just what I needed to hear. And yet . . . "Then why won't you look at me?" The words came out soft, aching.

"I'm . . . struggling with this," he said, the words rough. "Because I see that bite on your neck and I know it's exactly what you want, but it makes me an asshole because it makes me furious. I want to put my fist through a wall, and I know I should be congratulating you."

Strangely enough, his fury made me feel better. I could safely tell him about the unhappiness and vague discomfort I had about my chosen path. I moved toward him, smoothing my hands over the shoulders of his jacket, admiring the way it hugged his large frame. He'd dressed up for me? A flush of desire crept over me. "You don't have to congratulate me," I told him softly. "I didn't enjoy it."

He turned and gave me an agonized look, and the breath sucked out of my throat. His dark eyes were tortured, his face drawn into harsh lines. The circles under his eyes told me that he wasn't sleeping well, either. "What am I supposed to do, Marie? I want to rip his head off for touching you." His eyes gleamed, catlike. "Instead, all I can do is sit here and try and support you, because I can't stop you. If it's what you need, I want you to get it. I just need to know where that puts me."

I reached over and unplugged the fryer. My hand stole under his jacket, slipping around his waist. "It puts you in my arms. That's exactly where I need you to be. Here. With me. Kissing me. Touching me."

His jaw remained clenched. I felt the urge to kiss it and gave in to it, wrapping my other hand around his neck and drawing his face down so I could brush my lips over his unshaven cheek. He was stiff in my embrace, but not pulling away.

Angry, but wanting to be here with me. Conflicted.

I knew how that felt.

"Thank you," I said softly, and kissed his hard mouth, pressing my body against his.

He grabbed my ass and pulled me against him, hard. His dark eyes stared into mine. "Don't thank me just yet. I'm feeling rather territorial," he rasped, his gaze going to my neck. "Fighting the urge to throw you down and mark the hell out of you to stake my claim."

Liquid heat poured through me. Mmm. I stroked my hand up his shirt under the jacket, feeling the play of muscles and feeling the odd need to purr like a kitten. "Then don't fight it."

A low animal growl started in his throat. "Marie."

I leaned in and traced my tongue ever so lightly against the tight seam of his lips. My body pulsed with need—need for him, need for the promise in his voice. I brushed my breasts against his chest, my nipples hardening deliciously at the friction. "I'm yours, Josh."

For tonight, anyhow.

His hand went to the back of my neck and he was holding me, pinned, and his mouth swooped over mine. It was a hard, branding kiss. This wasn't the light, playful flirting we'd done before. This was a claim of territory, of possession, of ownership. It was delicious.

"You sure you want to say that to me?"

"Absolutely," I breathed.

Chapter Thirteen

*H*e grabbed me behind the knees, swinging me into his arms as if I weighed nothing. I yelped in surprise and flung my arms around his neck as he swept down the hall to my bedroom.

Well now, this was more like it.

Josh carried me to the bed and gently laid me down atop the blankets. "If you don't want me, Marie," he began, stripping off his jacket, "you'd better speak up now."

I sat up in the bed, my fingers going to his belt. "Oh, I want you. More than anything."

His fingers tangled in my hair and he growled with need, the sound shooting desire straight to my core. Blood pulsed, thick and heavy in my veins. I loved that he was so overcome at the thought of me touching him. I loosened his belt, then tugged his pants down, then his briefs. When his cock was free, I wrapped my hands around it and sighed in pleasure.

"This is my favorite part of you," I said, teasing.

He drew his lips back in a half snarl, half grin,

pushing at my hands. "Why don't you show it how much you like it?"

Desire pulsed through my body. My nipples ached with need, but not nearly as badly as I ached between my legs. I felt the sudden urge to slide my hand between my own legs and play with myself. But that meant I'd have to take my hands off him, and that was the last thing I wanted to do. I wanted my hands all over him. Wanted him kissing me. Touching me.

I might not have another chance to touch him after tonight. I felt like somewhere out there, an hourglass was slowly losing grain after grain of sand. Who knew how much longer I had? And I was going to let nothing pass me by this night.

Especially not Josh.

I wrapped my fingers around his length and gave him a seductive smile, then slowly licked my lips.

"Mmmhmm." His eyes were avid as they gazed down at me.

I licked the head like I would a lollipop. A long, slow lap of my tongue, savoring every moment and drawing it out. At his tortured groan, I began to swirl my tongue around the crown. I wasn't an expert on blow jobs, but this seemed like common sense. Take him in my hands and mouth. Drive him crazy. Simple enough.

"Suck it," he breathed, his hand fisting in my curls. "Suck on me, Marie."

An eager flutter in my belly, I ran my tongue along the head again, then took him deeper into my mouth. He pushed his hips even as I took him deeper, and I loved the feeling of him filling my mouth, the feeling of him butting against the back of my throat.

"Jesus, Marie. Your mouth is amazing."

I worked him deeper, then released him to stroke the wet length again. "Do you like that?"

"Hell, yes. Do you?"

"Mmm," I said in response and put my tongue on the head of his cock again. My fingers went to my panties, and sure enough, I was wet with need. "See how much I like it?"

His eyes glittered and his nostrils flared, as if taking in my scent. "Seems unfair for me to have all the fun," he said and pulled away.

I whined in response, only to have him grab me by the waist. He fell onto his back, dragging me down with him. "Undress. Quick."

"But—"

"Just do it," he said, and playfully bit my arm.

I yelped, backing away and stripping off my clothing. He ripped off his shirt and kicked away the remainder of his clothing pooled at his feet. I tossed mine onto the floor as well. Then his hot hands were on my waist, dragging me down against him, and Josh's mouth was on mine, kissing me wildly. I moaned when his tongue stroked into my mouth and thrust against my own. He tasted so good.

"Take my cock in your mouth, Marie," he whispered when we broke the kiss.

That sounded good to me. I slid down his big

body and shifted to the side, grasping his cock in my hand and running my lips along it.

He reached out for my thigh and tugged on it. "Give me your hips, Marie."

I looked up from the attention I was lavishing on his cock, dazed. "What do you mean?"

He gave me a feline grin. "I want your hips. In my face. Come straddle me."

A hot blush crept over my cheeks at the mental image. "Josh, I—"

Then he was grabbing my hips and hauling me bodily over him. I barely had time to get my balance, my knees on either side of his face and me feeling a little ridiculous. My blush was scalding my cheeks.

"Very pretty," he said in a husky voice that sent shivers down my spine. I felt him run a finger along the seam. "Spread your legs for me, Marie."

But spreading my legs meant that my hips would descend on his waiting face. I felt so open and exposed. So vulnerable. His hands gently held my thighs, encouraging me, and when I hesitated a moment more, he nipped at the inside of a thigh with his sharp teeth. "Open for me, Marie."

I sank down, my entire body tense with need and a strange sense of anxiety. My hands clutched at his cock, wrapped around the thick length.

His tongue stroked through the slick folds of my sex and I jolted, my entire body fluttering. Oh, that was . . .

He did it again, and I felt the rumble of his purr under my body even as I jolted again. "You taste amazing, Marie. So sweet. I could lick you for hours."

I'd probably turn into a helpless pile of mush if he did. I forced myself to concentrate on pleasing him instead, and took the head of his cock again. It was wet with pre-cum, and I licked it clean, pleased when he groaned in response. As I swiped at his cock with my tongue, he continued to lick my sex with long, smooth strokes of his tongue. It made me want to wriggle with ticklishness, but it wasn't unpleasant. It wasn't relaxing, either, though.

Then his tongue speared against my clit. I gasped, only to have my mouth suddenly full of his cock as his hips thrust forward. Distracted, I sucked him deep, working him with my tongue. He continued to flick his tongue against my clit in small, swift licks that made me want to squirm away as much as it made me want to bear down on his face. It felt . . . amazing. I whimpered in response, my mouth full of his cock, and he thrust again, raising his hips.

"Love the taste of you, Marie," Josh whispered against my female flesh, nuzzling at me. When his tongue stroked the length of my sex again, I raised my hips, involuntarily following his tongue. He chuckled at my response, and then I felt him thrust his tongue deep into my core even as he thrust into my mouth.

My senses in overload, I worked the length of his cock with my tongue and my mouth, but the feel of his tongue thrusting deep inside me was distracting me beyond my limits, and my movements were jerky and abrupt. Josh didn't seem to mind—when I stopped working, he would thrust his hips up a little, pushing into my mouth again, and I would start anew, sucking and licking at him. The torture of his mouth was incredibly distracting, making my entire body drawn and tense with need.

I felt his hand lift from one of my thighs, and as his tongue speared deep again, I felt his thumb graze my clit, rolling it against the pad of his finger. Oh, my God. That was . . . I rocked my hips against his face, hard, no longer caring about being shy. His purr grew louder, and I could feel it in his tongue as he stroked it inside my sex, the faintest hint of vibration deep in his throat. Stroke, vibration, thumb on my clit. Stroke, purr, thumb on my clit. I was lost in that chain, barely realizing that I wasn't fulfilling my end of things and only licking wildly at his cock. All of my attention was on his mouth on my sex.

His thumb rubbed my clit hard, just as he stroked his tongue deep again. I gave a sharp little cry and came, the orgasm ripping through me with startling intensity. He murmured something that sounded like praise, his thumb still rubbing my clit, drawing out the crashing waves of the orgasm as I writhed over his face, lost in need.

When he stopped, I gasped for breath, only to find him sliding out from under me. His hands grabbed my hips, his movements almost rough, and hauled them into the air, my cheek pressed to the bed as I lay on my stomach. I felt him raise up behind me, felt the hard probe of his cock against my sex.

He thrust in a finger, and I bucked my hips. It felt tight but so good. He hissed in response. "So wet." He pushed again, and it felt . . . thicker. Two fingers. Then he scissored his fingers inside me, and I gasped at the sensation. "Are you ready, Marie?"

I nodded, feeling tension building in my body all over again. I wanted another orgasm; needed more from him.

He gripped my hips and I felt him nudge at my entrance—and this time he pushed in, and it was big and hot. I bit my lip as he pushed in, inch by inch. It felt deep and thick, and like he was stretching me. Delicious and full and intense.

When he stopped moving, he stroked my buttock and thigh. "Am I hurting you?"

I gave a tentative wiggle, more of a tease than anything. I felt his big body over mine, his knees up against my spread ones. His cock was buried deep inside me. "It feels amazing."

"Good," Josh gritted, and then he thrust.

I gasped again. That was . . . incredible. "Keep going!"

He pushed deep and began to slowly stroke into me with quick, hard thrusts. His hips pistoned his cock into me, stroking over and over. The surge deep inside me made the tingle inside me build again, and I rocked my hips back against his next thrust, needing more force, more friction, more everything.

He groaned, his fingers digging into my backside as his thrusts became harder, rougher, less controlled. "You're mine," he growled, and punctuated each word with a hard drive into me. "Say it, Marie."

"Yours," I breathed, and was rewarded with another hard stroke. His touch was branding me. Owning me. And right now, I wanted to be owned. More than anything else, I wanted to be his. "All yours."

Josh gave a feral snarl and his fingers dug into my hips. Claws pricked at my skin and I gasped at the bite of pain.

"Josh!"

He came with a snarl, rocking into me hard, pushing my entire body forward into the mattress. His strokes slowed and he rocked into me one more time, breathing hard, and I wriggled against him again, still needing more. *"Please,* Josh."

His hand moved between my legs, cupping me. Teasing me. "Say you're mine?"

"Yours," I sobbed, pushing against his hand with deep-seated need.

Josh dipped a finger into the curls of my sex and began to slowly rub my clit. I stiffened and came hard, again, my sex clenching, body rocking with need.

Eventually I stopped shuddering and was left gasping in the aftermath. Josh pulled me against him, tucking my head under his chin. He pressed a kiss to my hair and hugged me close, and I felt the rumble of his purr low in his throat.

I felt warm and happy at his side. Sated. Elated.

A weird emotion crept up inside me. Contentment? The aftermath of lust?

It wasn't love . . . was it? I couldn't afford love.

And yet, I kept feeling it.

Josh kissed my hand. "You hungry?"

I chuckled. Food was the last thing on my mind, but shifters needed to eat constantly. I'd seen how much food tiny Sara could pack away. "Not really, but I am open to suggestion."

"I'll finish making you the *poutine*," he said, sliding off the bed and pulling me with him.

We showered first, quickly soaping each other up and chatting about small things. He was tender and affectionate, kissing me constantly and wrapping his arms around me as we washed and then toweled each other off. By the time we made it back to the kitchen, we were both worked up again.

It took a few hours to get the *poutine* made, but it was decent. Not quite at the level of French-Canadian cuisine, but he got major points for effort. After we ate we collapsed into bed, where Josh made slow, delicious love to me again.

And then he fell asleep. I dozed for about ten minutes, and then my brain snapped awake, just like it always did. Frustrated, I slid out of bed and wrapped my robe around my body, heading for my puzzle with a yawn. No sense in waking Josh up.

I had just put together a corner when I felt him place his hands on my shoulders. He pressed a kiss to the side of my neck. "Can't sleep?" he asked in a drowsy voice.

"Understatement of the century," I said with a wry half smile. "You can go back to sleep. It's okay."

But he only pulled a chair next to mine and looped his arm around my waist, pulling me close. His chin perched on my shoulder, and he watched me as I pulled another piece out of the pile of corner pieces and studied it.

Wrapped around me. Not chatting in my ear. Not taking over the puzzle. Just being with me. Letting me know that I wasn't alone.

It was good that my tumbled hair hid my face, or he might have seen the tears that pricked my eyes.

"Tell me about your mother," he said quietly. "What was she like?"

I thought for a moment, turning a puzzle piece in my hand without really seeing it. "She was exuberant. Larger than life. Everything she did was big. She laughed big, smiled big, and threw the worst temper tantrums I've ever seen." I smiled fondly at the memories. "And she loved my father an insane amount. When he had to travel for business, she'd just wilt. And when he was back, she perked right up again. They were wonderful together, and so happy. And we all used to love to go on vacation, wherever we felt like driving to that weekend. I was lucky to have those times with them."

"And she was French-Canadian?"

I nodded. "Quebecois. Her family was a very small but old one. Very Catholic and old Quebec. They didn't speak a word of English, and my father and I didn't speak French, so we were never super-close to them. My dad only knew a few phrases here and there. My mother, though, she was very quick to spout off in her native language. She cussed in French whenever she was mad, and I picked it up," I said with a faint smile. "There's nothing that feels quite so good as ranting at someone in a foreign language."

He grinned and kissed my shoulder. "Sounds sexy when you do it."

I shook my head. "Mine are watered down. She could cuss a blue streak."

"How did your parents meet?"

"She rear-ended him in a parking lot and cussed him out. He thought she was fascinating. The rest was history."

"So it runs in the family, that women are attracted to men that drive them wild? I see." Josh gave me a teasing look. "It explains how you've fallen into my arms despite complaining the entire time."

I snorted.

He reached over me to move a puzzle piece into place, and it felt easy to sit there with him. Natural. Like this was something all couples did.

He kissed my shoulder. "It must have been really hard on you and your father when she passed."

I nodded. "It was a slow and painful death. At the end, she didn't recognize anyone. She was lost in her own mind and tortured. The worst thing is being relieved when someone passes away because you know they're no longer in pain." Even after all these years, it was still hard to talk about. "I . . .

thought my dad would never recover. But he's moved on, and I'm happy for him. Even if I question his taste in women."

Josh laughed. "Posey is cute in a garish sort of way."

That was the right word for her. "She makes my father happy, so I like her well enough. I'm just glad he has someone this time—" I stopped when his expression grew dark.

"Marie," he whispered huskily.

I shook my head, not wanting to talk about it. I was closer to a cure than ever before. "You're right. I'm just being morbid. Pass me that corner piece, would you?"

When I got to work the next evening, I was exhausted but content. I'd taken some caffeine pills to give my slumping body a boost, but my mood was terrific. I still had Josh. Through everything, I had him. And I was so close to getting Andre to turn me. I'd figure out the repercussions once I had this whole mortality thing off my plate. All in due time.

"Marie, can I talk to you for a second?" Bath called from her office.

"Sure," I said, tossing my purse down on my desk. "Let me just log in—"

"Actually, let's talk before you log in." Her voice was cool. "Come in here, please."

Unease flashed through me. I glanced over at Ryder's desk, which was empty. Her purse hung on the back of her chair, so she was here somewhere. Were we going to be asked to leave? Dread curled in my stomach.

I walked into the small office and wasn't surprised to see Sara sitting in one of the chairs across from Bath's desk. She looked unhappy, a drawn expression on her dainty features, her wild, newly pink hair tucked behind her ears.

Bath shut the door to the office and gestured for me to sit.

I did, feeling sick to my stomach. "Is something wrong?"

The two sisters exchanged a glance. Bathsheba cleared her throat and clasped her hands on her desk, looking solemn. "Marie, I want you to know that both Sara and I have nothing but affection for you. You were in my wedding. I count you as a friend. I really do."

I could almost hear the "but" hovering in the air. "I count you as a friend, too."

"This is very hard for me to say." She paused, studied her hands, and sighed. "It's come to our attention that someone has been using the database for their own needs during work hours. A client came to us and said that he'd gone out on a date with a woman, only to find out when she arrived that she was human."

Damn. Damn. Damn. It was probably the vampire Josh had chased off. The horny one with an affinity for the shocker. I'd been afraid that would come back to haunt me.

Both Sara and Bathsheba were looking at me expectantly. It was on the tip of my tongue to tell them the truth. *I have a fatal disease. I'm looking for someone to turn me before I die.* But . . . the words wouldn't come out of my mouth. "I . . ." I tried to force the words out, but they wouldn't come. "I . . . I'm sorry."

They both looked disappointed.

Bathsheba said, "I'm sorry to say that because of how precarious things are in the Alliance right now, this makes things difficult for us. Combine that with the fact that vampires have difficulty trusting the Alliance anyhow. They think that the agency is fooling them to drum up business, and they're not happy. A client is seeking legal action for misrepresentation."

I was aghast. "You're being sued by a vampire?"

"I doubt it'll ever go to court," Bath said, "but it will cost us an arm and a leg to settle."

"I'm sorry that I've caused the agency so much trouble," I said softly.

Sara added, "This is also making the Russells look very bad, and the were-cougars can't afford to lose control of the Alliance."

I shook my head, confused. "What do you mean, it's making the Russells look bad?"

"You're mated to Josh. I see his mark on your neck. I smell him all over your skin."

"I'm *what?*" I stared at her, appalled.

"Mated." Her brow furrowed. "He bit you on the neck, right? That's a claim. He's staked you out as his personal property." Her gaze narrowed. "Has he tried to turn you?"

"No," I said quickly. "I won't let him."

Both sisters exhaled sharply, looking relieved.

"Good," Sara said. "If he turns you, all hell will break loose. We have to do damage control, spin things as positively as possible. Hopefully a few months from now, when everything has died down. Beau's mated to a human and it hasn't caused too many ripples. I'm sure Josh mating with one won't be ideal, but it won't be seen as too abusive of power."

Mated. What the hell? Fury at Josh, who had never pointed this out to me, began to build. He'd known exactly what my plans were, and he'd snuck this up on me.

Just before nibbling on my neck, he whispered, "Marie, I can't be with you without . . . putting some sort of claim on you."

I hadn't realized exactly what that had meant. Damn it.

"That doesn't change the fact that we have to fix the situation here today," Bathsheba said, looking upset. "And I'm sorry, Marie. I hope you don't take this personally, but you're fired."

I arrived home less than an hour later, with a box containing all the stuff from my desk. I had worked at Midnight Liaisons for well over a year, and I'd enjoyed every minute of it. I'd made friends. I'd met Josh. It had given me hope when I'd had none.

And now that chapter was over. I stared at the small box of my things. Pencils, personalized Post-its, the bow from the box of chocolates that Josh had dropped off that day.

Fired.

No more access to the database. No more vampires. No way of getting in contact with Andre or any other potential dates.

I was fucked. Panic began to set in, and I headed for the medicine cabinet to dose myself with anti-anxiety medication. I'd figure a way out of this. Josh would know what to do. If he didn't, I'd—

The phone rang.

I raced for my purse, fishing out my phone quickly. Ryder's name was on the caller ID. My heart sank a little at the sight. "Hello?"

"Hey," she said quietly, her voice muffled and a little hollow. "I'm in the bathroom at work. I just heard. Savannah's sitting at your desk. What the hell happened?"

"Sara and Bath found out," I said, curling up on the couch and digging my fingernails into my palms so I wouldn't cry. "Some vampire I went out with sued the agency, so they fired me."

"Oh, God. I swear I didn't say anything."

"I know you didn't. The vampire ratted on me."

"What are you going to do? Do you need money?"

I smiled despite the panic in my belly. "No, I'm okay. Thank you for offering, though. I'll file for unemployment or something." I'd have to file to extend my medical insurance, too. I chewed my lip, thinking hard.

"Okay. Do you want me to come over after work? Want to talk about it? We can go out for breakfast. I'll buy."

"It's okay. I think I'm just going to lay down and . . . nap." I choked on the last word, a big fat lie if there ever was one.

"Is there anything I can do?"

"Actually . . ." I bit my lip. Was it too much to ask of our friendship? "Would you mind looking up someone in the database?"

"You want the phone number of the vampire you were dating?"

I held my breath. "Something like that."

"I already checked his profile, and he sent your fake one a message. Said he wants to meet tonight. Has a surprise for you."

My heart pounded. "A surprise?" Maybe he'd decided to turn me. Hope made the world suddenly bright again. "Give me his number. And thank you, Ryder."

"Hey, what are friends for?"

Andre didn't answer his phone. I remembered that he hated phones, though, so I left a text message stating that I wanted to meet him. And for the next six hours, I checked my phone like crazy.

Nothing.

Just when I was ready to give up hope, my phone

buzzed with a text. I scrambled for it and picked it up with shaking hands.

My bodyguard will pick you up at Konstantine's. Be there in a half hour. I think you'll like my surprise.

Yes!

I scrambled to my bathroom and checked the makeup I'd put on in the hope of meeting with Andre. I checked my hair and tugged at the neckline of my simple black dress. I shuddered at the faintest mark of his bite still on my neck, now scabbed over. If he was turning me tonight, that meant he'd have to bite me again. A wave of revulsion crashed over me, quickly pushed away by an overwhelming sense of elation. Just one nasty bite . . . and then I had eternity.

No more worries about my health. About hallucinations. About any of it. Hope and need pushed through me, so strong that it made me stagger. *Please, God, let this work.* I said a quick prayer, kissed my mother's Virgin Mary figurine for good luck, and ran to the front door. I had just enough time to make it to the restaurant. I opened the front door and—

Josh was there, his hand raised as if about to knock. He eyed my sexy dress, my high heels. A grocery bag was in his hand again. He raised his eyebrows at my outfit. "Where are you running off to?"

I reached up and gave him a hard, fierce kiss of excitement. "I'm going to see Andre. He says he has a surprise for me. I think he's going to turn me!"

I flung my arms around him in excitement. "Isn't that great?"

He didn't hug me back. "Marie—"

I pulled away, shaking my head. "Josh, I love you, but I don't want to hear it right now. Not when I'm so close to reaching my goal. After this I'll have eternity! I'll live."

"You love me?" He gave me an odd look.

Whoops, had I said that? I gave him another quick kiss. "I do. I love you. I'll prove it when I get home."

But he slowly shook his head. "You don't get it, Marie. If he turns you . . . I won't be here when you get back."

"Why not?" He wasn't going to go all principled on me now, was he? I'd thought we were past that. "Josh—"

"Marie, if you pick this vampire, you're picking him for all eternity. Remember that I told you how seriously they take that? He's not going to let you walk back out the door and into my arms."

I stared at him. I hadn't thought further than getting turned. How stupid of me. How shortsighted.

His face grew tight with anger. "Just because you choose to go after this plan of yours with blinders on doesn't mean I will. If this guy wants to turn you, it's because he wants an eternal companion. I don't want that to happen. We'll find another way."

We? "You're not the one dying," I said bitterly. "I'm not about to turn back now—not when this is in my grasp. You can't ask me to choose between you and dying, Josh. That's unfair."

"I'm not asking you to," he said quietly. "I'm asking you to trust me to find another way. We'll go to more doctors. See a specialist. Check with the Alliance doctors—"

"Don't you think I've tried everything? Don't you think I know what my options are? I don't know how much time I have, Josh. The hallucinations, the anxiety, the insomnia—they're worse than ever. I can't keep doing this. You can't ask me to keep going in the hope that something will change."

"Just give me a week, Marie. That's all I ask. You say you love me. Do you love me enough to trust me for another week?"

I stared at him. Another week of misery. Of sheer exhaustion. Hallucinations that told me that my brain was shutting down. Of dragging myself through every hour of every day.

Another week in Josh's arms.

But what if Andre didn't want to wait? What if he changed his mind?

I couldn't risk it. I leaned in and gave Josh another kiss. "I love you," I told him softly. "I do. But I'm not changing my mind."

He stared at me, his face cold. "I'm not going to sit back and let you ruin your life, Marie. This is a mistake. I know things about vampires that you don't. This one's not a nice guy. I don't trust that he's going to turn you. He's just using you as his personal soda fountain—"

I suddenly remembered that *Josh* had bitten me, too. "At least he didn't put a mate mark on me and then lie to me about it."

"Fat lot of good it's doing," he said angrily. "Especially since you're determined to run headlong into a vampire's arms."

"How could you do that to me? Stake your claim on me like I belong to you?"

"Last night you were quick to say you were mine. Are things different now that you've had a chance to sleep on it?"

Tears of frustration threatened to spill from my eyes. "Please. I have a chance at more time. You can't ask me not to take it."

"And I won't," he said, moving in to brush my tears away with his fingers. Then he kissed my forehead. "Let's talk about it."

He pressed more light kisses to my face, my nose, my cheek. Light, loving kisses of affection. God, I loved his kisses. He moved past me and gestured at the kitchen. "You should see what I brought you."

I nodded, pretending that I was just about to follow him. When he moved into the kitchen, still talking, I tore down the stairs and raced across the lawn to my car. I got it started in record time and was backing out of my parking space just as he appeared at the head of the stairs, looking utterly furious.

I mouthed, "*Sorry*" as I peeled out of the parking lot.

After tonight, I'd have all eternity to make it up to him.

Chapter Fourteen

The sedan pulled up to a posh brownstone in an exclusive part of Southlake Town Square.

Not exactly what I'd pictured for a vampire, but it did scream "money."

The driver nodded at the house on the end. "We're here, miss." He watched me with attentive eyes, his nostrils flaring every now and then to catch a scent, which told me he was some kind of shifter. He was big and burly, like half the shifters I knew of.

"Thank you," I said quietly and opened the door, stepping out onto the curb. I moved to the steps of the brownstone, studying it. The exterior was neat and well maintained, with a box of white flowers hanging at one window. Very homey.

It didn't scream vampire, but maybe that was the point.

I knocked, feeling anxious. What if I turned around and Josh was there to try and "rescue" me from the situation again? What would I do then?

But the door opened, and a smiling, beautifully dressed Andre gestured for me to enter. "Welcome, Marie. I'm so glad you could make it."

I smiled brightly and stepped inside, feeling a bit like a fly that had stepped into the spider's web. But that was silly, of course. I'd told him I'd wanted to be turned, and now I was here at his place. This had to be leading to something.

The interior of the house was just as elegant as the exterior, reminding me of something from an English painting—heavy, ornate, and austere. Deep cherrywood floors complemented the mahogany furniture. An oil painting hung on the far wall, and it looked like Andre in old-fashioned clothes, his hair in a long queue. That was . . . weird. "Nice place," I said, since he was watching me expectantly.

Andre inclined his head at my compliment. "I appreciate fine things."

I nodded again, unsure what to say to that. "I'm glad you wanted to see me again."

"I did," he agreed. His smile seemed a little more toothy than usual, and alarm bells went off in my head. "I am glad you could come tonight. Did you have to change your plans?"

I glanced around at his immaculate, barely-lived-in-more-like-a-museum home. "Actually, I had an opening in my schedule."

"So no one is expecting you back?" he asked, moving toward a bottle of wine on the dining room table.

There went those alarm bells again. I followed behind him, hesitant. What to say? Did turning take a while? Was that why he was asking? "Well," I hedged. "Actually, a friend is waiting for me. He wasn't happy that I left, but you are my priority."

"Oh? He?" Andre's lips thinned.

Damn. "Just a friend," I said quickly. "No one important."

"He must not be, if you came to be with me in the middle of the night," he said slowly, as if measuring out the words. "This pleases me."

I didn't care if it pleased him or not. "You said you had a surprise for me?" Might as well cut to the chase.

Andre grinned, and his teeth were definitely elongating. He poured me a glass of wine and held it out. "Shall we enjoy a nice drink first?"

I took the glass, and when he gestured toward the couch, I sat, still uneasy. To my surprise, Andre sat next to me. He didn't have a wineglass. "I thought you said you wanted a drink?"

"Oh, I do." He reached out and brushed a curl of my hair off my shoulder.

Skitters of alarm raced through me. *This is what you wanted,* I told myself. *It's what you wanted. What you wanted.* I downed a big gulp of wine, feeling it burn in my throat. He was staring at my neck avidly, and I realized . . . that I didn't want to feed him. The thought made my skin crawl with revulsion.

When he leaned in, I flinched away.

He pulled back, frowning at me. "Do you not want to be here with me, Marie?"

I set the glass down, wanting my hands to be free for some reason. "Not at all. I just . . ." I forced a vulnerable look to my face. "It really hurt the last time. I'm a little frightened."

A lot frightened.

He puffed up with pride, a pleased-with-himself smile curving his fanged mouth. His teeth grew to an enormous size, and he ran a finger down my bare shoulder, as if eyeing a tender morsel. "Then shall I lick you this time, my pet? I assure you that it won't hurt that way."

Oh, ugh. When he leaned in, I leaned away again. "May I know what my surprise is first? Or is the bite my surprise?"

He gave me a confused look. "The bite?"

"Are you going to turn me?" I asked baldly.

"Ah." He barked a laugh. "No. Here it is." He pulled a long velvet box out of an interior jacket pocket and offered it to me.

A necklace? I stared at the box, disappointment crashing through me.

"Perhaps if I enjoy tasting you again, we will move on to other things," he continued. His tongue flicked out between his fangs, as if licking his lips.

Other things? Like . . . sex? And then what? If I had sex with him—ugh ugh ugh—and kept feeding him, then *maybe* he'd eventually decide to turn me?

"Do you plan on turning me at some point?" I asked softly.

He arched an eyebrow. "You do realize that vampire law states that any vampire who turns another must give away half his fortune to his fledgling? I'd have to like someone quite a bit to turn them." He chuckled humorlessly, his cool hand skating down my arm. "That doesn't mean I don't like you, of course. It just means that I need to get to know you better first."

He'd had four hundred years to get to know other girls, and he'd never turned anyone.

And he wasn't going to turn me. I was just a convenient drink that he'd keep dangling the carrot in front of until one of us got bored. He'd give me a few more baubles and then call it a day, moving on to the next girl.

I wasn't a potential mate, as Joshua had feared. I was the vampire equivalent of a booty call.

And now I realized the biggest flaw in my plan. Since there was a hefty fee associated with turning a vampire, someone would really, really have to be in love with me to turn me.

And I was in love with Josh.

The surge of disappointment made me want to throw up. I wasn't going to be turned after all. There wasn't going to be a Get Out of Jail Free card. I was done. I was dying.

I was dead. It was just a matter of time.

Tears pricked at my eyes and I swiped at them, getting up from the couch. "I . . . don't think I can do this."

"Do what?" Andre got to his feet, his eyes taking on a menacing gleam.

"Feed you. So unless you want to turn me right now, this drinking fountain is closed for business."

"Turn you? Tonight?" He laughed hard. "I'm

afraid that I'd need a bit more persuasion before thinking along those lines, my dear."

And there was that carrot again. "I *need* someone to turn me," I told him through clenched teeth. "I'm dying."

"Then perhaps we can come to an agreement," he said in a silky voice, taking a step toward me. "You feed me, and we'll . . . talk about it."

Yeah, right.

I shook my head. "I'm leaving."

"You're making a mistake," he said warningly.

"This entire thing was a mistake," I told him, my throat raw with unshed tears. My entire life was crashing down before my eyes. I'd been fired from my job, the only access that I had to the Paranormal Alliance. The one vampire that stood a chance of turning me was just using me, and the man I loved had asked me to trust him and I'd run away.

And I was still fucking *dying*.

"Good-bye, Andre," I said, heading toward the door.

"Marie," he warned, walking quickly behind me. "I'm not going to like it if you try to leave."

Alarm raced through me. That sounded ominous. Even worse, it sounded like he was enjoying it. *Vampires are predators,* Josh had told me. *They like to chase down their prey.*

And here I was, running from him.

I picked up my pace. I just needed to get down the steps. He wouldn't attack me out in the open.

But when I put my hand to the door, the knob

wouldn't turn. I jerked at it, confused. "What—"

Andre's heavy body crashed into mine. He wrapped an arm around my neck, cutting off my air, and hauled me up against him. He was incredibly strong. My feet lifted off the ground and I kicked in alarm, realizing I couldn't breathe.

"I told you I wouldn't like it, little pet," he said, and sank his teeth into my bare shoulder.

I screamed, but it came out as a gurgle, his arm was so tight around my neck. I couldn't breathe. There was no air. Panic shredded at me as his teeth sank deeper into my skin, like claws ripping at my flesh. He sucked hard, blood running down my shoulder.

I twisted violently against him, but it was no use. My lungs ached and panicky lights began to flash behind my eyes. It wasn't going to end like this, was it? Choked to death by a feeding vampire? I kicked feebly.

The world began to edge with black, and I dug my fingers at his arm, trying desperately to free myself. I . . . couldn't . . . breathe . . .

Then everything went black.

A hand patted my cheek. "Are you okay?"

I stirred, my head throbbing, my throat aching. My shoulder felt like it'd been scraped raw. I opened my eyes into a dark room, lit only by a small night-light on the far side.

At my side, the person scuttled away and I sat

up, turning to look at her. As I did, chains clinked and I frowned, putting my fingers to my neck. There was a metal collar around it with a chain attached. I looked over at the woman. "I'm chained?"

"We both are," she said, and moved into the light of the night-light.

It was a human woman, her hair hanging about her in a tangled cloud, and what I could see of her face was hollow and unhappy. She wore a metal collar and a dirty bikini top.

She smelled, too. Like unwashed skin. I wrinkled my nose and scooted backward, hissing at the waves of pain the movement sent through me. I gingerly touched my shoulder and winced. "Asshole," I muttered, trying to examine it in the low light. It felt raw as hell, but I couldn't tell how bad it was. "Where are we?"

"In a wine cellar," the woman said. The dim glow of the night-light revealed the long chain attached to a hook in the wall. "He keeps his meals down here."

"Meals?" I repeated stupidly. "Who are you?"

"I'm Lily Faust."

The name didn't ring a bell. "Is Andre keeping you here . . . to turn you?"

She gave a mirthless laugh. "No. I'm his lunch when he can't find anything else." She raised one arm to the dim glow of the night-light, and I saw that her arm was riddled with bites. Big, ugly ones.

"Oh, my God," I said. "He's going to keep us chained in here?"

"For a short time," she said softly. "Then I imagine he'll get rid of one of us. He's brought a few others down every now and then, but . . . I never see them after he takes them away. I don't know if he lets them go, or something worse."

Considering he kept a girl chained in his basement to feed on? I was going to go with "something worse."

I stared up in the darkness. A crack of light upstairs told me that a light was on somewhere. "Are we . . . still in his house?"

"I don't know," Lily admitted. "I went out on a blind date with what I thought was a nice guy, and the next thing I knew, he was choking me. I woke up here. I've been here for . . . a while."

I swallowed hard. "How long is a while?"

"What month is it?"

Oh, God. "May."

She shuddered. "Six months. I suppose I should count myself lucky. The others never even last a few weeks."

I didn't *have* months, and an hysterical laugh bubbled in my throat.

"What's so funny?" Lily stared at me.

"I'm dying," I choked out. "Fatal disease." When she scooted away, I added, "Not contagious. I just find it ironic that he kidnapped a dying woman. Guess he's in for a rude surprise."

"Is there anyone who's going to come looking for you?" she asked. "My family's dead. I don't have anyone, and I was at college. I think that's why he snatched me. Easy pickings."

I thought of Josh. His look of betrayal as I'd run

away from him tonight. God, I was an idiot. He'd known something was suspicious about Andre; he'd warned me not to go.

Just trust me. We'll find a way.

And I'd thrown that trust in his face. I totally sucked at this relationship thing. "I don't know if anyone will come looking for me."

She sighed heavily, and I felt like echoing it.

"When will he be back?" I asked.

"He comes every day," she said dully. "I guess when he's hungry and needs something to snack on."

I tugged at the collar around my throat, then looked up at the crack of light up the stairs that led out of this place. "Someone will come looking for us," I told her, forcing bravery into my voice. "We can't just go missing."

Except my dad wouldn't know where I was. Ryder, either. Bath and Sara would just assume I was avoiding their calls, since I'd been fired from the agency. If Josh didn't come looking for me . . .

I stopped that line of thought. He *had* to come.

Had to.

I extended a hand in the darkness toward Lily. "We're going to get out of here."

She clasped her hand in mine, and I noticed how thin and fragile her hand was. "You don't have to try and cheer me up. I've been here for six months. I know what our odds of being rescued are."

A voice called my name, stirring me out of the darkness. "Marie," I heard. "Marie!"

Hope surged in my chest. Josh!

But Lily still slept undisturbed, huddled against me. Was . . . was it just a hallucination? I'd had several of them since being chained down here. I didn't know how many hours had passed. Endless, tense hours, waiting for Andre to return.

"Marie!" he bellowed.

I licked my dry lips. Maybe this was real. "I'm here," I called, my voice faint. I was thirsty and hungry, and weak from the loss of blood. When I tried to struggle to my feet, it was extremely difficult.

There were footsteps somewhere upstairs, then I heard a hand try the doorknob.

Lily woke up and gasped, scuttling into a shadowy corner of the room in terror.

A large body slammed against the door. Once, twice. Then it crashed open.

"Marie?" Josh asked, and I saw his glorious, wonderful silhouette, haloed by the lights.

"I'm here!" I said, still struggling to stand up. The chain at my neck felt as if it had weighed a hundred pounds. "Josh, I'm here!"

"Thank God." He fumbled for a light switch, then cursed and moved down into the darkness. His eyes gleamed like a cat's in the night, scanning the room. They lit on me, and I heard a feline growl start low in his throat. "Baby. What did he do to you?"

I was enveloped in warm, strong arms. I clung to him, burying my face in his chest as he kissed my hair, stroking it back from my face. I even cried. "You came after me!"

"Of course I did. Are you crazy? I've been worried sick about you." His hand went to the collar at my throat, and the low, ominous growl started in his throat again. "What the fuck is this?"

I couldn't seem to stop shivering, even with his warm arms enveloping me. I was so tired and cold and weak. "He's keeping us down here. Like snacks."

He lifted his nose and scented the air. "I thought I smelled someone else. Who's here?"

"Another human girl," I told him.

In the darkness, I heard Lily whimper. I didn't know if it was a whimper of fear or a whimper of acknowledgment.

"I'm getting you both out of here," Josh said roughly. He pressed a quick kiss to my forehead, then grasped the chain again, eyes gleaming in the darkness. "Where's this linked to?"

"The wall," I told him as he began to follow it.

He grasped the chain where it was attached to the wall. I knew Josh was strong, but was he *that* strong? His muscles bulged and I heard him groan . . . and then I heard the brick crack. A second later, the hook in the wall ripped free and the chain fell limp to the floor.

"That was amazing," I breathed. "Josh, you're wonderful!"

He cast a flashing glance back at me. "If that was all it took to get you to finally acknowledge my awesomeness, I'd have done feats of strength for you long ago, baby."

I gathered my chain, rushing forward. "Now get Lily's. Hurry!"

As he tugged at it, I moved down the length of chain to the deepest shadows of the room. I held my hand out to Lily and was relieved when she took it, her own trembling.

"He . . . he's not human—" she said quietly to me, clearly afraid.

"No, but he won't hurt you. You're going to be safe and free."

She clung to my hand as her chain ripped free from the wall.

"Let's go," Josh said, extending his hand.

I walked toward him, my steps weak and slow. Lily clung to my side, shaking with terror. I wanted to tell her to buck up and be brave, but she'd been held captive and feasted on by a vampire for the last six months. I was guessing that trust didn't come easy to her.

"Are you okay?" Josh asked, coming to my side. His glowing eyes flicked over me, studying me in the almost darkness. "Do you want me to carry you out—"

The floor creaked upstairs.

We froze. Lily sucked in a breath.

The growl started low in Josh's throat.

Terror flashed through me. "Josh," I whispered.

"I'm going to change, baby," he said softly. "Don't be frightened, okay? I'm going to change and take care of him, and then we're going to get out of here."

I nodded, tugging Lily tighter to me. This was going to be difficult for her to see and hear.

Josh dropped to all fours, and I heard the sudden, violent crack of bones as Josh's growl continued. Alarmed, Lily slid behind me. I had to pretend everything was okay, even as I strained to see Josh. How long would it take?

I heard a rustle of movement. Something wet and raspy licked my hand, and then I watched the big cat step into the light flooding down the stairway.

"Be careful," I whispered. "Please be careful."

He climbed the stairs and into the light.

Almost immediately, we heard the sound of snarls. Something heavy slammed up against the door, banging it shut, and Lily and I jumped with alarm.

Josh was strong. He was a bodyguard. He knew a lot about vampires. He'd be just fine.

I repeated this mantra as the sounds of fighting continued upstairs. Lily's fingers dug into my arm, and I forced myself to disentangle from her death grip. "I need to see what's going on."

"No," she begged me. "Stay with me. I'm scared."

I shook my head. "He might need my help."

He probably needed my help like he needed a hole in the head, but I wanted to be ready if he did.

I climbed the stairs slowly, my long, dragging chain in one hand, the banister clutched in the other. Just climbing the stairs was killing me; it was alarming how weak I was.

To my surprise, Lily was at my side, helping me push to the door. I turned the doorknob, then eased it open a crack.

The room was in shambles. A white couch was tipped over in the center of the room, the wooden tables overturned. Broken vases littered the floor. A picture was askew on the far wall, and a rug was rumpled up against the fireplace. An enormous tan mountain lion streaked past, its claws digging into the hardwood floor. It pounced, knocking something—or someone—out of the way.

Then a man's shadow approached from the hall, and I realized that Andre wasn't alone. A bodyguard? Maybe they'd know Josh!

The mountain lion growled, and Andre bit out a curse.

"Get off of him," a voice called from the hall. An enormous man came into sight; his skin was pale, like a vampire's. Oh, no—this was bad. Josh wouldn't stand a chance against both Andre and that vampire behemoth.

I glanced back at Lily and raised a finger to my lips, indicating silence.

She nodded.

I eased the door open, clutching my chain against my chest so it wouldn't clink and give me away. I tiptoed out just in time to hear Josh's yowl as the second vampire landed on top of him.

"Snap his neck," I heard Andre shout, "Kill him!"

Fuck *that*!

Josh gave a snarl of pain and I heard something crack hard, spurring me forward.

"Get off of him," the vampire bodyguard growled again.

I had to do *something*. I stared at the chain in my hand, then moved closer until I was in striking distance. No one had noticed me yet.

The bodyguard was still yelling at Josh. "Get off of him!"

The cougar gave a low, muffled growl, his teeth sunk into Andre's throat, making him writhe on the floor.

The bodyguard raised his nightstick to strike Josh again, and I lashed out with my doubled-over chain, snapping it against the back of his head.

It cracked loudly; the vampire groaned and fell to the floor, unconscious.

I slid weakly to the ground, unable to remain standing anymore.

Distracted, Josh turned his attention to me, and Andre heaved his body, bucking off the cougar in a last burst of strength. The cougar dug for traction and flung himself back at Andre, but the vampire blocked him, sending him into a nearby table, where his head hit the corner.

He went limp.

"Josh!" I screamed, crawling forward.

Andre brushed at his bleeding lip, panting hard. As I stared, he drew out a gun.

No! I tried to move forward, but my movements were sluggish and slow. I had to do something, though; Josh needed me!

A small, dirty figure flew forward, something raised in her hand. Lily held it high and then stabbed downward, straight through Andre's heart.

He gasped, clutching his chest, and toppled.

I stared. A thick pencil jutted out of his back. No—three pencils, rubber-banded together to make a thick makeshift stake. They must have been sharpened to a deadly point.

Andre didn't move.

Lily dusted off her hands, then leaned over the vampire to examine him. When she was satisfied he was dead, she spat on his fallen body. "I've been holding on to those pencils for months in the hopes that they'd work. They went through his skin like butter."

"Thank you," I said weakly, and collapsed to the floor.

"Are you okay?" she asked, rushing to my side.

"Josh," I said, all my concern for him. He was so still. Fear clenched my body. "Is he . . . ?"

She crouched next to him, pressing her fingers under his nose. "He's breathing. I think he conked his head pretty hard." Her fingers hesitated, and she touched his fur. "He's a . . . cat?"

"Shapeshifter," I said tiredly. "I'll explain later." At her frightened, uncertain look, I decided I needed to explain a little more right now. "There are a lot of creatures that hide their true nature. Josh is one of the good ones. We're safe with him."

She nodded uncertainly, glancing down at his still body. "So . . . what do we do with him?"

I didn't know.

I stared at his unconscious form. At the body-guard who was equally unconscious. At the dead vampire with the pencil sticking out of his back. We needed help.

I thought about calling Ryder, but she was at work. If I called her to help me dispose of a vampire body, she'd get fired for sure. And this was my problem.

I needed someone I could trust, who wouldn't ask too many questions. Who would help without blaming.

I spotted a table nearby and a phone atop it, and I moved toward it slowly. "I know someone who can help."

Lily nodded, biting her lip anxiously.

"Go find some rope and tie up the guard," I told her. "We don't want him attacking us when he wakes up."

She nodded and raced off, her chain dragging on the floor. I finished dialing and waited for the phone to ring.

Five rings, and then a sleepy voice picked up on the other end. "Hello?"

"Daddy?" My voice cracked a little.

Chapter Fifteen

*M*y dad arrived less than a half hour later. In that time, we'd tied up the guard and dragged him into a nearby room, then pushed a dresser in front of the door to put a little space between us and him. We were exhausted and it was slow going, but fear pushed us onward. Lily had to do most of the work, since I was too weak to do much more than feebly shove.

Andre remained dead. Really dead. And Josh was still out, which worried me.

My father, bless his heart, showed up without Posey. He asked no questions, just moved to my side and hugged me. I melted into his warm, strong hug, fighting my weepiness. I needed to be strong right now.

He stared at the dead vampire for a long moment, then looked at me again. His gaze went to the collar around my neck, and the chain.

"Marie-Pierre . . . ?"

"It's a long story, Dad," I told him. "For now, we need to get Josh out of here."

"And Josh is the . . . cat?"

I nodded. "He'll change back later, if we can get him to wake up. Right now we've got to get him home and call the Alliance doctor."

I could have called the Russells, but I didn't trust them to not frighten the hell out of Lily. Plus, I didn't know what to do about the vampires—live or dead.

"Do we . . . need to dispose of the body?"

I stared at my dad in surprise. "You'd help me dispose of a body?"

He hugged me again and rubbed my shoulder. "I'm your father, honey. Of course I would."

Well, geez. I nodded, my throat tight, and gestured to Josh. "Just help me get him in your truck and to a doctor. We'll figure out the rest later."

But I didn't know where Josh lived. "His wallet. It's probably in his pants."

Lily and I both turned to look back at the wine cellar, and dread piled up in my stomach. I didn't want to go back there, and I guessed Lily felt the same.

I looked to my father. "It's in the cellar. I can't . . . I don't . . ." I gestured at the chain around my neck helplessly. "Can you . . ."

My dad patted my shoulder. "I'll go get it. You girls wait here."

I moved back to Josh's side, stroking his face and fur as we waited. Dad came back a couple of minutes later with car keys, a wallet, and Josh's clothes piled on his arm. "His car must be out front. One of you should probably drive it wherever we're going."

"I'll do it," I told him, staring down at Josh. He was so quiet and still. "Let's just hurry."

We pulled up to an enormous house out in the country about an hour later. The big, looming two-story house had several lights on, and by the time we made it down the gravel driveway, me in Josh's sedan and Lily and Dad in the truck with Josh, a few men had stepped out onto the porch.

I recognized Everett, Ellis, and Austin. This wouldn't go over well. Not only did I have their unconscious brother with me but I also had two humans who now knew about the Paranormal Alliance.

I put Josh's car in park and hauled myself out of the driver's side. I immediately staggered, feeling that awful lethargy coming over me again.

"Marie?" Austin moved to my side, propping up my elbow. "What are you doing here? Something wrong at the agency?"

"Josh is in the truck," I told him. "We have to get a doctor. He's unconscious."

The Alliance doctor was there in a matter of minutes, with Beau not far behind him. Both looked grim as they entered Josh's room, where the cougar was stretched out on the bed. The other Russells paced nearby, watching us.

I wanted to be in there, but Austin was hovering outside the door protectively, and I was willing to bet that he had instructions to let no one pass—including me. I was okay with that, as long as they made Josh all better. I clasped my hands against my chest to keep them from trembling. He'd been so still and quiet when they'd hauled his limp body out of the truck.

If he died . . . I felt a sick lurch. I thought of Josh's cocky smile, his eyes shining with merriment as he teased me. His long lashes. His big shoulders. His big arms holding me tight. The kind way he always gave Carol a ride home at night. Tears pricked my eyes. Why had it taken me so long to realize what a great guy he was?

I should have trusted him.

If I had to die, I could accept that. But Josh? Vibrant, sexy, gorgeous, funny Josh? He needed to live, and I clenched every muscle in my body, as if thinking it hard enough could will it into being.

Everett and Ellis hovered over Lily and my father and me. It made Lily terrified, and she huddled in a corner of the room, ignoring the offers of food and drink. She hugged her legs to herself, ignored everyone's attempts to calm her, and stared around her with wide eyes, trembling.

My father calmly sat at my side and rubbed my shoulder. And even though Everett and Ellis glared, I explained to my father why Josh was a cougar, and who the dead man was.

The harder part was telling him why I'd been seeing a vampire in the first place. I couldn't bring myself to explain that I was dying. There'd be time enough for that later.

To my relief, my father didn't ask questions. He only nodded thoughtfully. "And this is secret? All this?"

I nodded. "No one's supposed to know. At all. It endangers everyone."

"But everyone at your job knows?"

I winced. I'd tell him some other time that I was fired. "They do. Everyone at the agency had to sign a hush order before we could get accepted into the Alliance as auxiliary members."

He nodded, then looked at Ellis and Everett, who were still frowning at us. "You got one of those hush orders for me?"

Everett and Ellis exchanged a glance. "I'll get Beau," Ellis said, disappearing into Josh's room.

"Dad," I began.

He patted my hand. "Now listen, Marie. You're tired. We're all tired. There's a lot going on right now. Posey's expecting me home, and I don't want to worry her. So let me sign one of those hush orders and then we can all get some sleep."

"You don't have more questions?"

He chuckled and tousled my hair, just like I was a child. "I have a lot of them. But I'm guessing that the less I know, the better."

I nodded, blinking hard. "That's probably best."

Dad smiled at me. "I like Josh. And you trust him. I know you don't trust easily, so when you do, I trust your judgment."

"I love him," I said softly, burrowing into his arms for a hug.

"I know you do, Marie," he said softly. "But

there's nothing you can do for him right now. Let's go home and we'll come back tomorrow."

I shook my head, pulling out of his arms. "I want to stay. I want to see Josh when he wakes up."

He nodded. "If you want. Your little friend can come home with me, though—"

"She stays," Everett said in a flat voice. "Everyone stays until Beau says so."

Beau emerged a short time later and had a private discussion with my father. I sat on the floor next to Lily, feeling the need to comfort her with my presence even if she didn't want me there. Nondisclosure contracts were produced, and my dad signed one willingly. Even if Posey asked, he'd never say a thing.

And suddenly, I realized . . . it was all right to tell him. I was dying, and that was okay. My dad would be terribly sad, but he would be by my side until the bitter end. Just like he had with my mother. Tears brimmed in my eyes.

Life wasn't about being alone so that no one would get hurt.

It was about loving the ones you had, while you had them. My dad loved me. I loved him, too. It would devastate him when I died, but more so if I hid it from him until the bitter end.

Once the papers were signed, my father gave me another fierce, warm hug. I declined his offer of going home again, determined to see Josh as soon as they'd let me. When I was out, I'd call him, I promised.

We'd go to breakfast and then I'd let him know everything. A strange feeling of relief swept through me. I didn't have to go through this alone, after all. I gave him a hug and he left.

To my surprise, Beau didn't like the idea of Lily leaving. "She stays until we figure out what to do with her. In the meantime, you and you," he said, pointing at the twins, "need to go to that address and clean things up. Austin's going to contact the vampire liaison and let them know what happened. She'll meet you there. I suspect there's going to be a lot of explaining over the next few days, and we need to make sure everything is in order."

I struggled to my feet. "Can I see him?"

"You," Beau said firmly, "need to rest. You're so tired you can't even stand up straight. We'll talk in the morning."

I lay in bed, staring at the ceiling, thinking of Lily and Josh. She'd been terrified at the thought of being dragged into a strange room and had fought Beau, kicking and screaming. They'd had to call in the doctor to sedate her.

I didn't know what was going to happen with her. She was pretty messed up. What did you do with a human girl as damaged as that? They couldn't turn her loose, like they had my father.

Even though my father had signed the nondis closure, I knew they'd be watching him carefully for the next while, just in case.

I drifted in and out of a light doze, my body so exhausted that the room was hazy. Hallucinations flashed back and forth, as they always did when I was exhausted. The walls wavered, then shifted to my own room. Then they changed to blood. Then spiders. Then back to blood, the plain white walls streaming crimson as I stared at them.

My mother had been institutionalized a few months before the end, and I was heading toward that.

I hoped I had enough time to tell Josh that I was sorry and that I loved him.

My hallucinations turned again, and I whimpered when the walls of the guest room changed to Andre's cellar. In the dark, it was suffocatingly real. I still had the collar around my neck, too, since we'd had to put off going to a locksmith until the morning. It wasn't a good feeling, and it was clearly feeding my dreams.

"Marie!" Josh called.

I squeezed my eyes shut, my mind clearly replaying my rescue from the cellar.

"Marie! Where is she, damn it?"

I heard an unfamiliar feline snarl, then footsteps pounding through the hallway.

"Now, Josh—" began a calm male voice, only to be cut off by another angry snarl.

I sat up, rubbing my eyes, trying desperately to piece my confused mind back together. Was this a hallucination? Or was that really Josh? Desperate with hope, I started to get up to see for myself.

Then the door was flung open, and a tall, broad silhouette stood in the light.

And oh, God, he looked so good that I didn't trust my eyes. I rubbed them again. "Josh?"

"Marie," he growled, the sound fiercely possessive. He stalked into the room and moved to the bed.

Relief hit me so hard that I began to tremble, tears spilling from my eyes. "Oh, Josh—"

He tangled his hand in my hair, tugging me forward and pulling me against him. My arms went around him as he sat on the edge of the bed.

"Marie," he half-growled, half-whispered. "Baby. You okay?"

I nodded jerkily, unable to stop running my hands over his body, reassuring myself that he was okay. My Josh. I'd nearly lost him. The tears kept spilling forth and I couldn't seem to stop them. A muffled, choked gasp escaped my throat. "I thought . . . I thought you . . ."

"I'm here, baby," he said, pressing a kiss to my temple. "I wouldn't leave you."

I clung to him, needing to hear him right now. To touch him. "I love you," I whispered.

A figure loomed in the doorway, blotting out the light again. "Josh, we need to talk," Beau began. "This situation—"

"Leave us!" Josh said, leaping from the bed and snarling protectively, standing over me.

I flinched backward, staring at him in surprise.

That fierce, furious response was so unlike him.

Beau raised his hands in a peacemaking gesture. "Before you do anything crazy—"

"I said leave us," Josh said in a dangerous voice. "Now." He took a menacing step toward the door.

Bewildered, I stared at them. What was going on? Josh was acting like Beau had trespassed or something. As I sat frozen in the bed, Beau nodded and walked away. He called something too low for me to hear, and then it was lost as Josh slammed the door shut.

He turned back to me, his eyes gleaming green with his cat.

"Are you okay?" I whispered, wiping at my cheeks.

He moved back to me in the bed, his gaze possessive as he looked over me. "Did he hurt you? Tell me."

I shook my head slowly.

Josh exhaled sharply, and his big shoulders sagged with relief. He tugged me close, and I went gladly into his arms again.

"I'm sorry," I said, unable to keep from crying. "I should have listened to you. I should have waited. I just—"

"It's okay, baby. You're just scared." He stroked my hair, holding me.

Scared? I was terrified of dying. But now there was something that frightened me even more—the thought of losing Josh. "I shouldn't have gone."

"No, you shouldn't have. But I understand it."

Fresh tears brimmed. Of course he did. He'd been with me, every step of the way.

"I was just so close," I said softly. "I . . . was afraid to wait. The hallucinations are getting worse. It's like right before my mother had to go into the hospital—"

He pressed a kiss to my forehead, his fingers wiping away my tears. "You should have told me."

"I didn't want to acknowledge it," I confessed. "Because if I do, that means I accept that the end is inevitable. But . . ." My breath shuddered. "I need to face it. I'm going to die."

There. I'd said it.

"No," he growled low in his throat. "You're not."

I shook my head. "It's too late, Josh. And it wasn't even a good idea. I don't want to be with any vampire." I laid my cheek against his shoulder, feeling exhausted with the weight of it all. "I just want you."

"You're not going to die," he stated, his voice rough with emotion. He tilted my chin back and stared into my eyes, his green-glinting ones inhuman in the moonlight. "Do you trust me?"

There was a feral growl in his voice.

Goose bumps raised on my skin. "Josh, what do you—"

"Do you trust me?" The question was harder, flatter.

And I realized what he was asking.

I thought of the tiger girl. I thought of Greenland. I thought of Josh and his big family, and the way he laughed and joked with his brothers. He would lose all of that if he went into exile with me.

"I can't ask that of you," I whispered. "Josh, I can't ask you to give up your life—"

His fingers went under my chin, held my gaze to his. "The first thing any relationship needs is trust."

If I said yes, there would be no turning back. I ran a hand down his arm, caressing his skin. "Just promise me that you won't regret this a few weeks from now, when we're exiled."

He growled low in his throat. "Marie—"

"I trust you," I said softly.

"Good," he replied, just as softly. Josh leaned in and kissed the tip of my nose, oh so gently. "I love you."

I smiled, closing my eyes at his tender touch.

So I missed it when he grew fangs and sank them into my neck.

I gasped, jerking in surprise at the bolt of pain.

He held me close as his teeth pulled out of my skin, then he began to lick slowly, sensually. "I'm sorry. I can't turn you without it hurting a little." He tugged at the collar of the pajama top I was wearing, exposing the shoulder closest to him for his attention. "The first bite usually doesn't take."

A little twinge of anxiety flared through me. "Oh . . . ?"

He continued to lap at my neck, and his tongue felt oddly . . . rough? That was a little strange. Not in a bad way, just strange. He continued to stroke my skin with his tongue, and in between lapping, delicious swipes of his tongue, he commented, "Sometimes it takes a lot of bites. Sometimes it doesn't take at all."

"Oh," I said, feeling a weird mixture of disappointment and anxiety. "So I guess . . . you'll have to keep biting me?"

In response, his teeth sank into my skin again, this time just above the collarbone. I jerked in response, pushing at his shoulders. It hurt, even though he shortened the bite and began the soothing licking a lot faster. "I have to do this, Marie," he said softly. "I don't want to hurt you, but it can't be helped."

I nodded shakily, my skin hot and uncomfortable where he'd bitten me. He carefully licked each wound, taking great attention with it.

I was glad it was dark, since I didn't want to watch. I shrugged my pajama top a little lower, letting it hang at my elbows and revealing a large quantity of bare skin to my lover. Then I tugged at the metal collar still around my throat. "I wish I could take this off. I keep thinking about what happened."

"Don't think about it, love," Josh said softly, kissing my shoulder. "I'm here with you now. I'm not going to let anything happen to you. Let me take care of things."

More than anything, I wanted him with me. Whatever happened, we were in this together.

I let my hands fall from the collar and relaxed, trusting him.

He continued to lap at my bare skin, and it soothed the pain. It also made my pulse start to pound, centered right between my legs. I blushed at the thought. Was I supposed to be turned on by him biting me? Probably not. I said nothing, determined to let him concentrate. "Is . . . is it your saliva? That does the turning?"

"It's a lot of things," he murmured, pressing a kiss on my bare shoulder. "But mostly the bite."

"H-how does that work?" I hated the wobble in my voice when he moved to a new, bare patch of skin and began to nuzzle at it. I felt dread at the thought of his bite, yet anticipation at the sensual licking afterward. "Is it like a venom of some kind, like a snake? Or—"

"Shhh," he told me, and kissed my shoulder. At my shiver of response, he sank his teeth into my skin.

I whimpered, resisting the urge to claw away. But then he was pulling his teeth free, and he began to lick the spot on my skin for long, long moments.

"Maybe it's something in the saliva that mixes with the blood," I said in a low, husky voice. Each swipe of his tongue was making my nipples get harder. I tried to distract him—and me. "And that's why you need to . . . lick me."

I was getting hot and bothered just at the thought of all that licking. The bite wasn't bothering me nearly as much now, especially since it came with all that decadent, sensual rasping of his tongue.

Josh leaned back into my neck and inhaled my

scent. He groaned low, then leaned in to lick and suck at my neck. "Ah, Marie, I can smell how turned on you are."

I froze as he nuzzled my neck, preparing the next spot. "Sorry," I whispered. "Just ignore me."

"Hell, no—it smells amazing. I want more of it." His hand slid to caress one of my thighs, stroking along the inside of it and sending my nerve endings flaring madly. "Let me touch you, baby."

I nodded, swallowing hard as his other hand skated down past my neck and over my shoulder, tugging down the wide vee of the borrowed nightshirt I wore. "Who gave you this?"

"I—I don't know. One of the twins?" I hadn't paid much attention to it. I'd been too distracted by the thought of Josh lying hurt, Josh possibly dying.

"Don't like it," he growled against my neck, and pressed a hot kiss there even as he ripped at the nightshirt. Buttons popped off, clinking as they smacked the wall and floor. The shirt parted, exposing my bare breasts to the low moonlight. He growled low against my throat and reached to cup one of my breasts, his big hand encircling it.

I gasped, shuddering against him. That felt so, so good. His thumb flicked over the peak and I whimpered. I almost didn't notice when he sank his teeth into the curve of my neck and quickly withdrew, lapping and sucking at the skin. His thumb continued to roll my nipple, teasing the stiff peak as his other hand slid up my thigh.

I moaned, tangling my hand in his hair.

He hissed when I touched his temple. "Watch the wound."

I jerked away. "Are you okay? I'm so sorry."

He just continued kissing me. His hand gently pinched the inside of my thigh, close to my sex. "Stay still." His voice was low, husky, and thick, as if he was struggling to keep control.

I moved my hand down to his thigh, digging my nails into his jeans when he pinched my nipple and sank his teeth into my neck again. It stung and burned, but between the licking and his teasing caresses, I was having a hard time caring about the bite.

The hand on my thigh slid farther up, and he cupped my sex. "I love how wet you get for me," he growled.

My hips pushed against his hand involuntarily.

He growled low again and sank his teeth into my collarbone once more as two fingers slid down to my clit and stroked. I jerked in his arms, whimpering again.

Josh withdrew again, lapping at the bite as his fingers stroked through my slick flesh. "Quit jumping."

"I can't," I panted, arching a little when he rolled my nipple against his thumb again. "Feels . . . too good."

He chuckled, giving my burning skin a long sweep with his tongue that made me moan again. "Flatterer."

"Stop . . . touching me . . . if you want me to

stop . . . jumping," I said breathlessly. His fingers stroked up to my clit and began to circle, and I spread my legs wider. "Oh, God, that feels . . ."

"Good?" he prompted between licks.

My fingers dug into his clothed thigh. "I want to touch you."

He pressed a kiss to my neck. Once, twice. "I can see that we have a small problem, then. Because I'm not going to stop touching you, and you're not going to stop twitching, are you?" His fingers stroked and circled at my clit, and I arched against him. "So what should we do about this . . . ?"

"Get naked," I breathed, writhing when his hand squeezed my breast. God, that felt incredible. "Get naked and have lots of sex. Bite later."

"How can I resist such a demanding woman?" he said, nipping at my shoulder again. He slid his hand away from my sex, making me whimper in protest. "Get on your knees."

A hot bolt of desire rushed through me at the command. I got on my hands and knees in the center of the bed, full of need and energy. My entire body throbbed with want, and I looked over at his silhouette in the darkness, trying to see him. I only heard the clink of his belt and the rustle of his jeans as they fell to the ground. Then the bed sagged and his warm hand skated over my back.

He lightly pressed a kiss to my buttock. "Lean forward, baby. I think I need to wear you out before I have my way with you."

"And how are you going to wear me out?" I asked

breathlessly, leaning forward until my cheek hit the mattress.

His fingers glided between my parted legs, stroking my slick flesh again. "Part your legs for me, Marie. I want your knees wide."

I did as he asked, spreading them wide on the bed. I felt his big hands on the backs of my thighs, then he tugged at my legs, dragging me down, confusing me . . .

Until I felt his hot, open mouth on my flesh. He'd slid under me, his head between my legs. Now I was pinned against his mouth, held down by his big hands.

I shrieked at the first delicious stroke of his tongue against my core.

"Shhhh," he said, nuzzling my flesh. "You've got to keep it down, baby. I don't want anyone coming in here to rescue you from me."

I didn't want that, either!

He licked my flesh again, making me squeak, then lifted his head. "Is this bothering you? Do you want me to stop?"

Oh, no. That was the last thing I wanted. I grabbed a pillow and stuffed it against my face. "Don't you dare stop, you *tête de cochon*."

"You say such sweet things, baby," he murmured in a husky voice, then his mouth dipped low again, his tongue stroking at my core.

I moaned into the pillow, my hips jerking in response. Oh, God. Oh, God. That felt so good. "*Ostie de tabarnak!*"

His tongue stroked there once more, then he shifted me forward and I felt his tongue rasp against my clit, sending a shock wave through my body. My toes curled in response and I bit down on the pillow, breathing hard. *Criss. Criss.* That felt so amazing. It sent jolts of pleasure coursing through my body, and each one built on the last as he continued to lick the slick little bud slowly and thoroughly, leaving me panting and biting the pillow. On his next lick, I shuddered and groaned into the pillow. "*Voyons,* Josh. Faster. Please!"

He ignored me, continuing long, slow, dragging licks that made every nerve ending in my body light up. I needed him to work my clit with fast, strong strokes to pitch me over the edge I was spiraling closer to, but he was determined to torture me, his tongue moving in new, exquisite ways. I flexed against his face, moaning hard. "*Please,* Josh, please! Harder, you *batarde!*"

But he only chuckled and continued. I was writhing against his face now, my hips jerking with every stroke of his tongue, my teeth clenched on the corner of the pillow, whimpers escaping me with every stroke, lost in a daze of pleasure.

Then his finger grazed against my core as he licked at me, and I gasped. When his finger stroked into my core, I arched. "*Criss!*" He stroked deep again with his fingers, and again, and sucked at my clit.

And I came.

My entire body clenched, my toes curled with

pleasure, my body shuddering from the intensity as he continued to stroke my clit with his tongue as his finger stroked deep inside of me. The waves of pleasure went on and on, until I was keening into the pillow.

He kissed the inside of my thigh. "You say the sweetest things when you're lost."

I was boneless with pleasure, unable to do more than clutch at the pillow as he grasped my hips again. The pleasurable aftermath of the orgasm was still racing through me when I felt his cock nudge against my core and then he sank deep, seating himself in my body.

I moaned anew. He was so big that he filled me up, making me feel impaled on his length. I loved the feeling. I loved him. And I wanted to tell him. "I love you, Josh," I moaned as he stroked into my body again.

"I know, baby," he said, his voice rough and low. "Keep it down. The others have really good hearing, and we can't let them know what we're doing."

He thrust hard, jarring me forward, rocking me toward another orgasm. The delicious tension began to rebuild with every stroke into my body. As with his tongue, he took his sweet time. And that slow, measured rhythm drove me utterly wild. I was writhing underneath him again, moaning his name, desperate for the new orgasm.

I clenched around him and he hissed a curse; his movements became rougher, stronger. I reveled in it, loving that he was spiraling quickly out of control. My hips rose to meet his, and then I shattered as another orgasm blasted through me. Shuddering ripples of pleasure rocked through me, and he shouted my name as he began to come, his strokes rough and wild as he went over the edge.

After, he collapsed on the bed, panting hard. I was still boneless, clutching the pillow, an entire corner wet from where I'd bitten down so much. My eyes closed, I existed in a sleepy, exhausted, delicious state.

I barely noticed when he got up from the bed. He pressed a kiss to my belly. "Be right back."

"Mmm, okay."

I heard him return a minute or two later; then I felt him grab my hands and pull them over my head.

My eyes flew open. As I stared, he wrapped a long silk scarf around my wrists and then began to tie them to the wrought-iron headboard.

"Josh? What are you doing?"

He kissed my lips lightly. "We have a long night ahead of us, baby, and it'll be best if you don't fight me."

"But . . . this?" I tugged at my wrists.

"Better safe than sorry." His hand went to one ankle, and I felt another scarf go around it. "Do you still trust me?"

I nodded, feeling a bit of alarm mixed with my languid daze. "I do."

"Good. Just remember that I love you."

"I will," I told him as he finished tying down my other leg. "I love you, too."

His eyes gleamed bright again in the darkness before he bent low.

And then the real biting began. The ones before had been love nips. These were raw and painful, and I yelped as he sank his teeth in.

"I'm sorry," he told me. "It has to be done."

Chapter Sixteen

*E*verything in my body ached. Everywhere.

Daylight streamed through the blinds, and I turned my head away. Josh slept against my side, one arm thrown possessively over my waist, one leg over mine, his body half-covering my own. A low purr rumbled in his chest.

He looked exhausted, I noted tenderly. He'd worked on my body for hours, licking and biting my skin over and over again, to the point that I felt raw all over. Some people took on only one bite, he'd explained, but he'd wanted to be sure that mine took. I didn't have time to waste, after all, and he wanted me safe. So he'd meticulously bitten and licked and bitten and licked every inch of my skin.

When the afterglow of endorphins had worn off and his bites had made me whimper in a bad way, he'd made love to me again, teasing me past the brink of madness and back into that dreamy, blissed-out zone where his bites had barely hurt and every lick had been an affirmation of how much he loved me.

Sometime before dawn we'd both collapsed, exhausted. I must have been extra tired, because for once I'd been able to sleep for a while.

I shifted underneath him, wincing at the pain that rushed through my body from my sore, stiff muscles. Another shiver ripped through me, and I winced. That one had felt harder than the last. Why was my body cramping like this? I winced and tried to stretch.

The skin on my arm suddenly burned hot, like someone had laid a curling iron against it. I gasped, twisting to see what was causing it. To my surprise, dun hair was pricking through my skin. I stared, and another shudder ripped through my body, this one harder. Bones cracked.

I began to panic.

"Josh," I yelped, wriggling under him. As I jerked at one foot, I noticed my toenails elongating into claws. I was turning! It worked!

Then a flash of mind-numbing pain ripped through me, and I screamed as my bones and muscles gave a horrific twist. It shouldn't have felt like that, should it?

Josh jerked up and looked at me with bleary eyes. As he saw my arm bristling with fur and my fingers curving with claws, delight filled his face. "We did it, baby!"

Another ripple tore through me, this one even more intense than the last. My body locked, and I heard bones snap and creak. "Help me!" I cried.

"It's okay," he said, stroking a hand down my

arm to soothe me. "I'm here with you. Everything will be all right."

I curled into a ball on the center of the bed. It smelled of my blood and sex and sweat, and when Josh leaned over to kiss me, I smelled his skin, wonderful and earthy and magnified a dozen times.

The barrage of scents made my stomach churn.

I hugged my knees close, waiting for the next intense round of pain, staring at my half-animal arm and trying not to freak out. "Does it always hurt like this?"

"Every change hurts, I'm afraid."

I nodded, biting my lip. "How . . . how long will it take for me to shift?"

He gave me a helpless look. "I'm sorry; I don't know. I've been able to change ever since I was born, so I don't think about it." Josh continued to stroke me, soothing me with soft touches. "I imagine the first time will be the hardest, but after that you'll get used to it."

That didn't sound too bad. But . . . my body wasn't changing anymore. I stared at my arm and my half-formed feet, and shuddered. No more ripples through me. Just the scents of the bed, and the room, and Josh nearby, watching me with concerned eyes.

The scents were too strong, too much. "I . . . I think I need to shower."

He helped me get up, my body feeling weak and fragile. This was supposed to help, but if anything, I felt worse. I had a brief, horrible thought: what if this didn't fix it? What if Josh had ruined his life for nothing?

I barely made it to the bathroom before vomiting.

Josh stroked my hair back from my face as I was sick. "What can I do to help?"

"Just help me shower," I told him, leaning heavily on him. "I'll feel better after I shower."

Except I didn't.

If anything, I felt worse. The strange tremors continued through my body over and over again, locking me with pain. Each time, I braced myself against the pain, to hold steady until it passed. And each time, it seemed to hurt more. My claws elongated, my feet and hands warping until they were half-paws, my lower arms and legs coated with a soft layer of fur.

And then, nothing. Nothing for long, awful hours.

When night came and I was no closer to changing fully, Josh tugged the sheets over my sweating, sick body and stroked my cheek. "I'm going to leave you for a few minutes, but I'll be right back."

"Promise?" I wanted to cling to his hand, but I knew that was silly.

He nodded, then kissed my sweaty forehead. "I love you. Everything is going to be fine. Trust me."

I did. I'd trusted him this far. He'd see me through this. I closed my eyes and bit down on my lip as another ripple of pain jolted through me, centered in my hands and feet, and I felt the bones creak a little more, give a little more. They were like white-hot balls of agony at the end of each limb.

I hoped it wouldn't be like this every time I changed. I didn't think I could take much more.

I heard Josh pad down the stairs, the wood creaking with every step. Heard a muffled conversation, and then a beep that sounded like a phone hanging up. The creak of the stairs as he returned, and then the delicious scent of Josh that told me he was back moments before he walked through the door.

He held my ugly, misshapen hand as I panted through another ripple of shifting. My body felt so weak that I was starting to think this was the end. Maybe I was too weak to change fully. Maybe my overtaxed body couldn't handle it. Josh was worried, too. His handsome face had deep lines around his mouth and eyes, even though he kept a cheerful expression for my sake. He told me a story of him and Beau as kids, and the biggest catfish they'd ever caught. He told me about the first girl he'd ever kissed, when he was seven, and being decked by another were-cougar for doing it. He told me all kinds of funny stories while his hands stroked my aching, rippling flesh, not showing the worry he had to be feeling.

After another round of pain stabbed through me, I heard the door slam below. Josh's senses immediately went on alert, and he covered me with the sheet, tucking it close around me. I heard the low murmur of a woman's voice, and then two sets of feet coming up the stairs, one much heavier than the other.

I marveled at my newly sharp hearing; shifters could hear everything around them.

There was a quick knock at the bedroom door, and I gave Josh a horrified look. Here I was in bed, naked, with mutant, misshapen hands and feet. "Send them away. Please."

He shook his head and gave me a kiss on the forehead. "This is the cavalry, baby."

Josh opened the door, and I saw Sara, dwarfed by the enormous Ramsey.

Sara's gaze rested on me, and her eyes flashed with anger as she looked back to Josh. "What did you do? Did you collar her?"

"No!" we both said in unison. I was appalled at the thought.

"Of course not," Josh added, scowling at them.

Sara stepped forward, stared at my twisted hands, then looked at Josh again. "What did you *do?*" she demanded.

"What had to be done," Josh said, his big shoulders tensing.

A low, rumbling growl emanated from Ramsey, then the big blond man charged across the room and grabbed Josh by his collar, hauling him bodily up against the wall. Josh was tall and muscular, but Ramsey was a brick house.

Josh bared his teeth, glaring at Ramsey. "Let go of me."

"You turned her?" Ramsey snarled. "Fucking idiot." He slammed a fist into Josh's jaw.

I screamed, but for some reason, Josh wasn't

fighting back. He simply glared at Ramsey, even as the other man shoved him against the wall again and shook him so hard that the pictures clattered to the floor.

"That's not going to solve anything, Huggy Bear," Sara said in a tired voice, and she moved to the side of my bed, crouching low. "You can knock his teeth out later. Are you okay, Marie?"

I gave her a wan smile. "I'd give you a thumbs-up, except I don't think I have a thumb anymore."

She took my hand-paw in hers as the two men continued to snarl at each other.

"You had no right to turn her," Ramsey growled.

Josh ignored him, his gaze on Sara. "Is she going to be okay?"

Sara's gaze moved over me, her eyes lingering on the collar at my throat for a long moment. Then she nodded firmly. "I've had worse. It just takes soothing the nerves and letting things happen naturally. She needs to relax." She put her hands on her hips and glared at the two men. "Which is not going to happen if you two continue to growl and beat each other up."

The big bear shifter let go of Josh, and he dropped to the floor, landing easily. He rubbed his neck, scowled at Ramsey, and moved back toward me again.

The bear shifter grabbed him by the back of his collar once more. "We're going to go talk. Outside."

"Thanks, Huggy Bear. Love you." Sara blew him a kiss with a smile and turned back to me.

Josh wrestled away from the bigger man's grasp. "I want to stay by her side. She's my mate."

Sara's voice was cold as she told him, "You're the problem right now, Josh. You need to leave so I can help her. Or do you want her to die?"

He flinched, his gaze returning to me, panting in the bed.

"I'm okay," I told him softly. "Go with Ramsey."

He gave a short, jerky nod and turned to go out the door. He and Ramsey had a shoving match on the way out, and I suspected it'd turn into a full-out brawl when they got outside.

Sara calmly shut the door behind them and turned back to me. I noticed her smell, light and sweet, with a hint of some kind of animal that I didn't recognize.

"Now," she said firmly as she sat on the bed next to me. "I want you to tell me if you're really okay. Did he hurt you?"

I stared at her, wide-eyed. "Hurt me?"

"I've never thought Josh would be the kind to turn a girl against her will, but you never know. What happened?" Sara's mouth thinned with displeasure.

I shook my head. "You're misunderstanding. I asked him to turn me, Sara. I . . . I have a disease. It's killing me."

Her face softened with understanding—and chagrin. "Oh, Marie. I'm sorry. I just . . ." She looked a bit embarrassed. "I guess I jump to conclusions when I see a girl in a bad situation. My hackles get raised and I get defensive. I'm sorry to accuse Josh."

"It's okay. He's been great through this. Really."

Sara snapped her fingers, eyes lighting up as something occurred to her. "Wait. Is this why you were looking for a vampire?"

I gave her a bitter smile. "Ironic, huh?" I told her about Andre and about Lily, who was still sequestered here. "At first I wouldn't let Josh turn me. Not after what happened with the tiger clan and the girl. I couldn't do that to him. I love him." My voice cracked on the confession. "But when we realized the vampire wasn't going to turn me . . ."

"He stepped in because he's got a massive case of white knight syndrome." Sara patted my shoulder. "It's okay, Marie. Just relax. Now listen: when I was turned, I didn't have anyone to teach me, either. These born shifters aren't the greatest teachers, because they're so used to it. Well, except Ramsey. He's good at that, but he's good at everything that requires patience and skill." As I watched her, a blush colored her cheeks. "Anyhow. I'm going to be here with you, and I'm going to walk you through it, okay? Just don't fight the change. Fighting it is the worst thing you can do."

"Don't fight it. Got it," I said, just as another set of jaw-cracking muscle spasms ripped through me again.

Sara waited until those were done, and when I was panting for breath once more, she leaned in and patted my shoulder. "So, let's talk about Kegels."

"Kegels?" I repeated, not sure I'd heard her correctly.

"Yup. I swear, they're useful."

A few hours later, I was a cougar. The change hadn't been swift, but Sara had gently talked and soothed me through the process, telling me all about her own trouble points with shifting, and how focusing my inner muscles would speed things along. Kegels, she'd said cheerfully, just like another wolf had told her.

So when my inner muscles had been all flexed and ready to go, I'd begun to sink into the next wave of muscle cramps, mentally encouraging and centralizing.

After that, it hadn't been nearly as bad. My body had sleeked into that of a dun-colored cat, with a small, rounded head and long tail. The hated metal collar had fallen off with my transformation, and I studied my paws and my tail with surprise. My senses were wildly different as a cat, too, the scents almost distracting in their strength. Sara's scent no longer smelled clean, either. It smelled like wolf. I hissed and was immediately embarrassed.

"There, there, kitty," she said with a grin. "You'll get used to the big bad wolf here eventually. We'll shift together for the next few weeks until you get the hang of it."

I paced around the bedroom, trying out walking on all fours. I'd expected my body to feel weirdly out of balance, but everything made sense, oddly enough. Even my tail seemed to have a life of its own, lashing and smacking the wall as I lowered my head and scented the floorboards. So many people's scents were here. Everything was just . . . overwhelming.

I thumped to the ground, suddenly exhausted.

"It's okay," Sara said, coming to my side. Her fingers moved along my head, and she scratched behind my cat ear. To my surprise, the sensation was wonderful—I hadn't realized how itchy it had been until then, and I leaned into her fingers. "After you've had a little time to get adjusted, we'll go outside and you can run for a bit."

I tried to reply, but it came out as a weird coughing noise.

She grinned. "Just nudge me with your nose if you understand."

I did.

Sara gave me one more pat, then got to her feet, stretching. "I'm going to run down and get a drink of water. You stay here and relax for a few, and when I come back, we'll take a walk around the house."

We did a walk around the house, and up and down the stairs. I caught all the different scents as we walked, Sara chatting up a storm next to me. The older scents of Everett, Ellis, and Austin. Lily's unwashed scent from her room.

But Josh was nowhere to be found, and neither was Ramsey.

I wanted to ask where they were, but I couldn't.

My cat form was many things, but it wasn't vocal.

When we'd finished pacing the house, I allowed Sara to lead me upstairs. "You're probably getting tired," she told me. "It's been a long day. Lie down and take a nap; being a shifter can take a lot out of you."

I couldn't say that I wasn't able to nap, so I figured I'd just lie down for a bit and rest.

But when I laid my head down, I immediately fell asleep.

I woke up, startled to find that it was dark outside. I sat upright, fumbling over my paws and ungainly body. Still a cougar, then. I was alone in the room, Sara's scent now fainter. Had I been asleep for long? I rose and stretched.

The next moment, my body shivered and my muscles revolted, shuddering hard. I braced myself for the change back to human—and then stopped. Bracing myself was what had caused the problems before. Instead, I thought of Sara's calm, easy words and let the changes ripple back over me.

The change back to human didn't take very long at all. It was painful and messy, but it only took a matter of minutes before I was collapsed on the wood floor, gasping, in my own body again. I touched my skin, marveling to see that no trace of cougar fur or claw remained.

How marvelous.

There came a soft knock at the door, and I caught

Sara's scent a moment before she spoke. "It's me. Can I come in?"

I moved to the bed to grab the sheet to cover me. For some reason . . . the bed was made. When had that happened? I pulled the sheet off and wrapped it around my body. "Come in."

Sara poked her head in and beamed at me. The scent of wolf filled my nostrils. "Oh, good, you're awake. And back to normal, I see."

I rubbed my bleary eyes, then wondered how well I would see with my new eyesight. I squinted at Sara's face, then sighed and reached for my glasses. Nearsighted as a human, perfect vision as a were-cougar. Guess you couldn't have everything. "It's all me again, yeah. Thanks for talking me through it."

She grinned, sauntering in. "Yeah, men see a woman in pain and they flip out. Sometimes you need another calm presence nearby. I'm just glad I could help."

Speaking of . . . "Where's Josh?"

Her smile was a little too bright to be natural. "He'll be along shortly."

I nodded, then glanced at the room. "Um, have you seen my clothes?"

She snapped her fingers. "Oh. I had them laundered for you yesterday. Just a sec."

Yesterday?

She left before I could ask her.

I glanced at the window, but it was dark.

Sara returned a minute later and presented me

with my clothing, neatly folded. "No detergent, since that sort of thing bothers the nose when you're new. You'll get used to it eventually."

I took the clothing with one hand, the other holding the sheet closed. "Um. What did you mean about yesterday? Was I out long?"

She laughed. "Out long? Girl, you slept for three days straight."

"Three . . . days?" I hardly dared to believe it. I dropped onto the edge of the bed. "I slept for three *days*?"

"And snored for most of them, too. I didn't think cats could snore, but there it is." She looked pleased. "I wasn't sure if you were going to stay in cat form the whole time, but we didn't want to wake you just for that, so we let you sleep."

Three. Whole. Days.

I'd slept. I'd finally *slept*. I swiped at a tear that slid down my face.

I was free. I wasn't going to die. I was healthy, and I was going to live! I laughed, though the knot in my throat made it come out more like a snuffle.

Sara looked worried. "Marie? You okay?"

"I slept," I blubbered. "Oh, my God, I slept."

"You did," she agreed, mystified.

I stared down at the bed and ran a hand over the rumpled covers. "Can I . . . can I sleep again?"

She laughed. "Sure, if you want to."

Oh, I did. I wanted to see if I could do it again.

But I wanted to see Josh, too, and share my excitement with him. I gave the bed another longing look, then glanced at Sara. "You'll wake me up when Josh gets here?"

She nodded and shut the door, leaving me alone with the bed. I stared at it for a long minute. *Please don't let this all be one massive and incredibly cruel hallucination.*

I slid into the center of the bed, nestling my head in the pillows and snuggling deep. Could I fall asleep again? My body was tense, as if I didn't quite believe it yet. What if it was just false hope?

But even as I worried, my eyes drooped closed and I fell back to sleep.

I woke up at dawn and felt incredible.

I was going to live. Glory *fucking* hallelujah, I was going to live! I danced flat on my back in the bed, grinning like a fool. And it was all thanks to Josh. Beautiful, wonderful, thoughtful Josh. I wept with joy as I dressed.

I was giddy with excitement, and for the first time in months I felt strong and healthy and powerful. I didn't even mind the were-cougar part. Turning into a cat would take some getting used to, but I'd have Josh on my side.

I wasn't looking forward to exile, but I pictured cozying up in a snowy cabin with Josh at my side, huddled under the blankets, and decided that it might be fun. Everything seemed like fun now.

I left the bedroom and went downstairs, my stomach growling loudly. Either I was starving or this, too, was amplified in my new state. Probably both. I found Sara in the kitchen, setting two plates at the table near an enormous stack of pancakes. At the sight of her, I was so overcome with giddiness that I enveloped her in a hug.

She stiffened at my touch, then relaxed. "I take it we had a good morning?"

"I feel amazing," I told her, unable to stop smiling. "I'm so happy I could burst." My stomach growled and I slapped a hand to it in embarrassment. "I might also be hungry."

She laughed and gestured at the table. "I thought you might be, so I made breakfast. No meat, though. You might want to ease off on that for the next few weeks until you get used to controlling your shifting. The predator in you gets excited by meat, and your animal side's harder to control when you're hungry."

I nodded as I sat down, soaking in the information. The pile of pancakes looked so good that I stabbed one with a fork and ate it whole, no syrup. I needed something in my stomach *now*.

Sara ignored my bad manners, pouring two cups of coffee and moving back to the table.

I glanced around. No scents of anyone but Sara and me. No Ramsey. No Ellis or Everett. No Lily. And no Josh. I missed him. "So where is everyone?" I asked between bites.

"Giving us some space," she said cheerfully. "A new shifter is under a lot of strain, and the others thought it might be best to keep your exposure to a minimum while you adjust."

"Is Lily okay? I can't see her going with the others willingly."

She grimaced. "Well. Lily is a problem. She's human, but she's seen too much for them to just send her home. The first night you were here and unconscious, Lily bolted. The twins gathered her up again. She's now being kept in a safe location until the Alliance decides what to do with her. They're meeting with the vampires this week to discuss 'the incident.'" She made air quotes.

"Apparently the vampires didn't believe the story until Josh pointed out that Andre had been keeping Lily captive for quite some time. Now they're bending over backward to try to smooth things over, but Beau's people are furious and questioning everything. As they should. It seems like this isn't the first incident with that vampire, and now the Alliance wants stricter guidelines for vampire interaction. There's talk of setting up a permanent liaison, which means that the dating agency would have to work with them." She grimaced.

I grinned. "Not my problem, now that I'm fired. And turned!"

"Yes, you are," she said with a small laugh. "And I'm sure you'll get the hang of it pretty quickly."

And she'd given up her time to teach me the ropes. I thought of her mate, Ramsey, and how they seemed to constantly touch when they were together, and I said, "I'm sorry. This must be a big chore."

She shook her head and reached over to pat my

hand. "Not at all. I had no help when I was newly turned, and I'm happy to be of assistance. Ramsey is patient. He knows I'll be back." A smile curved her face. "I gave him homework. He needs to improve his PvP skills in WoW, or else I'm going to totally school him the next time we play. And he's not a good loser."

I had no idea what that was, but it sounded like they enjoyed it. As she chatted about shooters and techniques, I ate methodically. When she got up to bring over more coffee, I noticed a massive, dark red mark at the base of her neck. I tried not to stare at it, but I couldn't help but ask, "What happened to your neck?"

She blushed bright red and clapped a hand over the mark. "Um. So that's probably new to you. It's a mate mark," she said with a hint of pride. "A man gives it to his mate when he wants to claim her before all others."

My eyes widened. I had forgotten about my mate mark. I got up and went into the bathroom, suddenly curious to see it on my own neck.

I paused at the sight of my reflection in the mirror. I looked tired, but not as hollow and wasted as before. The hunted look in my eyes was gone. I touched my hair. It was shiny for the first time in weeks, instead of dry and flat. Huh. My gaze dropped to my neck, and I brushed my hair back.

There, just below my ear, was a single reddish mark on my neck, like the world's largest hickey.

How was it that only shifters could see this? That didn't make sense . . . but then again, neither did turning into a cat. I thought of Josh's mouth on my neck as he'd kissed and nipped at me, and my body flushed.

Suddenly I wanted to tell him how much I loved him, to share my utter joy at being cured. He'd saved me.

I rushed out of the bathroom and almost smacked back into Sara, who had followed me. "Can I see Josh now? I want to talk to him."

She bit her lip. "There's a bit of a problem . . . He's been arrested for turning a human. And it's not looking good for him."

"But he changed me to save my life," I pointed out, even though I'd expected repercussions.

"The reason behind it doesn't matter," she said gently. "All the other alphas can see is that a Russell broke the rules, and Beau's backed into a corner. He can't let his brother get off scot-free while throwing down the hammer on anyone else who changes a human. It's just really bad timing. It just looks like the Alliance playboy decided to take a human play-mate."

"That's not it at all!"

"Unfortunately, Josh refuses to discuss any of it."

I sighed. "Well, he's not going into exile alone. I'm going with him."

She stared at me. "Marie. This is far worse than that. Josh deliberately flouted the rules set out by his own brother, so this is huge. He's going to be

made an example to others. We're talking permanently exiled from the Alliance, which would make
him fair game for any Alliance member. He'd be
completely unprotected—anyone could attack him
without repercussion."

I swallowed hard.

Chapter Seventeen

*I*t was three long, horrible weeks before the Alliance tribunal met at City Hall.

While we waited, I was kept under lock and key at the Russell house. Though only Sara and I were there, I could smell another shifter in the air the few times I was allowed out onto the grounds. We were being watched, even if it wasn't overt.

I wasn't allowed to go back to my apartment, so my father was allowed to occasionally visit me. Beau and the other Russells were carefully watching him, but I knew he would keep the secret. He didn't have to be told.

Sara told me that if anyone asked, I was to say that Lily and I had been alone that night, and that we'd dragged Josh to the Russells' without assistance. Lily was being kept at a secure location separate from me, and I knew she had to be frightened.

Sara was my shadow the entire time I stayed at the Russell house, always there with a helpful word. I shifted a few more times in the three weeks, each one messy and painful, but she assured me that was normal until my body adjusted. Shifting rarely pained her any longer, and she shared tips on easing into the process. When we made it to the woods she ran alongside me, her dog nipping at my cat's heels. It was good to not feel alone, and I was grateful to have her at my side.

I'd have rather had Josh, of course; I missed him terribly. He was the last thing I thought of when I went to sleep, and the first when I woke up. Was he safe? Was he under the same lockdown I was?

Would someone really kill him just for turning me? It seemed ridiculous, yet Sara was quite grave.

I refused to accept the possibility. There had to be a way to reason with them.

As I entered the small courtroom in Little Paradise, I stared at the seated council. Every face there was stony and stern, and every member glared at me. I clung to Sara's arm as she led me forward, soothing me with low murmurs. There would be no reasoning with them, I realized with dread.

I recognized some of the council members from the agency. The two werewolves at the end of the row were Alice and Jackson. There was an angry-looking man named Declan, who, I seemed to recall, was a were-lynx (and not a popular one). The leader of the were-tiger clan, Vic, as stern and fierce as ever. An older man I didn't recognize, who likely didn't use the dating service. The biggest clans in the area would be represented, and I mentally paired up the unknowns. Were-badger. Were-lion. Another man who smelled like a wolf, two others who smelled like cats that I couldn't identify, and one who I was pretty sure was a were-otter. All of the local alphas.

At the end of the long row of leaders was Beau, shuffling paperwork. He was dressed in a gray suit and tie, and his mouth was pinched and unhappy. Bath sat in the audience, her long blond ponytail wrapped around her hand as she anxiously watched her husband.

Sara nudged me toward a chair at the center of the room and I swallowed hard, my muscles leaping and tightening in alarm. I fought back the sensation, hoping I wouldn't go into a surprise-shift. That would be really bad.

I sat down in the chair and looked around at the sea of faces, but Josh was nowhere. My heart hammered in my breast.

Beau cleared his throat, then his piercing gaze scanned me impassively. "Thank you for joining us, Marie. I see that you are well. Have you had any problems with shifting after the first attempt?"

I shook my head, my throat dry. "I'm okay, thank you."

His gaze shifted to Sara, hovering over my shoulder. "How many times has she shifted since turning?"

"Four," Sara said, her voice small in the room. "Each time was successful, with no problems She should be fine with practice."

He nodded and glanced down the row. "Let

the tribunal record that the turning has taken successfully." He looked back to me and gave another crisp nod. "You may take a seat in the audience, Marie."

Confused, I stood up. "Do you want to ask me anything else?"

"You're not on trial," he said, his voice neutral. "Please have a seat."

I gave Sara a questioning look, but she only pressed a hand to my back and nudged me toward Bathsheba, and I sat between the two sisters. Bath smiled nervously at me, tugging at her long ponytail. Her scent was a mixture of human and cougar, and I noticed her neck was covered in mate marks.

Strange how these things were so obvious now.

"Let's bring in Joshua Russell," Beau said, his voice flat and emotionless.

My heart fluttered. I craned my head, desperate to see him. To catch a whiff of his scent. He appeared in the doorway a minute later, dressed in a plain black T-shirt and jeans. His hands were braced in front of him, handcuffed. My pulse spiked at that, and at the unshaven stubble on his jaw. A scowling Ramsey lurked a few steps behind.

Josh scanned the room as soon as he entered, and I held my breath until he found me. His dark eyes widened a fraction, that intense, possessive look came over his face, and his mouth curled in a hint of a smile.

Tears pricked my eyes. *"I love you,"* I mouthed at him.

His smile curved a little more.

Ramsey gave him a bit of a shove, directing him toward the chair in the center of the room.

Someone in the row of alphas got to his feet, and I looked to see it was Vic, the were-tiger leader. He crossed his big arms over his chest and scowled at Josh, who lounged in the wooden chair as if this had all been no big deal.

Vic glared down at him. "The council has met to determine what to do in regards to your situation. Given that your brother is the leader of the Alliance, he has asked that you not be given special consideration because of his position. To do so would undermine his status as an impartial leader."

Josh gave a jerky nod, as if he'd expected this.

Beau's face was tight, the edges of his mouth strained and pale. He was upset, and trying very hard not to show it.

"The council has met and discussed this for several days. We have weighed the evidence, and before we pass sentencing, we want to know one thing." His hard gaze leveled on Josh. "After all that has happened recently, we want to know why."

I held my breath.

Josh said . . . nothing. I couldn't see his expression, only part of his back, and I became intensely frustrated. What was he waiting for? Deciding whether to speak? Thinking his answer through?

"Because I love her," Josh said after a long moment, and my heart clenched.

"That's not enough," said Declan furiously. "Just

because you think with your dick doesn't mean you let it make the decisions for you."

"Quiet," Beau said in a lethal voice. "Vic has the floor."

The were-lynx leader's mouth thinned, and he went silent.

The were-tiger alpha glared at the row, and then turned back to Josh. "No other reason?"

After a long moment, Josh added, "She was dying. I wanted to save her."

"Humans die every day," the lone female alpha—Alice—said. "Supernaturals, too. It is a part of life. We can't go around saving everyone."

"I didn't want to save everyone," Josh ground out. "Just the woman I love."

"Did she ask you to turn her?"

"No," Josh said flatly. "She refused me. I insisted. When she wouldn't listen, I overpowered her."

I frowned at that. He was making himself sound like he was the one to blame for this. It was my fault—all of it was.

"So you coerced a human female into your bed, and when you found out she was dying, you decided to turn her? You let her into a secret, private Alliance without consulting anyone else?"

"I did," Josh said in a clipped tone.

What? "Wait," I blurted, getting to my feet.

Seven alphas scowled at me, the force of their displeasure so great that I staggered backward. I felt this odd compulsion to shrink back, as if desperate to please them. For some reason, their approval was important to me.

"We did not call on you," Vic began.

I forced the quiver in my stomach aside. This was no time to let my shifter hormones rule things. I shoved my hand into my purse, fishing out my wallet. Then I flipped it open and grabbed my Alliance ID card, walking to the center of the floor with the card raised. "I'm already Alliance. This ID says so."

"She's right," Beau said quietly. "She's been working at the agency for over a year now. That should be a consideration in this case."

"So what are we supposed to do?" Declan declared. "Just ignore the precedent that's been set? Run around turning human women just because we feel like it? Dilute the gene pool?"

A low snarl rumbled in Beau's throat. "My mate is human. Watch your tongue."

Alice raised her hands. "I want to know why it's so bad that she's been turned."

All eyes turned to her, and several withering scowls were now directed at her. I wanted to kiss the woman in gratitude. I edged closer to Josh, waiting for Ramsey to push us apart, but he didn't—so I laid my hand on Josh's shoulder.

He tilted his head and nuzzled my hand, letting me know he loved me. I felt a surge of love in response.

"We can't just go changing humans when we please," Declan snarled in her face.

The wolf alpha at her side—Jackson—got to his

feet and frowned at the man snarling at his mate. Alice put a hand up, calming him. "The problem with shifters is that we don't have enough women to go around, right? Why can't we be sensible about this? My pack was recently under attack for the simple reason that we have females and the other one did not. Power struggles over women in packs is not something new. Wasn't there a recent problem with another wolf pack and a female?"

All eyes in the room suddenly moved to Sara.

"There was," Beau admitted, his tone guarded.

"So why are we following their bad example?" Alice asked. "What's so terrible about turning someone if it's in a controlled, measured environment? Why can't someone be turned if they are vetted and double-checked? Does it matter if there's one more were-cougar? It's not as if we're fighting for game. We have supermarkets for that sort of thing."

Declan snarled, the sound feral and ugly. "What about that tiger boy? What happened there—"

"Wasn't controlled," Vic pointed out. "He didn't have my permission or the girl's. With both of those in place, I wouldn't have a problem with it."

"Nor I," said Jackson.

"Nor I," said another.

The lynx alpha shook his head viciously. "And what happens if our secret gets out? What happens if someone is turned and they go straight to the papers? Straight to the internet?"

"We're not saying that things have to be changed

overnight," Alice said, her tone calm and unruffled. "We're saying that we take control of things in a sensible manner. Do you think your clan members would go sneaking off turning someone if they knew all they had to do is talk to their alpha and have a few background checks run?"

Declan said nothing, his glare still clearly unhappy.

"I'm thinking it's going to become more and more difficult to keep things a secret in the future," Jackson said slowly. "The world's changing too fast. Maybe it's time we look at easing supes into mainstream society. Why should we hide what we are?"

Beau shook his head. "We're not ready to go mainstream yet. But I'm thinking a firm nondisclosure agreement and alpha participation in regard to vetting female members is not a bad thing. My wife is human. Her sister was *assumed* human. The other two who work at the agency are human. So how is it that Giselle—who wasn't the most reliable creature—was able to staff her agency with nothing but humans and no one had a problem with it?

"It's because they were discreet and signed a nondisclosure agreement," he continued. "She picked people she could trust and then gradually let them in on the secret, but she made sure she was protected first. That's how turning a human should be handled. It should be handled delicately and among those we trust. And if someday we're ready to embrace being out in the open with what we are, then we'll approach that."

Silence.

My palms grew sweaty, and I stared at the council, waiting. Under my hand, I could feel Josh was equally tense.

"Decision?" Beau asked. "Shall we put this to a vote? All those in favor of loosening the standards for turning humans?"

Six hands raised.

"All opposed?"

Declan's hand raised. "I don't like this," he bit out. "It's going to be abused. You wait and see."

"Anyone who wants to turn someone has to go through their alpha," Alice said in a smooth voice. "I have enough control over my pack to ensure that happens. You should, too."

Declan's scowl turned to her, but he said nothing else.

"It's settled, then," Beau said forcefully. "Share the news with your men. I'll leave it to each clan to govern their own people. We'll meet again in a month and reassess."

Vic turned to Beau. "And what about my clan members who are in exile?"

Beau clapped him on the shoulder. "Bring them home. We made a mistake. We should be teaching and educating, not trying to instill fear into men who are desperate for companionship. If they want mates, we need to give them mates. And I doubt every woman in the Alliance wants to take two husbands to make up for the slack."

"Not every supernatural acts like a were-fox,

thank you," Alice said in a lofty tone. "One mate is enough for most."

"Is that it, then? Is Joshua free to go?"

The alphas remained quiet. "No objections," one said at last, and my heart fluttered with joy.

I threw my arms around Josh, kissing his face wildly. He kissed me back, his mouth delicious on mine.

"I love you," I told him, cupping his face in my hands. "I love you so much."

"Marie, baby," he said softly, his gaze moving over me. "You look beautiful. And healthy."

"I'm sleeping," I told him happily. Tears pricked my eyes, and I couldn't resist kissing him again. "I'm sleeping every night."

"I'm so glad," he murmured, his voice husky with emotion. "So fucking glad."

Someone cleared his throat, and I glanced up, remembering that Ramsey still stood there. He held up a key for the handcuffs.

Once Josh's hands were free he took me in his arms, kissing me hard again.

"You shouldn't have taken the risk," I told him between kisses. "My life isn't worth yours."

"Your life is absolutely worth mine." He grinned down at me. "Though I have to admit that I'm glad Greenland is off the menu. I don't look nearly as dashing in a parka."

I laughed and wrapped my arms around his neck happily.

Another throat cleared and we looked over at Beau.

"Now that things are cleared with the Alliance, it's time to talk to your alpha. Because he's still furious at you."

Josh just grinned and tugged me close. "Yes, sir."

The lecture wasn't as bad as I thought it would be. It was mostly Beau reaming Josh out for being reckless and Josh accepting it without any protest, his arms wrapped around my waist as I sat in his lap. There was nothing Beau could say that we didn't already know, and by the time he finished venting, the two brothers were laughing and easy once more.

"Can I go home with my woman now?" Josh said. "You're wearing her out, and she's still fragile from turning."

Beau sighed heavily and rubbed his forehead. He looked as if he'd aged five years in the last few weeks. "Go home. Are you two going to be staying with us at the ranch?"

The arm around my waist tightened. "Actually, I thought I'd move in with Marie, if she'd have me."

"Marie would," I said in a pert voice, "except that Marie is probably going to lose her apartment now that she's unemployed. I understand that Bath had to make a point that the client information is safe, but it puts me in the unemployment line."

Beau nodded and looked at Josh. "This one, too, unfortunately. He's not going to be in much demand as a vampire bodyguard now that word's getting out about Andre. On the other hand, we will need an Alliance liaison to work with the vampire liaison. It needs to be someone charming but familiar with vampire bullshit. And having someone they're a little intimidated by would be helpful."

"That sounds like me," Josh said lazily. "Tall. Sexy. Intimidating. Good with vampires. I'll do it."

I snorted.

"I haven't given you the job yet," Beau threatened.

"Nah, but you will," Josh said with a grin. "You don't want me and Marie living on your couch."

"Great," I muttered.

"Actually," Beau began, then he crossed his arms and studied me. "I need an assistant, and I want someone in our clan because it requires confidentiality and trust. I thought about approaching Savannah, but Bathsheba's hired her on full-time at the agency, and she seems to enjoy it. Things are getting a little hectic back at the security office, and I'd rather spend my evenings with my mate, instead of handling all the Alliance paperwork myself."

I smiled, feeling hopeful. "I'm pretty good with paperwork."

"She's also pretty good at flaying people with her tongue," Josh said mildly.

I pinched him.

"I imagine that'll come in handy, given some of the people that call me on a regular basis," Beau said in a dry voice. "When can you start?"

"When do you need me?"

"Hold on," Josh said, moving protectively in front of me and raising his hands. "She's my mate, and she's still recovering from her illness. She needs a few weeks of rest before she thinks about going back to work."

"A few weeks is fine for her," Beau said. "You start on Monday. We have a little issue with the vampires that needs smoothing over."

Josh grinned. "I'm your man."

While Beau and Josh talked, I listened with only half an ear. I was sleepy, but it was a good kind of sleepy—not the terrible, dreadful kind of sleepy that meant I was going to have another bad night of insomnia. I yawned, enjoying the sensation.

Josh abruptly stood, taking my hand in his. "We'll finish this conversation later, Beau. My mate's tired."

"Oh, but I'm not—"

Josh gave me a direct, meaningful look. A rather scorching one.

I shut my mouth.

Beau chuckled. "Just call me when the weekend's over. We'll see about moving your stuff. Both of you go get some sleep. I'm going to go home to my mate. It's been a long day for all of us."

As we left the courthouse, I had the tiniest bit of fear that we'd be ambushed in the parking lot by the angry lynx alpha, that this wasn't just going to blow over.

Josh paused, staring into the parking lot.

My heart stuttered. "What is it?"

He gave me a wry grin. "My car's not here. I forgot that I rode with Ramsey."

"Oh. And I rode with Sara. Looks like we're stranded."

"Nah, wait here." Josh returned a few minutes later with a pair of keys and jangled them at me. "We're taking Beau's Viper. Bath's swinging by to pick him up."

My eyes widened as we approached the sleek sports car. "He's letting us take his Viper?"

He grinned. "I think he's worried that if we linger, Bath is going to want to chat about the new plans for the agency, and he'd rather just take her home and kiss the hell out of her. Like I plan on doing to you."

That sounded awfully good. "Let's get going, then."

As we drove, Josh told me about what he'd learned while being under house arrest with Ramsey.

It seemed that poor Lily was not so poor anymore. The Alliance vampires were horrified at Andre's actions, and the bodyguard we'd tied up had corroborated our story enough that Lily's crime of staking Andre was quickly swept under the rug. As hush money, the vampires had given her half of Andre's fortune in a trust account. The other half had been given to the local reigning vampire lord.

My father's name had never been mentioned in connection with the incident, which relieved me.

"That doesn't fix Lily's problems, though," Josh told me. "She's basically under house arrest until we figure out what to do with her. No one trusts her not to tell her side of the story, and she already ran once. When she's free, she'll be a rich woman. So we need to decide what to do with her until then."

Poor dirty, frightened Lily. "I want to help her. Any way we can. I feel responsible for her."

"The twins are watching her," Josh assured me. "But we'll go visit tomorrow, if you like, and make sure everything is okay."

We drove back to my place in record time and parked the car, then Josh swung me into his arms and carried me up the stairs. I clung to his shoulders as he unlocked the door, pushed inside, kicked it shut behind us, then moved straight for the bedroom.

I chuckled and leaned in to kiss his neck, inhaling his scent. He smelled different now that I was were-cougar. Delicious and rich and full of woodsy notes that tickled my nostrils like perfume. No one smelled as good as Josh. I ran my tongue along the cords of his neck. "You taste as good as you smell."

"You're going to find that a lot of your senses are more sensitive now that you're a were-cougar."

"Mmm, sounds good to me. Is there a downside to this?"

"An intense attraction to fuzzy mice, tuna, and an inability to tell the alpha no."

That didn't sound so bad to me, since Beau was

the alpha of our small group. "It's a trade-off, I suppose," I said lightly, running my fingers along the inside of his collar, then nipping at his neck. "I saw my mate mark."

"You like it?" he asked in a husky voice, depositing me on the bed.

I curled my hands into his shirt and dragged him down next to me so I could keep kissing him. "I do. Do female shifters give them to their mates?"

"Sometimes," he said, sliding a hand over my hips and resting it on the curve of my ass. "Did you see Ramsey's neck? It's covered."

I shook my head. The big were-bear wore his blond hair long and shaggy. I'd check for it next time. "I guess Sara likes him a lot."

"You could say that."

I ran my fingers along his neck. "So can I mark you? Lay claim so all those other nasty were-cougars in the area keep their paws off?"

"Well, seeing as how the only were-cougars in this area are either male or related, I don't think that's an issue. But I'm more than happy for you to mark me and declare me all yours."

I crawled over him, fascinated by touching him, the feel of his pulse underneath his skin. The scent of him was intoxicating. I moved in and licked his neck again, testing for just the right spot to mark him, and was rewarded with his groan of pleasure. "Am I going to like being a were-cougar?"

"Once you get the hang of shifting, yes. I'll be at your side every step of the way, guiding you. And then, when you don't need my help, I'll be at your side chasing away any potential admirers."

"I don't want anyone but you," I told him.

"Sweet Marie-Pierre," he said, and grinned at the face I made. "I'm glad you're all mine." He knotted his hand in my hair and tugged my face down for another long, sweet, licking kiss. "And I'm so damn relieved that you're better."

"Me, too." Then I sat upright, glancing around the room. "Oh, shit. My dad. I should call him and tell him everything is okay. He's worried for you."

Josh dragged me back down to his chest. "Call him tomorrow. Tonight, you're all mine."

"Only tonight?" I teased and leaned in to nip at a promising spot on his neck, enjoying his masculine shudder of response.

"We'll start with tonight," he said. "But I'm greedy, Marie-Pierre. I'm afraid I'm not going to be able to settle for less than every minute of the rest of our lives."

"I'm okay with that," I told him and sank my teeth into his neck.

That evening, as we lay in bed, Josh played with a curl of my hair, my chest propped on his. "I love you, Marie-Pierre."

I pinched his side. "You're cruel."

"For telling you that I love you?"

"No, for using that name. Telling me that you love me is just . . . confusing."

He sat up, jostling me from where I was nestled against him. "Confusing? What are you talking about?"

I rolled in the bed, moving away from him and wrapping up in the tangled sheets. "I don't know. I just don't see how you can be in love with me. Unless you fall in love with everyone you sleep with."

"Well, this is flattering," he said dryly. "You're so good with compliments, it's astounding that you're single, Marie. Absolutely astounding."

"I'm serious," I said. "You've dated dozens of women. Gorgeous women. I've seen some of your dates. They're bangin'. And you declare love for a skinny woman with enormous bags under her eyes and sleeping problems? You'll have to excuse me if I have a hard time believing I'm not some kind of charity case."

"Are you kidding me? You're skinny because you were sick. Emphasis on *were*. And it didn't take away anything from your appearance. I see a strong, determined woman when I look at you. That's beautiful."

"More beautiful than double-D cups?" I asked doubtfully.

Josh laughed. "I can't believe I'm reassuring you about your looks. Your figure is gorgeous. *You're* gorgeous."

I waved a hand. "It wasn't mainly my looks I was worried about. I want to know why you love *me*, and not all those other women you've dated."

"It's just you—everything about you. The way you flay me with your tongue in one sentence and then devour me with your eyes the next. It's your grit. Your refusal to give up when things look their bleakest. The way you won't back down from a challenge. I love all of that about you. It makes me want to challenge you even more, just to see how you react." He grinned. "It's why I loved teasing you in the first place."

I leaned in and gently kissed him. "I love you."

He pulled me in close, grinning. "Now say something dirty in French, just for me."

I laughed and did just that.

After a fierce round of lovemaking and a night of blissful sleep, I called my dad the next morning. We made plans to meet him and Posey for breakfast. I'd promised Josh that I'd tell my dad everything, though we were resolved to be careful about anything related to vampires or shifters, since Posey hadn't signed a nondisclosure like Dad had.

The diner was crowded this morning, but as soon as we walked in the door, Carol gave a cry of delight, throwing her arms out to hug Josh. He enveloped her in a bear hug and gave her a smacking kiss. "How's the most beautiful girl in the world doing?"

She batted at him with her notepad. "She's still immune to your bullshit, young man."

Oh, please. If there was anyone who loved his bullshit, it was Carol.

I was surprised when she moved to hug me. "You

look well, honey. Those dark circles under your eyes are gone."

"Thanks," I said. "I've been catching up on my sleep."

"Josh, honey," Carol said. "The manager ran out to the bank and I need a box of menus from the top shelf in the back. Could you be a dear and go help the cook get it for me?"

"Of course." He winked at her and sauntered back to the kitchen. "I'll be right back, ladies. Marie, baby, I see your dad over there." He gestured at the far end of the restaurant just before disappearing through the swinging door.

I glanced in that direction. My dad sat in the back booth with Posey, who was wearing enough makeup to make Mary Kay pause, and even though it was seven in the morning, her hair was in a huge, perfect blond bouffant. For some reason, though, she didn't fill me with the annoyed dread that she normally did.

Dad raised a hand, waving me over.

I began to step toward the table when Carol batted me lightly with the notepad in her hand, getting my attention. "I'm glad to see you back, missy."

I smiled. "You are?"

"You had him all tangled up," she said. "Every night he came in, he was stressed out about you. Said he couldn't charm you like he charmed everyone else. I never saw him so flustered over a girl."

Well, wasn't that adorable? I laughed. "Oh, he's

just saying that. I'm sure he tells you that about all the girls he brings here."

She shook her head and gave me a sharp-eyed look. "You're the only one he's ever introduced me to, honey. When I saw him come in with you, I thought, he's going to marry this one. He's asked you, hasn't he?"

Jeez, she was sharp. I felt myself blush and resisted the urge to touch the mate mark on my neck. "More or less."

"That's good," she said, patting my hand. "That's very good. You make him happy."

"And he makes me happy," I said softly.

It was true. When he emerged with that box of menus and shot me a cocky, confident grin, my heart melted all over again. I adored the hell out of that overconfident, arrogant, loving, caring guy.

And I planned on spending the rest of my life proving it.

Epilogue

"Wake up, sleepyhead," a voice murmured in my ear, rousing me from the most delicious dream.

I snuggled deeper into the pillows and didn't open my eyes. I mumbled, "Five more minutes."

There was a soft chuckle, then a hand pulled me against a large, hard male body. I felt Josh lean over me, and felt his warm breath on my ear a second before he began to nibble on it. "You naughty minx. You're always sleeping late, aren't you?"

"Mmm," I said, sighing with pleasure at a good night's sleep—and the delicious man teasing my ear. "I love sleeping."

"It's time to wake up," Josh murmured, then kissed my neck. "You know what today is?"

It took a moment for it to register in my sleep-groggy mind, and then I realized. My eyes flew open. "Oh, jeez. My picnic!"

He chuckled. "That's right."

"Oh, heck, I've got to get up," I said, all sleepiness vanishing from my body. Today the were-cougar clan was gathering in my honor. It promised to be a big party, and it wouldn't do if I showed up late. Plus, I'd promised Bathsheba that I'd bring a few dishes to help out with the picnic part of things . . . and I hadn't started. I'd meant to cook last night, but Josh had distracted me with flirty kisses, and before I'd known it, we'd fallen into bed early, though sleep had come hours later.

I tossed the covers aside and rolled away from Josh, intending to get out of bed . . . only to be snared at the waist and dragged back against him, my sleep tank top riding up to expose even more of my skin.

"Where are you going in such a rush, gorgeous?"

"*Tête de cochon*," I said affectionately. "I need to shower and start cooking."

He kissed my bare shoulder, sending shivers through my body. "You can do that later."

"But—"

He nipped my flesh, then stroked it with his tongue to soothe the ache.

A low heat pulsed in my belly and my limbs immediately went liquid. I whimpered. So unfair of him to play dirty. But when his hand slid to my panties and began to edge them downward, I leaned back against him and sighed with pleasure. "Think we'll be late if we stay in bed for a bit longer?"

"Definitely," Josh murmured, his fingers sliding under the silky fabric.

About two seconds later, I found that I didn't care.

We showed up to the Russell house about an hour after I'd promised Bathsheba that I'd be there. She didn't say anything when I showed up in the kitchen; she just gave me a knowing look that made me blush bright red.

Her scent was something I recognized instantly. The oddly unfamiliar tang of human, plus a slight undercurrent of the more familiar—and more comforting—were-cougar. There was an enormous mate mark on her neck, visible right under the strand of hair that she tucked behind her ear.

Josh kissed my cheek and moved toward the stove that Bath hovered over. "Anything I can help with?"

She turned to face him, a look of surprised amusement on her face. "A Russell offering to help in the kitchen? Never thought I'd see the day."

"Hey, my favorite ladies are in here right now," he said easily, taking the bowl I was carrying from my hands and heading to the fridge with it. "You just tell me what you want me to do and I'll do it."

"You can head back to town and get some extra beer. We've got a few extras coming today."

"Extras?" I gave her an odd look. "I thought this was just Russells. Were-cougars." Of course, she was here, so it wasn't like we planned on sticking to that rule fast and hard. Beau wasn't about to have a clan get-together and not invite his own wife.

"It started out that way," Bathsheba said, pulling a list from under a nearby plate. "But then we didn't know what to do with Lily, since she's still under surveillance, so Ryder volunteered to watch her if she could come, too. I couldn't exactly refuse that. And of course there's Sara and Ramsey, who are always included even though they're not cougar. Jeremiah's bringing Miko and Sam. And Savannah asked to bring Connor."

Josh scowled. "Did you tell her no?"

"I told her yes," Bathsheba said in a pert voice. "Now please, we need a few more six-packs of beer. Would you mind?"

He snagged his keys back off the counter and moved toward me, giving me a quick, hot kiss full of promise. "I'll be back soon, baby."

"Got it," I told him with a soft smile, resisting the urge to swat his ass when he walked away. I watched him as he left, then turned back to Bathsheba once he was gone.

She was smiling. "So . . . how are things with you and Josh?"

"Good," I said, though the word didn't seem to encompass quite enough. Life was incredible, and wonderful, and so full of wonder and hope and happiness every day that I pulled out my mother's Virgin Mary figurine and kissed it in gratitude every time I woke up. I couldn't ask for a better life.

And it was all thanks to Josh, that wonderful, beautiful man.

"Mmmhmm. Can you start making the potato salad?"

I moved to the small mountain of potatoes on the far end of the kitchen table. "So why is it that we got stuck with the cooking?"

Bath pulled out a bottle of barbeque sauce from the fridge. "Because if I let one of the men in the kitchen, they'd eat everything before it ever made it to the table."

"And you like being in charge," I teased, grabbing the potato peeler and attacking the first potato.

She gave a small sniff. "That's not it. I just—"

"Like being in charge," Sara chimed in, walking through the back door, a bag of groceries in her arms. "Marie had it right the first time."

I caught the waft of wolf-scent and resisted the urge to wrinkle my nose. I was still getting used to all the different scents.

"You hush," Bath said to her sister with a mock scowl. "Did you bring the dessert?"

"Three cheesecakes," Sara announced proudly. "All fresh from the bakery. Ramsey's carrying them in. He says I'm too small and they're too heavy." She rolled her eyes.

"It *is* a bit of a pain in the ass that there's no road," I mentioned.

"Beau likes his privacy," Bath said simply. "If there was a road nearby, someone'd be driving down it constantly. He doesn't mind a little walking to get here."

I supposed he had a point. "Here" was Beau's cabin in the midst of the woods, with no roads, no trails, no nothing, for at least a square mile. It had been quite a hike for me and Josh, since we'd been carrying food as well, but I'd felt healthy and strong and alive—and my shifter strength was quite a bit stronger than my wimpy human strength. It had been a long walk, but not a hard one, and I was pleased at that.

Bath and I cooked and made sandwiches while Sara sat on the counter and picked at the food, nibbling when she thought Bath wasn't looking. As we worked, we chatted and laughed, and more people began to wander into the kitchen as they arrived for the party. Eventually Josh returned with the beer, and instead of setting up outside with the other guys at the picnic tables, he headed toward me in the kitchen and picked up a potato peeler.

That was why I loved the man. Beneath that incredibly flirty exterior was a heart of gold.

Each person came by to give me their congratulations on my successful turning and subsequent absorption into the Russell clan. The twins showed up first—Everett and Ellis. Then Austin, then Ryder and Lily, whom no one knew what to do with. Beau moved back and forth between the house and the grill outside, smelling like smoke and cougar. Everyone was thrilled that I'd joined the clan, and I didn't see a hint of antihuman sentiment anywhere. It made me wonder if it was going this smoothly for all of the clans, or if it was because the Russells were such a mixed blend that it didn't matter to them. I couldn't see it being this easy for the poor tiger girl.

Sure enough, Jeremiah showed up with Sam—who smelled different and whom I'd never met, so I knew he wasn't a were-cougar—and Miko. Jeremiah congratulated me in his soft voice, then headed outside with the others as they passed through the house.

Bath gave me a prim look. "I hope you're not bothered by the fact that Jere has a boyfriend and a girlfriend?"

I wagged the potato peeler at her. "I worked at the dating agency, remember? I've seen weird, and that isn't weird. A were-snake and a harpy? Now *that's* weird."

Sara snorted, then plucked a deviled egg off the counter the moment Bath set it down. "That's not the weirdest pairing. Did you ever see—"

There was a knock at the door. Bath wiped her hands and headed to answer it, and Sara and I turned to look. The scent of wolf was definitely getting stronger. I wrinkled my nose a little, not used to the smell.

A man about Sara's age stood in the doorway—Connor Anderson. His dark hair was shaggy and hung in front of his eyes, but he had a gorgeous face. He also looked downright uncomfortable and kept glancing over his shoulder to the person standing behind him on the steps. "Hi."

"Come on in," Bath said warmly. "We're still making food. Everyone else is out back."

He stepped inside, and the smell of wolf accompanied him. A woman stood behind him, her hand clasped in his, and I waved at the heavily pregnant Savannah Russell.

Bath leaned over Savannah's enormous belly and kissed her cheek. "Why don't you two go out back and say hello to Beau? He'll be thrilled to see you."

I hid my smile. Bath was a sly one. Sending them out to Beau meant that they'd be under the leader's watchful eye, which meant the other Russell clan members—Ellis, Everett, Austin, and my own Josh—wouldn't be free to show just how much they disliked Connor. Savannah gave Bath a grateful look. I watched as they entered the living room, heading to the back of the house, Connor hovering over Savannah as if she might break. Adorable.

There was another knock at the door, and I looked over at Josh in surprise, mentally counting heads. Wasn't everyone here by now?

"I'll get that," Bath said, a hint of a smile.

"Were we expecting someone else?" I asked, curious.

Josh reached out and stole a cube of potato from my pile of diced vegetables. "Wait and see, baby."

A familiar, warm, human scent filled the air, and I gasped in surprise at seeing my father. Happy tears filled my eyes, and I launched myself at him. "Daddy! You're here?"

He wrapped me in his arms. "*Ma petite puce*. It's good to see you, too."

I hugged him close, so full of joy that I could burst.

"It's a family gathering for you," Bath said, "so it wouldn't be right if your father wasn't here. And thanks to the nondisclosure agreement, I didn't see a problem with it when Josh mentioned it."

I looked back at Josh. "You are the best thing since sliced bread."

"I know," he said smugly.

"Why don't you take your father outside and introduce him to everyone?" Bath suggested.

I smiled up at him and looped my arm through his. This day just got better and better.

When the food was ready, everyone piled out to the tables. I sat to Beau's right, Josh's arm looped around my waist, and I felt a little embarrassed when a dozen beers were raised—and a glass of water from Savannah—and all eyes went to me.

"To our new sister," Beau said. "Our clan grows daily, and I, for one, am thrilled."

"Hear, hear," Josh said, then leaned in to kiss me.

I returned his kiss and looked down the table at the faces there. My father, directly across from me. Josh. The twins. Jeremiah and his dates. Ryder and Lily. Bath and Beau. Sara and Ramsey. Connor and Savannah. So many people in my life now.

Ice Queen Marie had disappeared— better yet, she'd been absorbed into a large, eclectic family. I wasn't allowed to hold myself apart any longer.

I'd gone from having nothing to having every thing.

"Can we eat now?" Josh asked. "I love Marie and all, but those ribs look incredible, and I'm starving."

I laughed, and the entire table erupted with groans.

Everyone dug into the food, and within a half hour, the plates were cleaned. Some people sat around the table, sharing conversation.

One of the twins showed up with a football in his hands. "We've got enough people here for a good game. Who's up for it?"

"Flags?" Connor asked.

"Flags are for pussies," Everett retorted. "Tackle football. How about you, Marie, since you're the guest of honor?"

A month ago, I'd have been too weak to do more than walk across the room. But now? I was brimming with health and happiness. I put down my napkin. "Why not?"

"Excellent. You can be team captain. Josh can be the other."

We moved to the front of the group, and Josh gave me a wicked grin. "How about my team is shirts and yours is skins?"

I rolled my eyes. "How did I know that was going to come out of your mouth?"

"Because you know me, baby."

"Indeed. Well then, let me pick first." I glanced over at the people who were still sitting. "Who all's playing?"

"I am," said Bath.

"No," Beau said stubbornly. "You're too fragile."

Her lip curled, just a little. "You're kidding, right? You're going to play the 'human' card on me? Humans play football all the time."

"Not my human."

"Beauregard Russell!"

"Fine," he said in a menacing tone, then cast a look down the table. "If anyone tackles my wife, I'm coming after them."

"Beau," Bath said warningly.

"I'll take her," I chimed in. "She can be our quarterback."

"So unfair," Josh protested. "Now you really do have to be skins."

I smacked him on the arm.

Football was a blast, but a total blowout. Josh had managed to let me pick Ramsey for my team—a deliberate move, I suspected, since it was supposed to be my day and all—and with the massive were-bear on our side, it was more or less a massacre. We learned early on to give Bath the ball and then let Ramsey barrel everyone else out of the way as they charged down the zone. Pretty soon, we were winning by four touchdowns. It wasn't a very fair game, though. Every time I'd break free, Josh would be there to tackle me.

Something told me he just wanted to drag me into the grass, and I didn't mind.

Sara was on Josh's team, and on the next pass, she caught the ball. I moved to tackle her, but sure enough, Josh was there again, leaping on top of me and dragging me to the ground before I could touch her. His hands were everywhere as we rolled in the grass, and I laughed.

"You know, if you wanted to cop a feel, you could just ask," I told him between breaths.

He grinned down at me. "It's more fun this way."

A high-pitched squeal caught my attention, and I turned to see Sara launch herself bodily at Ramsey, as if her slight form could knock him down. I'd say one thing for Sara—she was small but fearless.

She was so much smaller than Ramsey that he just caught her out of the air, turned around, and began to run toward our end zone with his mate trapped in his arms, laughing and still clutching the ball. A moment later, Ramsey scored for our team.

The sidelines—Savannah, Lily, Ryder, and my dad—erupted in laughter.

"We concede," Josh announced. "Having Ramsey on a team is like having five extra players."

"I win," I crowed, rolling onto him on the grass.

"Yes, you do." He grinned up at me.

Desire rolled through me, and to my surprise, my claws popped. I yelped as I felt hair follicles tingle and come to life, a sure sign that I was about to change. Even though I'd been a were-cougar for a little over a month now, I still didn't quite have the hang of everything. It would come with time and I didn't need to worry about it, but it was still embarrassing.

"Looks like it's time for a run," Josh announced.

"Mr. Bellavance, why don't you and I and Lily

and Ryder go inside for some coffee?" Bath said brightly. "I think the others want to spend some nature time out here." With a knowing glance at her mate, Bath shepherded the humans out of the clearing, and suddenly it was just shifters.

A familiar scent neared, then Beau was kneeling beside me from where I sat atop Josh, struggling to hold my claws in until the humans were gone. "Don't fight it, Marie. It's a natural part of your life now. It's time to run with your clan if you're ready."

I nodded, my throat suddenly dry. This would be my first run with the entire clan, plus a few others. Performance anxiety struck me. What if I couldn't shift fast enough for them? What if they had to stand around and wait for me while I struggled to turn? That would be humiliating—and painful.

All around me, shifters began to strip off their clothing, tossing it to the ground. Clothing always had to go first—it got too easily destroyed by animal claws and shifting bones. The last thing you wanted was to turn into a cat and end up partially strangled by your bra because you didn't take it off first. But still, stripping down in front of a group of strangers wasn't something I was used to. I hadn't grown up in a shifter clan, where stripping down in front of others was as natural as breathing.

Off to one side, I watched Sara fling off her top, and Connor was helping Savannah unbutton her maternity dress. To one side, the twins were shucking their jeans and talking about football scores.

Ramsey was pulling his shirt over his head, and the others were undressing as well. No one was paying a lick of attention to me.

So why was I so nervous?

"Hey," Josh said, grabbing me by the waist and turning me toward him. As if he could read my thoughts, he said, "Don't think about it, okay? Just think about changing."

I nodded and stared down at my clawed hands. I'd end up scratching myself if I pulled my T-shirt over my head. "Could you help me?"

His eyes gleamed, catlike. "Help you undress? Marie, you flirt."

"*Tabarnak.* You know what I meant. Just do it," I said, laughing.

"Yes, ma'am." His hands slid under my shirt, easing it over my head, and I kept my gaze on him and his gorgeous body. Better to look at him than the others, lest I have a modesty freak-out and embarrass myself in front of my new clan.

Within moments I was stripped of everything but my skivvies, and Josh was helping me with those, pressing little kisses on my skin as he did. I blushed, thinking of the others who might be watching us, but then my shift kicked into high gear and I forgot about everything else.

I wasn't sure that changing into a cougar would ever feel normal, my entire body transforming and realigning, my spine shifting and curving, my hips moving downward and tilting, my legs completely changing to the backward bend of the feline's, growing fur, claws, and fangs. It forced me to concentrate on allowing it to happen naturally, and by the time the transformation was complete, I lay in the grass, panting, in full-on cougar form.

I wasn't sure how long it had taken, but a gentle hand stroked my side and down my fur. "Everything good, baby?"

I opened my eyes and saw Josh's handsome face, always tinged with a bit of concern for me. He hadn't shifted yet; wouldn't until he was sure everything was okay with me. Sweet man. I licked his hand in affirmation, then head-butted it.

"I'll take that as a yes," he said with a grin and began to pull off his own clothing, fur sprouting as he did. Josh, born as a shifter, could transform much, much faster than I could.

I waited, adjusting to the thicker, more vivid scents in my shifted form. All around me I could smell the others—an eclectic mix of cougars, bear, and wolves. Not a normal pack, for sure. The scent of humans lingered in the grass, but the smell was getting old already, and I knew the others were inside, likely having a coffee with Bath as she kept them distracted from what was happening out here.

And then Josh was licking my ear, his rough cat tongue affectionate. I got to my feet and faced the clan, fully transformed.

The clearing was filled with animals. Beau and the other Russells had transformed into sleek cougars, though Savannah's sides bulged with her pregnancy. The two wolves paced a fair distance away, and Ramsey's massive bear form was already crashing into the woods.

Beau lifted his muzzle, scenting the air, then turned and loped into the woods. When the others fell in behind him, I joined their ranks, Josh a few steps behind me. I'd read up on cougars after I'd been transformed, and unlike wolves, we weren't pack animals. It was family more than it was pack. It was comfort and togetherness.

We ran through the woods, and I lost track of time. The cougar side of me relished the wildness of running through the woods, tracking prey, and playing with the other cats. There were predator games of hide-and-seek, and following scent trails made messy by wolf and bear.

Hours slid away, and when I looked up, the sky was dark, the moon glowing, and Josh and I were on the trail of a nearby skunk. The human in me didn't want to catch it—not really—but the animal side of me found the strong scent and the promise of prey irresistable.

A short time later, the trail went cold. When Josh split off from the rest of the cougars and turned into the woods, I followed him, curious.

We ran for some time, alone, and then he flopped to the ground, rolling in the leaves and deadfall, his belly up as if he wanted his stomach scratched. I wanted to laugh with amusement, but the only thing that came out of my throat was an odd, cat-like chuff. I was surprised at the sound . . . and then my fur rippled and I braced myself, my body slowly changing back to human.

Long minutes passed and I concentrated on the shift itself, fixated on the slow, smooth return of my fingers and bare white skin. When it was done, I collapsed on the ground and glanced over at Josh, surprised to see that he'd changed back to human form as well.

"I think we lost our skunk," I told him mournfully.

"You didn't really want it," he told me with a grin, reaching over to slide his fingers on my sweat-slicked belly. "Think of the heart attack Bath would have had if you'd returned to the house smelling like skunk."

"You have a point," I said and yawned, snuggling closer to his naked, sweaty form. Leaves and dirt were sticking to our bodies, but I didn't care. I liked Josh's scent—sweaty or clean, he smelled delicious to me.

"You did well, baby. I'm proud of you." He leaned in to nuzzle my cheek. "What made you shift back now?"

"I wasn't trying to," I told him, running a hand over his gleaming shoulders. "I think I learned the hard way that cougars can't laugh."

He chuckled, nipping at my shoulder. "No, they can't." His hand covered my breast. "I'd rather be human right now . . . for other reasons."

He flicked my nipple with his thumb, and I sucked in a breath, immediately scanning the woods for others nearby.

"No one's here," Josh told me in a husky voice. "They headed in. We're the only ones still out on a run. They wanted to give us some alone time." And he continued to stroke my nipple, his touch working it into an aching point.

I leaned in to kiss him, biting at his lower lip in a way I knew he liked. "But we're all sweaty and covered in dirt."

"There's a stream nearby," he told me, leaning down to lick a bead of sweat off my breast. "If you're into that sort of thing."

"Mmm." My hands slid to his nipples and grazed them in retaliation. "Think we'll make it to the stream?"

"Maybe." He bit my nipple. "Maybe not. Do you care?"

"Not really," I told him and rolled the two of us until he was under me and I was sitting atop him, straddling him. His cock was trapped between my thighs, a hot length of promise. "I find that I'm caring less and less with each minute."

"Me, too," he said with a grin.

So we "didn't care" for several hours into the night, and on until morning.

And that was perfectly fine with both of us.

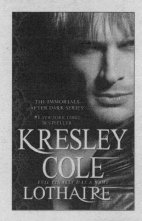
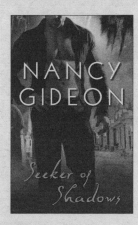

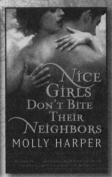

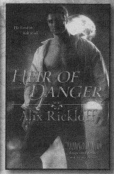